Dragon's Fire

Also by Jane Johnson

The Secret Country
The Shadow World

Dragon's Fire

Jane Johnson

Illustrated by Adam Stower

SIMON AND SCHUSTER

First published in Great Britain in 2007 by Simon and Schuster UK Ltd
A CBS COMPANY

This paperback edition published in 2008

Simon & Schuster UK Ltd
Africa House
64-78 Kingsway
London WC2B 6AH

A CIP catalogue record for this book
is available from the British Library.

ISBN: 978-1-41692-590-3

1 3 5 7 9 10 8 6 4 2

Typeset in Garamond by M Rules
Printed and bound in Great Britain by
Cox & Wyman Ltd, Reading, Berks

www.simonsays.co.uk

Contents

CHAPTER ONE

Bad News

'No, no, Iggy, you're hopeless! How on Earth are we going to convince the neighbours you're just an ordinary cat if you can't even manage to chase a ball like a normal kitten?'

Ben shook his head at his cat in frustration. Some new people had recently moved in next door, and Iggy had complained that the woman kept giving him funny looks, as if she knew more than she was letting on, so Ben had been trying to teach him how to behave like a 'normal' cat.

Now Iggy – known in another world as Ignatius Sorvo Coromandel, or the Wanderer – sat and watched as Ben got down on his hands and knees and tried unsuccessfully to fish the last ball of screwed-up newspaper out from under the dresser where he'd just hit it. All this paper ball chasing was getting really, really annoying. He'd played along with Ben for a while, catching the ball, juggling it, running around, batting it from paw to paw like some clever furry footballer; but now he was very, very bored. He'd managed to get rid of about a dozen of the irritating newspaper balls now – just out of Ben's reach beneath the carved Welsh dresser with all Mrs Arnold's best china on it – and Ben *still* hadn't worked out that he was doing it on purpose. Which was probably because Iggy had perfected the 'oops-nearly-had-it-that-time, what-a-butterpaws-I-am!' technique of knocking each new ball just a bit too hard so that it shot across the floor and under the dresser.

Games. Humans seemed to love them. He couldn't imagine why. Safely unwatched, the little black-and-brown cat yawned grotesquely, then stuck his tongue out at the boy's back.

'I'm not an ordinary cat,' he rasped, his voice all sandpaper and vinegar. 'And I ain't no kitten.'

Ben pushed himself back upright and stared at his friend crossly with his mismatched eyes, one a sensible hazel-brown, the other an odd and vivid green. 'Well, *I* know that, and *you* know that, but you're supposed to be undercover! Cats with special wayfaring skills from the Secret Country are a bit hard to come by. You might find yourself getting caught and sold off . . . to some horrid petshop or something.'

Iggy sniffed. 'That's not funny, Sonny Jim.'

Ben had, in fact, rescued the little talking cat from Mr Dodd's Pet Emporium, a strange shop full of peculiar and remarkable animals, many of whom had been smuggled in from the Secret Country of Eidolon, where all the magical and extinct creatures live. But that had been before Ben had known anything about the Shadow World; or Mr Dodds (who in the Secret Country walked eight feet tall and had the head of an enormous dog); or that his own mother was Queen of Eidolon, which made *him* a halfling prince – half of this world (since his dad was human) and half of the other: hence his different coloured eyes.

'Look, just one more try, eh?' said Ben, trying to sound reasonable. It was for Iggy's own good, after all.

'There's no more newspaper,' Iggy growled. 'You used it all up.' He gave Ben a smug sort of look: though because of all his fur it was a little hard to judge his expression. Cats use their eyebrows a lot to express themselves, and they have the gift of being able to see exactly how another cat is using its eyebrows, but humans are a bit stupid like that and find it hard to tell just where a cat's eyebrows finish and the rest of its fur begins.

Ben laughed. 'You don't get off that lightly: there's *always* more newspaper. It's under the sink.' And off he went to the kitchen to fetch some.

Iggy watched the boy's retreating back furiously. Under the sink. He might have known. Everything that didn't have a proper place anywhere else in the house got kept under the sink. Sometimes he thought it was where *he* belonged. Iggy sighed and ambled over to gaze boredly out of the window.

Something moved, fast, a movement he caught just out of the corner of his eye. He blinked, then looked again, but all he could see was a falling leaf, a red-and-gold twist of fire, spiralling down out of the old oak tree to join a thousand other autumn leaves on the shaggy grass beneath it. Time was passing, in this world and the Shadow World. Who knew what might be happening in Eidolon now?

He stared at the tree, as if it might give up its secrets to him; but nothing else seemed to be stirring out there.

'Come on, Ig, pay attention!'

Ben held out another ball of newspaper and Iggy sighed. Turning his back on the window, he tried to look alert and interested, but it was pretty hard. The ball went up into the air and he batted at it half-heartedly.

'Oh, Iggy, honestly!'

The thing had got itself caught up on the little cat's claws. Ignatius Sorvo Coromandel shook his paw in irritation, but all that happened was that the paper ball started to unravel itself. He stood on a corner and pulled at it with his teeth. Nothing happened. This was not very dignified, particularly for a cat of his prestigious heritage. His father had climbed the highest mountain in Eidolon, and his mother had been a great explorer; but here was their one and only son, the Wanderer, with a piece of dirty newspaper stuck on his paw. He growled at it; but that did not achieve anything at all. He gave it an extra-hard tug and, with a sudden roar, the paper ripped away from his grasp and lay there on the carpet, defeated at last.

'Grrr!' said Iggy, standing over it. 'Grrrrr!!'

Ben shook his head. His friend had clearly gone quite mad. 'Oh, Iggy, for goodness' sake, do stop it. It's only a bit of paper!'

But the little cat's muzzle was screwed up in an expression of sheer loathing. Ben sighed and bent to pick up the offending scrap.

'Oh no . . .'

There, square in the middle of the newspaper, on what had clearly been the front page of the *Greening & Bixbury Times*, was a grainy black-and-white photograph of someone horribly familiar. And under it ran the story:

LOCAL PRISON BREAK-OUT

'That's the beast who hit me over the head when I came through the wild road!' Iggy growled. 'Grrrrrr!'

The wild roads run between our world and the Secret Country, and only a few folk know where their entrances can be found, or how to travel along them. Ben had travelled the wild road into Eidolon through the great stone in Aldstane Park many times now, more or less safely.

'Yes, that's Awful Uncle Aleister,' Ben concurred, studying the photo with a sinking heart.

'What does it say?' the little cat demanded in his gravelly voice. 'He's still safely in prison, isn't he?' The fur had started to bristle on his neck.

Ben started to read:

'Ardbar Prison was last night the scene of a dramatic jailbreak. At around nine o'clock inmates report hearing a tremendous noise. "We thought it were a gas explosion at first," said Rodney Lightfoot (serving eleven years for cat-burglary), "because the kitchens're in a right dodgy state here." Then someone said, "It must be a bomb!' and then the power failed and all the lights went out. It were mayhem."

Prison Governor Collier takes up the story. "We implemented emergency measures and my officers immediately sealed the perimeter and encouraged the men to return to their rooms, where we locked them in for their own safety. However, when the back-up generator kicked in and the floodlights came on, we found there was a huge hole in the east wing and that one of our inmates was missing."

Prison officer Mr A. Tookey had come off duty earlier in the evening and headed as usual for the Red Lion public house. On returning to Ardbar to retrieve items he had left in the staffroom there, he made a bizarre sighting: "There was smoke and dust everywhere; but out of the middle of it came a massive great ugly woman – at least I think it was a woman – I mean, some of the girls around here are pretty big, but even by local standards she was a real monster, about nine foot tall, with a load of orange and black hair and great big . . . er—"'

'Grizelda!' exclaimed Iggy. 'That's got to be a description of that awful ogress who hangs around with the Dodman!'

Ben nodded grimly. 'It does sound rather like her.' He read on:

"'Anyway this, um, thing came out of there with a portly-looking chap tucked under her arm. Then all the smoke and dust and stuff swirled out on the perimeter field, and I thought it was a helicopter or something. Except it was really quiet, and those choppers generally make quite a racket. But when the smoke cleared I got the shock of my life: it was a bl***y great monster with a pointy head and these huge, batlike wings, just like this picture of a dinosaur I used to have on my bedroom wall when I was a lad! And then the woman-thing sticks the chap on the dinosaur's back and off they all go, up into the sky."

There were no other witnesses to this strange account, and other regulars at the Red Lion report that the officer had "been really hammered" and was prone to exaggeration when "under the influence".

"Last year it was flying saucers," said barmaid Sally Ellery, rolling her eyes.

However, the *Gazette* can report that our reporter spotted some enormous footprints in the grounds outside the walls of the east wing that did not resemble anything he had seen before. We called in dinosaur expert, Professor Hugh Juggley-Twitt, to examine the evidence.

Professor Twitt was initially circumspect in his assessment. "They look rather similar to casts made of footprints found in the Mid West of America which may date back to the late Cretaceous period. But those prints belonged to a species of flying dinosaur called a Pterosaur which has been extinct on this planet for the best part of

150 million years. So, obviously, these can't belong to anything like that! It must be a hoax."

We pressed the Professor for his opinion of what else might have made the marks, but he laughed nervously and said something about his reputation going up in smoke if we quoted him further, and left in a hurry; but not without taking several photographs of the footprints, "for future reference".'

'Wow!' said Ben. 'A dinosaur! Do you really think it is?'

'It's probably all a big mistake.' Iggy wasn't going to be drawn on the subject. 'What does the rest of it say?'

But there was no rest, for here the report was torn.

Ben glared at Iggy accusingly. 'What have you done with it?'

Iggy glared back, then spread his empty paws at Ben. 'I haven't got it! That's the whole of the bit you screwed up to make a stupid ball for me to chase.'

'Well, where can it be, then?'

The little cat shrugged. 'I haven't eaten it, you know.'

Ben stomped off crossly through the door into the kitchen and rootled around under the sink till he found the rest of the newspaper. He brought it back, and got down on his knees beside Iggy. Smoothing out the paper ball, he matched it up to the torn front page, and read on:

'The missing prisoner is Mr Aleister Creepie of King Henry Close, Bixbury, jailed earlier this year for selling dangerous animals. If you see him please do not approach him but contact the police at Bixbury's Incident Room at once.'

Ben and Iggy exchanged anguished glances.
'Oh, Iggy. It's true. Awful Uncle Aleister's escaped!'

CHAPTER TWO

Bag-o'-Bones

At that moment, the front door opened and Ben's father came striding in, followed by a thin, heavily-perfumed woman with long red hair and a lot of teeth and a gangly youth wearing a pair of jeans so ridiculously loose that it looked as if they'd fly off him if he sneezed. Ben wondered if maybe he'd got locked out of his house, trouserless, and had to raid a fat neighbour's washing line. Except that they *were* the neighbours. Ben's family lived next door to them. Ben didn't like them much. There was nothing he could put his finger on, exactly, to explain why. They weren't as nice as old Mr and Mrs Thomas who used to live next door. Something about them just gave him the creeps. He turned around to gauge Iggy's reaction to the visitors, only to find that he had vanished. Or almost. The tip of his tail stuck out from under the sofa, the tuft of black fur a bit of a giveaway against the cream shagpile.

'Ha!'

The scrawny youth, belying his lazy appearance, was on it in a flash, grabbing it with both hands. There was a terrible commotion, involving considerable hissing and spitting (most of it from Ignatius Sorvo Coromandel), then the cat flew out of the living-room window like a giant furry bullet.

The red-haired woman started to sneeze and sneeze.

'Oh dear,' she said at last, clutching Clive Arnold's arm. 'I'm most terribly allergic to cats; and poor Robert is, too.'

'Poor Robert' did not seem to have suffered any particular ill-effects following his set-to with the Wanderer; and it seemed rather perverse to chase cats if they made you ill, but Ben decided not to point this out. Besides which, how could anyone who claimed to be allergic to things wear so much horrible perfume?

Mr Arnold patted her hand solicitously. 'Don't you worry about that, Maggie. I'm sure Iggy will be perfectly happy to live outside.'

Ben fixed his father with an appalled stare. 'What do you mean?' he cried, all thought of Uncle Aleister suddenly flying from his head. 'Iggy can't live in the garden, he lives here!'

'Now, now, Ben,' his father chided. 'We can't have Mrs Bagshott sneezing her head off, can we? It's not very fair on her if she's going to be coming in all the time to look after us.'

A fleeting image of Mrs Bagshott's head flying through the air and out of the same window through which Iggy had exited like a great big firework distracted Ben for a moment; then he said stiffly, and probably rather rudely, 'We don't need looking after. That's what Mum does.'

For a moment Mr Arnold looked a little dazed, as if he had somehow forgotten the very existence of Isadora Arnold.

Mrs Bagshott smiled at Ben. It was not a very nice smile: there were altogether too many teeth involved in it. 'While your poor mother is away, Ben dear. Just to give your father a hand with the cooking and cleaning and all.'

'Ellie can help with that,' Ben said crossly, and rather chauvinistically, though he didn't really mean it: Ellie's idea of cooking was scraping burnt chicken nuggets off baking trays she'd forgotten in the oven; and her room was such a tip it really should have been the subject of one of those television programmes where fierce women came around wearing aprons and rubber gloves and threw all of your most prized possessions away. 'And anyway, Mum'll be home soon.'

Mrs Bagshott leant towards him, so close that he could see what looked like pale blue veins under her gaunt skin and he could smell her breath, which was vile, and her perfume, which was enough to make you gag. 'I wouldn't be too sure of that, young man,' she said softly.

Somewhere upstairs, a baby started to cry.

At the sound, Mrs Bagshott stiffened. Her pale eyes gleamed. Then she turned on her heel and kissed Mr Arnold on the cheek.

'I'll be back soon,' she promised, though to Ben it sounded more like a threat.

'Come along, Robert!' she called imperiously, and turned to leave, almost cannoning into Ben's older sister Ellie, who had just come through the front door.

In what seemed like a rather bizarre dance routine, each of the two stepped first to one side of the narrow hall, then the other, trying to get out of each other's way and failing; then Mrs Bagshott took Ellie by the shoulders and pushed her out of her path before clacking away on her ridiculous heels.

'What was Bag-o'-Bones doing here?' Ellie demanded, dumping her schoolbag on the floor.

'Don't be so rude, Eleanor,' Mr Arnold said sharply. 'Mrs Bagshott is a very kind lady. She's offered to help around the house while Mum's . . . away.'

'What have you told her?' Ben asked fiercely. 'About Mum?'

Mr Arnold looked vague. 'Oh, nothing much. That she's travelling for a bit.'

Ben and Ellie exchanged glances. 'I hope that's all you told her,' Ellie said grimly. 'I don't trust her, and I don't like the way she keeps sniffing around. She's after something.'

'Like a starving old dog,' Ben added helpfully, warming to his sister.

Ellie snorted with laughter. 'And her skinny son looks as if he could do with a bone or two to gnaw on!'

The usually mild-mannered Mr Arnold flushed a dangerous puce colour. 'Stop it! I won't have you speak about Maggie like that. She's . . . she's a lovely lady.'

Lovely? Ben stared at Ellie, who rolled her eyes. 'She's an ugly, smelly old bag,' she said, very quietly. 'She reeks of disgusting perfume and I don't want her in the house when Mum's away.'

There was a moment of terrible stillness, as if something massively heavy hung in the air between them all, ready to smash on the floor.

Clive Arnold's face contorted with anger. 'You'll do as you're told when you're in my house, young lady: I'll have none of your princess antics here!'

At this, Ellie tossed her head. 'I'll not stay where I'm not wanted,' she announced. 'I don't know what's come over you lately, Dad. If you change your mind and want to discuss matters civilly, I shall be in my room.' And with that, she grabbed her schoolbag and flounced off upstairs.

Ben watched her go silently. It wasn't often that he and Ellie agreed, but things had got a bit strange ever since the Bagshotts had moved in next door. Before that, they had had perfectly nice neighbours – an elderly couple called Henry and Maud Thomas who wouldn't say boo to a goose (if there had been any geese wandering around Bixbury to say boo to). They had always been kind to Ben, even when he had burnt their garden shed down, and broken their garage window with his football (he never had been very talented at sport); and he rather missed them. No one seemed to know where the Thomases had gone, and their house had never had a 'For Sale' sign outside; but then, quite suddenly, Bag-o'-Bones and Boneless Bob had appeared. It hadn't taken long for Mrs Bagshott to appear at their front door with a bottle of wine ('I do so believe in the importance of being a *good* neighbour,' she'd wheedled, batting her over-made-up eyelashes at Mr Arnold); and after that she'd been around all the time and the evenings now rang regularly with the sound of her awful, cackling laughter.

There was a movement outside the living-room window, and then a small dark shape appeared on the sill. A bloom appeared on the glass as Iggy pressed his nose against it. He looked very cold.

'Dad,' Ben started, 'now that Mrs Bagshott's gone, can Iggy come inside?'

'I think Maggie's got a very good point, Ben. Animals are dirty creatures and shouldn't be kept in the house. She keeps her house spotless.'

'How do you know? Have you been in it?' This seemed to Ben almost as big a treachery as allowing the horrid woman into their own house.

Mr Arnold shook his head. 'Actually, no, er, not yet: but you can just tell.' He blinked, and ran a hand over his face. He was beginning to look more like himself, less red and strained. He stared around as if it was the first time he had been in his own front room. Then he said, 'Why's Iggy out there on the windowsill looking half-frozen?'

Ben frowned. 'You said he couldn't come in.'

'Did I? I wonder why I said that?'

Ben decided to avoid mentioning Mrs Bagshott. It seemed as if Dad had been having a bit of a problem with his memory ever since she had appeared. 'Can I let him in, then?' he asked.

'Of course.' Mr Arnold looked confused, as if this was a most bizarre question to ask him.

Ben moved towards the living-room door. His foot slipped on the piece of newspaper he had been reading to Iggy. He bent and picked it up. 'Dad—'

'Yes, son?'

'Did you know about Uncle Aleister?'

'Uncle Aleister?' The confused look was back again.

Ben flourished the newspaper article at him. 'He's escaped. From prison.'

Mr Arnold didn't say anything. He just took the torn article from Ben's hands and studied it. 'Ah,' he said at last. 'Oh yes, I remember now.'

'You knew?'

His father nodded minutely.

'And you didn't say anything? You didn't think to warn Mum?'

Mr Arnold set his jaw. A tendon began to twitch in his neck. 'Mag— er, Mrs Bagshott said it would only worry her.'

Ben's skin crawled. What on Earth had his father been discussing with the Bag-o'-Bones? Another thought occurred to him. 'Dad, exactly when was it that Uncle Aleister got out?'

Mr Arnold tried to hide the newspaper from Ben; but the date was clear on the masthead.

'That's over a week ago!' Ben's eyes grew round with alarm and outrage. 'So an ogress blasts her way into the prison on some great big monster the Dodman's managed to get hold of to rescue Mum's horrible brother and you haven't warned her?'

His father looked flustered. Then he said, flatly and without any intonation at all, as if it was something that had been drummed into him by rote, 'It wouldn't do her any good.'

'She's got to know!' Ben shouted wildly.

Upstairs, Baby Alice began to wail even more loudly.

Mr Arnold took his son firmly by the arm and shook him, quite hard. It didn't hurt, as such, but it was so unexpected that Ben cried out. His father had never in all his life laid a finger on him, even under great provocation (like when he'd spent three months making a perfect scale model of a World War II Spitfire and had just finished painting it when Ben had helpfully put it on a radiator to dry, then forgotten about it, so that when he came back it was a nasty gooey heap, and the radiator was ruined).

'Now you've woken your sister! Shame on you. Maggie's quite right: you and Ellie are a pair of troublemakers and need to be taught some lessons! You shall go to your room and have no dinner; and I may think twice about letting you have any breakfast as well.'

And with that, Mr Arnold marched Ben up the stairs, never once easing his vicelike grip on his arm, thrust him into his room, and turned the key in the lock outside.

Ben stared at the keyhole in disbelief. He didn't even know there was a key to his room. In fact, until just now he would have sworn there had been no lock . . .

Something very odd was going on here. Something very odd indeed.

CHAPTER THREE

An Escape

After a while something tapped the window, making Ben jump. But it was only Iggy, teetering uncomfortably on the narrow window ledge. How he'd managed to get up there, Ben couldn't quite imagine. The little black-and-brown cat miaowed piteously and pawed at the glass. When Ben didn't move to open it quickly enough, Iggy ran a single wicked claw down the pane so it made a sound like a wailing banshee. He watched Ben spring into action, and flung himself through the gap, spraying water everywhere.

'Ugh!' said Ben. 'You're as bad as a dog. Perhaps old Maggotty Bagshott is right and it *would* be better if you lived outside.'

Iggy fixed his erstwhile friend with a sardonic amber gaze and began to perform a complicated grooming process. His normally scruffy fur was looking even more unkempt than usual, sticking out in little spikes, as if he'd gone all retro-punk and applied a load of hair-gel to it before coming in.

'You look horrible,' Ben grinned.

'*You'd* look horrible if you'd been shut out in the rain,' the little cat growled. He even sounded like a dog, sometimes.

'Oh.' Ben hadn't noticed it was raining. He stared at the window, where rivulets coursed steadily down the glass. The sun had gone down and now it looked grim and wintry out there. In the Shadow World of Eidolon now it would be summer; and his mother would be in the dappled Wildwood, facing a terrible threat as the Dodman massed his terrifying army.

'Iggy, we must get a message to Mum.'

Iggy looked at him askance. 'You mean you want me to go and find her?' He puffed out his chest proudly. 'After all, I am the Wanderer. That's my job.'

Ben snorted. 'No, that's not what I meant. You're hopeless on your own: you'd get lost. No, we'll both have to go.'

Nowhere in either world was safe any more. There was war in Eidolon; and now even his own home was under threat. He could not explain to himself, let alone anyone else, exactly what sort of threat he thought that Mrs Bagshott and her horrible son might pose, but his instincts told him something needed to be done, and that his mother was probably the only person who could do it. He watched a dribble of rain make its convoluted way down the dark pane to join the pool on the sill below and the world inside his head felt as gloomy as the world outside.

Iggy followed his gaze. 'But I've only just got dry.' Cats hate to be wet.

'All right, then,' said Ben. He pushed himself up off the bed, crossed the room and dragged a waterproof out from his wardrobe. 'I'll go on my own.'

The little cat sighed. 'Hadn't we better tell Eleanor?' he said, playing for time. Even five more minutes in the warm and the dry would help.

'I suppose so.'

In the next-door room, music thumped softly. Ben made a face. His sister was playing a CD by a new band called the Secret Agents, and he didn't much like them. He tapped on the wall.

No response. He tapped harder. 'Ellie!'

He heard the sound of footsteps, then the music went off. He tapped again. 'Ellie, can you hear me?'

Nothing. Then a door opened and the corridor floor creaked. The doorhandle to his room moved; but of course the door didn't open. The handle rattled harder.

'Ben? Why have you locked yourself in?'

Ben rolled his eyes. Honestly, girls could be so stupid some-times. 'I haven't locked myself in. It was Dad.'

'Why?'

'I said we had to warn Mum about Uncle Aleister—'

'What about him?'

'Old Creepie's escaped!'

'Escaped?'

'From prison. Over a week ago. It was in the paper.'

'I didn't see anything in the newspaper about Awful Uncle A.'

'I think Dad hid it. Under the sink.'

There was a pause as Ellie took this in. Then she said, 'Perhaps Bag-o'-Bones did it.'

That wasn't a nice thought.

'Ellie, Iggy and I are going to Eidolon. To find Mum and tell her.'

There was a moment's silence. Then Ellie said, 'I want to come, too.'

'You can't. Who'll look after Baby Alice? You can't leave her to the mercy of old Maggotty.'

'We'll take her with us.'

Ben rubbed his face wearily. This was turning into an expedition, and he didn't want to be its leader. 'She'll cry and alert Dad. And anyway, we can't take Alice into the middle of a war: we have to keep her safe, remember what Mum said? She's Eidolon's last hope.'

An ancient prophecy in the Secret Country told of three children, and everyone seemed to think that he and Ellie and Alice were the ones it referred to:

> *Three children from two worlds*
> *Three to save the day*
> *One with beauty's spell to tame*

One bravely to bring flame
And one with the power to name.

Ellie had already decided that she was the one who held beauty's spell. Ben was not so sure, though Darius the Horse Lord and the minotaur had seemed unusually impressed by her. He didn't even think his sister was particularly pretty, let alone beautiful. As to the other two talents the prophecy referred to, Baby Alice wasn't old enough even to hold a match properly, let alone 'bring flame'; and although she had uttered a few words, the last time had been several weeks ago, in Eidolon. Ever since returning to Bixbury without her mother she had remained steadfastly silent, except to wail like any other baby from time to time. And he didn't have the faintest idea what he had to offer, especially since Mr Jones, his history teacher at school, said he was so forgetful it was a miracle he could remember his own name.

'Anyway,' he reminded Ellie through the keyhole, 'you can't even see properly in Eidolon.'

This was true. Ellie had brown eyes, like their father, and for some reason they didn't work very well in the Shadow World. Ben had one brown eye and one which was bright green, like their mother's. He found that if he looked at things in the Secret Country with his hazel-coloured eye they were a bit blurry, but came into sharp relief if he looked at them with the green eye, or his Eidolon eye, as he liked to think of it. Both of Alice's eyes were a wild, otherworldly green; but who knew what a baby could see?

'I don't want to stay here on my own with old Maggotty Bagshott and Boneless Bob.'

'Ellie, you need to be Mum's spy, her secret agent. How will we know what's going on at home if no one's here to witness it? Anyway, it's pouring with rain. Alice will get sick. And your make-up will be ruined.'

There was a sniff from the other side of the door. 'I suppose you're right,' she said at last.

Ben breathed a huge sigh of relief. It was bad enough having to worry about Iggy getting lost or into trouble, let alone being responsible for his blind-as-a-bat sister and a baby. He bent down and applied his hazel-coloured eye to the key-hole. On the other side, Ellie dabbed at her face with a tissue. 'Anyway,' Ben added with annoying reasonableness, 'if you've got a cold here, you'd be horribly ill in the Secret Country.'

'I haven't got a cold,' Ellie mumbled indistinctly.

She moved out of sight, and seconds later he heard the door to her room close.

'You are an idiot,' Iggy growled softly.

'I am?' Ben thought he'd handled it all rather well.

'She's not got a cold. She's crying. It's a bit much when even a cat from another world can tell the difference and her own brother can't.'

He had a point. Rather than think about it any more, Ben shrugged his way into his waterproof jacket. It was rather noisy: like putting on a bag of crisps. He hoped his father wouldn't hear. Then he pushed open the bedroom window, and got a faceful of rain. 'Ugh.'

'Why don't we wait for it to stop?' Iggy suggested hopefully.

It was tempting, but Ben shook his head. 'Come on, Iggy, don't be a wimp.' And with that, he flung one leg over the sill, then the other, and pulled himself on to the drainpipe.

He had forgotten about the drainpipe. Even on a dry day it could be slippery and awkward: in the rain it was positively treacherous. He missed his footing, grabbed desperately with both hands and slid, at enormous and terrifying speed, down to the ground.

'Ow!'

Iggy, who appeared to have found his own way down not involving drainpipes or falling, butted his head against Ben's knee. 'Are you all right?'

Ben got gingerly to his feet. One of his ankles was stiff and throbbing, but it took his weight. He nodded bravely. 'Let's go.'

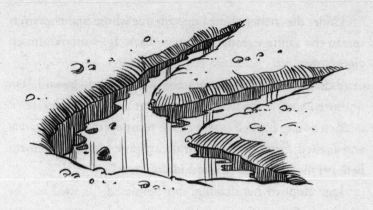

CHAPTER FOUR

The Aldstane

In the daylight, Bixbury was like any other small English town, bustling with traffic, with cars and motorcycles and buses, carrying people to work, to school or to the shops; but in the dark it was a very different sort of place, almost a secret country of its own. Shadows haunted the abandoned gardens, streetlights cast weird shapes into the deserted roads; bushes rustled furtively and rain pattered on to leaves. Once, an owl planed silently overhead, its long white shape like a reverse shadow against the sky. On a neighbouring street, something tipped over a dustbin with a crash. Ben nearly jumped out of his skin, but it was only a fox raiding the bins outside the Ganges Tandoori.

Under the shelter of the huge ash tree whose branches overspread the railings around Aldstane Park, Iggy shook himself vigorously.

'I don't much like your weather in this world,' he said. 'I'm not sure I shall come back when you return.'

Ben swung himself up on to the most overhanging branch and looked down at the little dark figure on the pavement beneath him. 'It must rain in Eidolon, too.'

Iggy stopped his shaking and pondered. 'It used to,' he admitted. 'Before the Queen left. Now all it does is thunder and throw down great hailstones in the winter. I can't remember the last time it rained in the Shadow World in the summer.'

Isadora, Queen of Eidolon, had met Ben's father, Clive Arnold, on a visit to this world fifteen years ago. She had fallen in love, and abandoned her realm for him. She had stayed here long enough to have three children – and to become increasingly ill as the effects of a magicless world took their toll upon her. But the kingdom she had left behind had also suffered. In the time she had been away, others had turned her absence to their advantage: her brother, Aleister, for one; and his associate, the Dodman, who, owning no magic himself, wished to see all things of magic destroyed so that he could take Eidolon for himself. It was why Isadora had eventually returned, to try to put things right. It was why Ben and Iggy had to find her and tell her the odds had changed once more.

Ben's mood was sombre as he tracked across the soaking grass of Aldstane Park with Iggy trooping bravely along at his heels, lifting his feet as high as he could to avoid getting too wet. Into the darkness of the rhododendron bushes they went, and the rain came down harder and harder, hammering against the great glossy leaves like a drum tattoo. The undergrowth got thicker and thicker, and the night darker still, until at last there seemed there was no moon and no starlight at all. Sighing, Ben dug in his pocket and pulled out his torch. The clearing in which the Aldstane was hidden was close now, he knew; but it was always hard to find, even on the brightest day.

He switched on the torch and swung it from side to side, but all he could see were wet bushes and brambles and fallen leaves. He turned around in a circle, then shrugged.

'I must have lost my bearings. What do you reckon, Iggy?'

But Ignatius Sorvo Coromandel had wrinkled his nose up and was looking agitated.

'Come on. You're the Wanderer. You're supposed to be able to navigate and find things.' Though he knew that Iggy rarely lived up to his name. 'Where's the Aldstane, Ig?'

But Iggy's tail was quivering and held low. He looked anxious.

'There's something wrong,' he said quietly, and the growl seemed to have gone right out of him. 'It smells wrong.'

'What do you mean, "wrong"?'

'I can smell Old Creepie. And something else . . .'

The hairs rose on the back of Ben's neck. He swung the torch wildly around, just in case Awful Uncle Aleister was lurking in the vegetation; though it seemed highly unlikely that anyone with any sense would be out in this weather.

'It's okay,' Iggy said, regaining some of his bristle and bluster. 'The scent's not recent.'

'I bet he went back to Eidolon through the wild road here, through the Aldstane,' Ben said, feeling a bit braver now. He stared around, following the torch beam until it came to rest on a hawthorn arch amidst the rhododendrons. 'Through here!' he cried, recognising where he was at last.

He could almost smell the leaf mould that surrounded the stone; he could imagine how its rough crystals would feel beneath his fingertips as he traced the ancient letters carved into its surface.

He ran forward, through the arch, being careful not to trip over the bramble runners that littered the ground; and suddenly came to such a violent halt that Iggy cannoned into the back of his legs and almost knocked him down. It was just as well he didn't, or Ben would have fallen headfirst into a great big hole.

They stood on the edge of the hole, uncomprehending. On the other side of it, the bushes had been flattened and trampled, the earth churned up by something vast and unforgiving.

But of the Aldstane there was no sign.

'Oh, Iggy. It's gone! The Aldstane, it's gone!' Ben's voice rose in despair.

'Yeah,' the little black-and-brown cat drawled, 'I think that's a fair assessment of the situation. Hole in the ground. No stone. Yep. It's gone. Gold star for observation.'

Ben glared at him. 'That's not very helpful.'

He stomped over to where the bushes had been flattened and shone the torch around, examining the damage. The rhododendrons here had been ripped apart, gashed and crushed by something huge. Had the council driven a bulldozer into the park to remove the Aldstane for some strange reason of their own? He cast the torch beam around the churned-up earth and leaf mould, but instead of the trackmarks which might have been made by a JCB, he found . . . something else.

'Look at this!'

Iggy walked slowly around the ragged hole to where Ben stood. He stared at the footprint, wrinkled his nose, then started to groom vigorously. Ben watched him, bemused. Iggy inspected a front paw disconsolately. 'Look at the mud on that,' he muttered, wiggling his dirt-caked toes. 'I'll never be clean again.'

'Oh, Iggy, for heaven's sake! Is that all you can think about? My mum's facing a terrible war, our only way into Eidolon has disappeared and all you do is worry about your fur being a bit grubby?'

'It's not just "grubby",' Iggy sniffed. 'It's wrecked.'

'I don't know how you can tell the difference. You're the colour of mud at the best of times.'

Iggy fixed him with a hard stare which reflected flat and hostile in the yellow light of the torch. 'I didn't sign up for any war.' The fur was bristling all the way down his spine, Ben saw now. He was scared. The instant of fury he had felt at the little cat's apparent indifference to the fate of the world vanished.

'Oh, Ig, I know. This is pretty big stuff.'

'You ain't kidding,' Iggy growled. 'Have you ever seen one of those things? They're . . .' he stretched his paws wide, gave up. 'They're vast.'

'What things?'

Iggy snorted. 'Dinosaurs.' He stared down into the huge impression left in the churned-up ground. It had filled up with muddy water, but even so it was unmistakable.

Ben shivered. 'Dinosaurs?'

He gazed at the footprint. It was the biggest one he had ever seen.

'Dad took me to the Natural History Museum once,' he said at last, remembering the giant skeleton that had taken up most of the main hall there.

'Believe me, you don't want to meet one of *these* on a dark night.' Iggy stared around, as if half-expecting a dinosaur to come creeping silently out of the shadows.

'So you reckon it really *is* a dinosaur print then?' Ben asked, squinting at it.

Iggy regarded him with his head on one side. 'Well, let me think. Just a leetle bit big for a cat – and oh, look –' he stretched out a paw gingerly and held it over the middle of the print, where it looked like a leaf floating on a pond '– only three toes – I've got four, plus this dew-claw . . . Dog? Ner, no nasty little dog claws. Just whopping great big ones. Bear? Jolly big one. Any escapes from the local zoo lately?' And before Ben could say anything, he shook his head. 'Nah, didn't think so. Which leaves us with . . . dinosaur.'

Ben felt a certain strange excitement rising in him. Imagine, a dinosaur in Aldstane Park! Wait till he told Adam. Then he realised that he probably wouldn't be doing anything quite so ordinary as going to school and telling his best friend dinosaur stories. Not for a while, at least.

He thought hard. Someone had removed the Aldstane. Deliberately. With a dinosaur. It must have been Awful Uncle Aleister. And he must have done it to stop anyone getting into the Secret Country. Or getting out. He shivered, thinking of his mother.

They *had* to find the Aldstane. Perhaps if they found it they could put it back. Without thinking this through, Ben strode off into the night, wielding the torch beam like a sword. Iggy watched for a split second, then bounded after him. He certainly didn't want to be left on his own here in the dark.

About thirty feet away they found the Aldstane, lying on its side, in the middle of a bramble thicket. The standing stone, which had once looked both majestic and eerie, with its time-pitted skin, its ancient carvings and brooding presence, now looked defeated and sad. Muddy and manhandled, it lay face-down, so that its runes – which showed, if you looked very carefully, the letters EIDOLON and a smudged chalk arrow pointing down into the earth – were hidden. Now it looked like a discarded lump of old granite, a fallen war memorial, a tumbled giant. Ben felt a hard lump in his throat.

'So now what?' growled Iggy, breaking the mood. 'I don't think we're going to be lifting *that*, do you?'

Ben shook his head miserably. Rain dripped off his hood, his nose and chin. 'So, what do we do now? That's the only way into Eidolon. Well, the only one we know about, anyway.'

Iggy was silent for a moment. Then he sighed. 'Not quite the only one.'

CHAPTER FIVE

Something Wicked

In another world, an immense figure tapped his claws impatiently on the stone battlements of a tall castle, the sound echoing through the night. His long moonshadow jutted horribly across the cobbles and ended in a massive dog's head.

The figure turned to address its companion: smaller, slighter and full of spiky angles.

'I have another task for you.'

'I am not yours to command,' the second figure said sharply. 'Even though you managed, somehow, to summon me again.'

She cocked her head and the moonlight fell across her face,

which was long and thin and as white as bone. The witch, for this is what she was, studied the Dodman silently with her pale, cold eyes, until he felt sure she was trying to put some sort of spell on him. He stepped swiftly back into the shadows, as if by this simple action he could somehow dodge her sorcery.

Maggota Magnifica smiled, showing her teeth, which easily matched those of the dog-headed man for length and sharpness. Then she tossed her long red hair. 'Don't you trust me, Rex?'

It was her special name for him and he hated it. She said it was the old name for a king, and that he should be flattered, but he could always detect an undercurrent of mockery in her voice when she used it. In the Other World there were pet dogs called Rex. He had heard their owners admonishing them outside the petshop: 'Now then, Rex, stop your barking. It's only a cat, and it's in a cage, so what good will barking do you?'

'Of course I trust you,' he said insincerely. 'What information do you have for me from the Other World?'

'The man, Clive Arnold, is of no threat. There's not an iota of magic in him. The older girl is interesting, but her magic is weak. The boy has possibilities . . . Yes, the boy has hidden depths, I think.'

'And the baby?'

Maggota spoke quickly; too quickly. She waved a hand. 'Of no consequence,' she lied. 'It's just a baby.'

'I want all three of them: to make sure.'

'All three? Isn't that just a tad greedy, my Rex?'

'All three!' he barked. 'I don't want that infernal prophecy hanging over my head while I'm trying to take my kingdom.'

She cast a sardonic eye at the dog-headed man. 'Afraid of the prophecy are you? Poor Rex. In that case, I'll do you a deal,' she offered.

'Deal! I don't do "deals"!'

'You will for me, or you will regret it. You shall have the boy and the older girl to do with what you will. But give me the baby.'

He regarded her curiously. 'What would you do with the little squawling thing?' Then he laughed. 'Don't tell me you've become broody in your old age?'

'Old age!' the witch spat. 'I'm in my prime!'

At this, the thing which till then the Dodman had thought to be a rather ugly scarf around the witch's neck raised its head and hissed at him, and he saw that it was in fact a particularly repulsive-looking snake, with an orange frilled crest and red-and-white bands around its body.

'Go back to sleep, Robert, my love.' It regarded her with its beady eyes, flicked out its forked tongue, then tucked its head back in its coils. She smiled affectionately. 'No, no, you are quite right: you are my baby. Do not fear being replaced. A witch is nothing without her familiar.'

The Dodman watched this display with disgust. 'Bring me all three children. I shall kill the boy and the girl. The baby you shall have, when the time is right.'

Maggota's eyes flashed. 'The time shall be my choice. Promise me truly or it shall be the worse for you! I shall bring the sorceresses out of the south and they will make your life a misery such as you could never imagine.' The Dodman opened his mouth to speak, but she sent a little spiral of power through the dark air and he abruptly found he could not open his mouth at all. In fact, he could not move. His jaws worked furiously as he tried to break the spell: to no avail.

She walked around him, shaking her head. 'Rex, Rex, Rex. You forget your origins, but I do not. I know perfectly well why you summoned me to do your dirty work for you. You are a thing with no magic, and a thing with no magic cannot use a magic thing.' She gave him her ghastly grin. 'Isn't that right? Cynthia may have brought you the Book, but you cannot use it. And that is why you have not been able to summon the Arnold children. You are too stupid to hold the power you think you hold, Dog-Head. Now, remember your promise to me. And when you know in your black heart that you will hold to it, you will find the spell releases you.' She leant in towards him, so close that he could see the scraps of meat caught between her fangs, and kissed him on his shaggy brow. 'And remember: I do this because it suits me, and because it amuses me. But if you try me too far, you will regret it deeply.'

She clicked her fingers and sizzled away into the night air, leaving behind her a faint aroma of rotten flesh and perfume.

'Oh, for badness' sake, Father, don't be such a coward! They won't really hurt you: they're ghost-dogs!' shrieked Awful Cousin Cynthia. 'Now, get me out of here!'

'Here' was a small and very sturdily constructed cage which

sat at the foot of the Dodman's throne in the Great Hall of Corbenic Castle, which the dog-headed man had renamed Dodman Castle, in his own honour. Cynthia was crammed into the cage so tightly that her nose stuck out the front and her toes out the back. When the Dodman sat on his throne, he liked to put his feet up on her. Sometimes he rested the Book of Naming on top of the cage and put his feet up on that, too, just to add insult to injury, for Cynthia had brought him the Book in return for a promise: that she should have the kingdom once it was won; after all, she was of the royal blood, being Queen Isadora's niece. She hadn't reckoned, although of course she should have done, on the untrustworthy nature of the dog-headed man, who had no royal blood in him, indeed no magic at all, and not an iota of honour either. He'd crossed his dog-claws behind his back even as he spoke the words of the promise: so even in Eidolon they counted for nothing at all.

And now she had lost her broomstick and her familiar too. Without them she was powerless.

'My dear, I'm perfectly well acquainted with the Gabriel Hounds: I grew up with them, you know. Back, back, you monster!'

This last was addressed to a spectral-looking dog which had slunk up silently, its fangs bared in a ghastly grin. At the sound of the voice, the hound's grin widened. It paused, sniffed, then wrinkled its muzzle and started to growl. It remembered Aleister Creepie of old. Even as a boy he'd been cruel and spiteful: tying their tails together when they slept, and sticking thorns in their noses. Ghost-dogs have long memories, especially for those who have harmed them; like most spirit-creatures they don't really have anything to do in the present other than nurse the grievances of the past, and where Old Creepie was concerned this hound had a list of grievances as long as its leg . . .

'Hurry up! Quickly, he'll be back soon!'

'I'm trying, I'm trying, Cynthia dear. But it's an infernally tricky lock, and these nails aren't well adapted to the problem.' In the Secret Country, Awful Uncle Aleister – who looked like the fat businessman he was in our world – turned into an ugly hunchbacked creature some way between a hobgoblin and a vampire. He had a big, fat, bald head and enormously long, but useless, fingernails. In Eidolon, the outward appearance of folk tends to give away clearly their inner, true nature. Thus it was with Uncle Aleister, and also with the sorceress known as Maggota who, in this world, appeared as maggot-ridden, deathly and grim as her name, whilst in the Other World – our world – she could appear (to Mr Arnold at least) to be a rather attractive redhead with an exotic taste in perfume and a sharp style of dress.

'Now, if we were in the Other World, I'd have you out of here in a trice, believe me!' said Old Creepie, but to be perfectly honest, he wasn't trying particularly hard to release his daughter because he was more afraid of the dog-headed man than he was of the little witch.

'Just like you managed to get yourself out of Ardbar Prison?' Frustration made Cynthia sarcastic.

'Now, now . . . *Ow!*'

The ghost-dog had got hold of him by the seat of his trousers and given him a nasty nip in the process, which is generally known to be a very painful place to be bitten.

Old Creepie shot upright, clutching his bitten bottom, and aimed a kick at the ghost-hound. His foot went right through its ghostly outline, but it yelped and yelped, causing all the other hounds to join in the racket. They milled around, growling and barking and ready to fight anyone or anything that got in their way. Except for the creature which now strode into the hall. Even the sight of the Dodman's face was enough to make them slink away, tails quivering between their haunches, into the safe places out of the reach of his hob-nailed boots.

It had taken the dog-headed man some time to capitulate to the sorceress's demands, and the battlements had been particularly – and possibly magically – cold, given that it was midsummer. When he had finally given in and been able to move, his limbs were almost frozen in place; and his nose was numb. None of this had put him in a pleasant frame of mind (if it could be said that he ever had such a thing). The Dodman had a great distrust of witches and their familiars. He did not understand their use of magic or their strange relationship; but he knew that one depended on the other. Which was why he had captured the creeping, slinking spy known as the Sphynx, which was young Cynthia's familiar, and separated it from its owner at the first available opportunity. Now it was in a safe place. A safer place even than its scrawny, wicked little mistress.

When he was in a foul mood (as he was now) it always

cheered him up to see Cynthia Creepie reduced to the status of caged animal. He remembered how she had brought him the Book of Naming and expected him in return to be her subject when he made her Queen. As if such a spiteful, ugly little wretch could be a Queen! Even though she was his sworn enemy, he had to admit that Isadora had presence and . . . well, nobility. Something about the way she carried herself, even under the duress of war or the burden of illness . . . the carriage of that beautiful head, that slender, but resilient body; the flash of those magnificent green eyes. There had been a time when he had (fool that he was) believed that Isadora cared for him, that he was not just some dog-headed pet for her, nor (in her eyes) a buffoon. He had, in his delusion, even dreamt they would be wed. But then she had not only deserted him, but her entire kingdom, and all for the love of a common man; a pathetic being from the Other World.

He could never forgive her for such an insult: he would show her how wrong and stupid she had been in choosing such a worm over him – the fine, the relentless, the powerful, the merciless Dodman! He would grind her magic to dust. He would destroy her kingdom, its woods and lakes and rolling hills. He would drive its denizens into oblivion. He would stake out her children (ill-begotten, crossworld creatures that they were) on the hard ground before her pleading eyes. His wedding gift to her would be the destruction of her last connection with the Other World: she would witness her three children crushed beneath the vast feet of an army of dinosaurs. A bolt of ice shot through him then: an aftermath of the witch's spell. *All right, all right,* he corrected his imagination; *two of the children I shall stake out for the dinosaurs, and the witch shall have the other.*

And after that? His vision always failed him at this pleasurable point. But he knew he would think of something . . . suitable. And at that moment his eyes settled on the grotesque figure of Old Creepie.

'Ah, Aleister!'

Aleister Creepie darted away from the cage containing his daughter like a beetle disturbed when its stone has been lifted. In the brilliant black sun of the Dodman's gaze, he quailed. 'I was just . . . er . . . checking that she was all right.'

'Of course I'm not all right!' Cynthia's sharp little fists hammered the floor of the cage. Spittle flew from her mouth. 'Let me OUT of here!'

'I see she can still caterwaul, so she must be as well as can be expected,' the Dodman declared smoothly, regarding his captive with something bordering on affection. Really, he was quite getting used to her there, below his throne. She was almost a piece of the furniture now.

He strode to Old Creepie's side and put a long, dog-clawed arm around his hunched black shoulders.

'Aleister, my dear, bad friend. It's so good to see you back where you belong again.'

'And not before time!' Aleister huffed. He couldn't help himself, however scared he was of his dog-headed associate. 'I mean, dear boy, it was your fault I was in that place. You might have tried a little harder, a little sooner, to rescue me. You've no idea what it's like, in prison. It's . . . well, the food was quite revolting. And then – why – it's been over a week since Grizelda got me out, and not a word from you.'

'Ah, yes, where is Grizelda? I have not seen her since I sent her for you.'

Aleister looked abashed. 'I . . . er . . .'

'What? Out with it!'

Old Creepie became flustered. He wrung his hands, but no words came out. 'I . . . ah . . .'

'For badness' sake, Creepie: has the cat got your tongue?' The Dodman thrust his unpleasant muzzle at Aleister Creepie. 'Because if you don't tell me at once, I can tell you the dog will have it!'

'You did tell me to cover my trail,' Aleister started with a whine.

'What have you done? Where is Grizelda? Where is my dinosaur?'

'To make sure we weren't followed, I had them pull out the Aldstane.'

'Good thinking.' The Dodman was surprised at this level of foresight from Old Creepie. 'Excellent. What did you do with it? Dragged it down after you? That must have made quite a crater when it came through the wild road. Hah! Probably flattened a few trees and some fairies in the process. I'd have liked to see that!'

'Ah, well . . .' Aleister was shifting awkwardly from foot to foot now, as if he wanted to go to the toilet.

'Spit it out!'

'I . . . ah . . . left them to do that while I got into the wild road. You know, authorities probably hot on my trail and all that . . .'

'You left them?'

Aleister nodded.

'In the Other World?'

A dark patch appeared on Old Creepie's trousers. 'Ah . . . yes.'

'YOU LEFT MY DINOSAUR ON THE OTHER SIDE?' the Dodman roared.

Aleister Creepie covered his huge bald head with his hands. 'And Grizelda, too. Don't hit me, don't hit me,' he begged.

The Dodman stared at him contemptuously. 'Well that's just wonderful. I tell you to cover your tracks and you go and leave a thumping great dinosaur and an ogress behind in a world in which neither belong. Very nifty!' He struck his forehead. 'With enough friends like you I could defeat myself in no time.'

Old Creepie frowned, confused by this tortured logic. 'I'm sorry,' he wheedled at last. 'I was trying to do the best thing.' He brightened. 'But at least the way between worlds is closed now. Isadora's right where you want her.'

The Dodman shook his head piteously. 'Really, Aleister, for someone with the royal blood of Eidolon running through his veins, you're remarkably ignorant about your own domain. There are a hundred wild roads; more. I dare say they'll find their own way back at last. There's no great hurry now: your little daughter has been most helpful in supplying me with many more such beasts.'

The Dodman bent down and waggled his fingers in front of his captive. Cynthia fixed him with her pale, gooseberry-green eyes. If looks could kill, it really wouldn't have done the trick, though the Dodman might have suffered a small pain in his forehead. She was weak from fury, and lack of chocolate.

'Some father you are!' the little witch wailed. 'How can you let him treat me like this? Get me out of here!'

Aleister Creepie coughed embarrassedly. 'I must say, Dodman, old chap, it's really not on to put poor little Cynthia in a cage like this, you know. I'm sure she annoyed you in some way: badness knows she can be most annoying sometimes –'

'Thank you, Daddy!' Cynthia hissed furiously.

'– but I'm sure she's sorry for whatever she said or did now that she's had time for reflection. Won't you let her out now, eh?'

'Oh, I don't think she's nearly sorry enough yet,' the Dodman said softly. 'Are you, my dear?'

CHAPTER SIX

In the Wildwood

'Cernunnos!'

A young centaur came cantering through the close-packed birch trunks, twisting neatly this way and that to avoid their barred silvery trunks. Golden light filtering down through the delicate leaves dappled his long dark hair and brown shoulders.

At the sound of his call, Cernunnos, Lord of the Wildwood, raised his antlered head from the contemplation of an elegantly white-flowered plant growing tall in the shade there.

'Darius, it's good to see you.' He waited for the centaur to come to a halt beside him. 'Look,' he said, 'wood asphodel. I haven't seen that bloom here for the best part of fifteen years.'

Darius regarded the flower curiously. 'Really?'

'It grows only where magic is strong and the air is pure. It is a plant peculiarly sensitive to magic.'

'The Queen was here, yesterday. She came for a walk, and she seemed most distracted. I am sure it wasn't in flower then.'

'How interesting.' A complex expression crossed Cernunnos's face. 'I wonder . . .' He looked deep in thought, his brows knitted together.

'My lord?' The centaur interrupted his reverie. 'I came to find you because I am worried about her. She is exhausting herself, and I cannot stop her. We cannot let her harm herself.'

'What is she doing?'

The centaur shook his head. 'I am not sure, my lord. She is doing nothing . . . *physical*; she sits still, but the muscles in her face twitch as if she is under great stress. She will say nothing to me. Perhaps she will tell you.'

They found Queen Isadora sitting on a fallen log in a sunny clearing. Her head was in her hands, but at the sound of their arrival she raised her face to them. She was paler than usual and blue smudges pooled beneath her vivid green eyes.

Behind her, in the shadows, lurked something vast. If it had stood up, it would have been as tall as the Dodman, with the head of a bull. At the moment it sat quietly resting its forearms on its knees, but it looked as if it might spring into action at any moment, and that if it did, the action would be swift and violent.

Cernunnos nodded to the minotaur (for that was what it was) then dropped to one knee beside her and took her hands in his, where they vanished inside his huge, woody grasp. 'My lady? You look tired. What have you been doing?'

Isadora smiled weakly. 'Not enough. Never enough. But perhaps they are safe now.'

Over her head, the Lord of the Wildwood and the centaur exchanged anxious glances.

'Who will be safe now, my lady?'

She smiled then, as if he had asked the most ridiculous question in the world. 'Why, my children,' she said softly. 'Ellie and Ben and Alice.'

'But the three are in the Other World,' Darius reminded her gently. 'They are safe there.'

She gave a small, bitter laugh. 'They should have been safe there, indeed, were it not for my own stupidity.'

'What do you mean, my Queen?'

The face she turned to him was ravaged. 'The Book,' she whispered.

'The Book of Naming?'

She nodded. 'It's lost.' She had been putting off this evil moment for as long as she could; she could put it off no longer.

'Lost?' Cernunnos thundered. 'What do you *mean* "lost"?'

'I hid it before the battle. You will recall how we had already decided we would not use it to Name my creatures and compel them to join us.'

The Lord of the Wildwood merely gave a curt nod to this: for he had agreed no such thing, it had been the Queen's

46

decree and he still could not find it in him to agree with her decision.

'Well, I hid it away, and when we got back to the Wildwood after our small victory all I could think of was Ben and Ellie, and making sure they got home safely to the Other World, so that I could concentrate on the hard decisions we must take in the war ahead of us.' She hung her head. 'I gave no thought to the Book for many days after that: there seemed so many other things to do – wounded creatures to attend to, reports to be had from our friends here and those who crossed the wild roads; and when at last I went to consult it, it was not where I had left it. Then I panicked, and thought I must have forgotten where I had put it, that I must have hidden it somewhere else. My memory is not all it was, I'm afraid. And so I searched, secretly, for I am ashamed to say I was almost more afraid of your reaction to the fact that I had lost the Book than I was for the consequences of losing it. And of course, I did not find it, though I looked everywhere.'

She sighed deeply.

'So then I sent out the cats to search for it; and I am afraid that yesterday one of them – my faithful friend Jacaranda – came to me with news of its whereabouts.'

The Lord of the Wildwood kept his voice low, but his eyes were stormy. 'Tell me, my lady: what did the old white cat report?'

'Cynthia took it. Cynthia Creepie. When she told me this I must admit I felt a certain relief, for although my niece is not what I would call a pleasant child, I do not think she is yet completely wicked. I hoped I might go to her and persuade her to return it, whatever her reasons for stealing it. But I fear that what Jacaranda told me next destroyed even that small hope.' She took a deep breath, then carried on swiftly, to get the awful thing said. 'I'm afraid she has given it to the Dodman.'

There was a shocked silence. Then Cernunnos threw back his head and gave a wild cry. It was a bizarre noise which rattled the very leaves on the branches overhead, and more of a deep-throated bellow than the high-pitched deer-shriek you might expect from a stag-headed man. The minotaur leapt to his feet as if he thought the Lord of the Wildwood might do harm to the Queen. Isadora quailed away, her palms pressed against her mouth. The centaur put an arm out to steady her; but even his sun-warmed face was pale.

Then Isadora seemed to gather herself. She stood straighter: the worst was surely over now.

'What's done is done,' she said at last. 'What remains to us now is to decide what to do about it.'

Cernunnos sat down heavily, as if his legs would not support him any more. His great antlers lowered till they almost touched the ground. He did not speak: could not trust himself to say anything that was not angry and could not be forgiven.

The minotaur watched him, his black eyes narrowed.

Eventually, it was the centaur who said, 'We must save our people. The Dodman will summon dragons and dinosaurs and all sorts of monsters to swell his vile army. We do not stand a chance. The small folk must find refuge; the rest of us must disperse far and wide. If we stay together in the Wildwood all we will do is provide him with a fine target. He will use the dragons to torch every tree that stands, and the dinosaurs to crush and rend everything that moves. Nothing can survive dragon fire or the teeth and claws of the tyrannosaur.'

At last Cernunnos raised his head. 'Might you now tell me, madam, what it is that you have been doing? I know that some of your magic has returned: I saw the asphodels where you walked yesterday.'

'I sent fading spells,' the Queen said quietly.

A spark of hope dawned in his bleak gaze. He stood up. 'Can you obliterate the entire Book?' he asked. 'It were better it were destroyed than be in our enemy's hands.'

She shook her head. 'It has taken a full day and almost all the strength I have to fade a single page.'

'And which page was that, my lady?'

She looked him straight in the eye, though his fierce antlered head towered above her. 'The page which lists the true names of my children.'

His great, woody hands balled into fists, but she stood her ground. 'That was a selfish act.'

The minotaur stepped swiftly between them. 'It was the act of a mother,' he said sharply. 'How can you blame her for it?'

Isadora turned her limpid green gaze upon the bull-headed man. 'It was the act of a mother *and* a Queen.' She turned back to the Lord of the Wildwood. 'Remember the prophecy,' she reminded him. 'It is the three who will save Eidolon. "Three children from two worlds." They are the future of our country, and so they must be saved.'

Cernunnos snorted derisively. 'The three! A silly, half-blind girl, a young lad and a tiny baby. Not one of them old enough or strong enough to bear arms. Not one of them possessed of true magic. What use are three halfling children to me? I need greater creatures than such at my command if we have any chance against the Dodman. A foolish rhyme is all that so-called prophecy ever was, and I will not place my faith in it, or in you, any longer.'

Then he gave her the curtest of nods, turned on his hoof and hurled himself off into the Wildwood.

The Queen stared at his retreating figure with dismay.

'Will he come back, do you think?' she asked. The way Cernunnos had spoken, as if he was in truth the ruler of Eidolon and not she, left her in little doubt of the answer.

Darius and the minotaur looked at one another in shock. Then the centaur shook his head. 'Cernunnos has been teetering on the brink of this decision for a long time, my Queen. He ruled the Wildwood during your absence: he finds it hard to share his power, and now he fears he has lost it all.'

'And will you leave me, too: you, minotaur, and you, Darius?'

The minotaur snorted. 'Never!'

Darius bowed his head. 'My Queen, no matter how bleak things may get, I shall not leave your side.'

'Then that is something. We had better follow and give comfort to those who have stayed behind or are now lost in confusion. And when we have gathered those who remain faithful, we must leave the Wildwood. By dead of night, tonight.'

CHAPTER SEVEN

The Minstrels

The rain was coming down hard now and Ben's waterproof was not living up to its name. He could feel a chill soaking into the shoulders of his jumper; cold water running down his back. They had been walking for what seemed like hours: at first through the suburban roads of Bixbury, where the streetlights gave the rain a watery orange glow so that it looked as if Lucozade was falling on to the wet cars and filling up the wide puddles; then the streetlights became fewer and farther between, until at last they vanished altogether. Now, there were no houses, no cars and nothing but hedges and trees that loomed up like giants, and it was darker than anywhere he had ever been before. He was (though he would not admit it to anyone, and certainly not to Ignatius Sorvo Coromandel) just a little bit afraid.

'Where are we going, exactly, Iggy?' he said, in as steady a fashion as he could manage, so as not to give the little cat the idea he might not entirely trust his wayfinding skills. Which, of course, he didn't. Iggy could get lost between the garden shed and the front gate: Ben was not at all confident that his friend had inherited any of his parents' expert explorer genes. Perhaps the Wanderer was really only an ironic sort of nickname for someone who got lost all the time.

The little cat didn't say anything; but he looked very purposeful, striding ahead of Ben with his tail in the air. He was as thin as a rat, his fur plastered to his skin, a state Ben knew he hated; but he didn't complain, which Ben thought was very stoic of him. He could feel runnels of rainwater trickling into the waistband of his jeans now, which was particularly horrible, and he definitely felt the urge to whinge himself.

Going home was becoming a much more attractive prospect than walking around in the cold night rain, but he knew it wasn't really an option. He had to find Mum and tell her what he had found out – about Uncle Aleister, the dinosaur, and the Aldstane. And, a little voice in the back of his head added, about Mrs Bagshott, too. The way she kept turning up. The fact that Dad seemed to like her visiting; that he talked to her about things he should not. The fact that he couldn't seem to see she was an ugly old hag. He hoped Ellie would be able to cope with her while he was gone.

If he ever got back to Eidolon again.

'Ig, where are we going?' he said again, a little louder and more firmly this time.

The little cat turned its reflective amber eyes upon him. 'To the Minstrels,' he said.

The Minstrels. A little shiver ran down Ben's spine that had nothing to do with the chilly rain. He had visited the Minstrels with his parents on his ninth birthday. Dad had driven into the countryside outside Bixbury in their old Morris Minor; Mum had packed a picnic. Ellie was around at Awful Cousin Cynthia's, playing at dressing up, since they were still best friends then, before Ellie had discovered where all the pretty feathers and bits of fur they used in their costumes came from (all the poor magical creatures Uncle Aleister had been shipping out of the Secret Country with the aid of the Dodman). And it was the year before Alice had been born, so it was just Ben and his parents and a wide summer sky at the start of the school holidays, and he had been very excited to have them all to himself, even though Mum hadn't been very well. She'd been complaining of headaches and not having any energy, and when it rained her joints pained her. Dad told him she was 'under the weather', which had confused Ben mightily, since wasn't everyone (who wasn't in a plane, or a spaceship, or a hot air balloon) under the weather? But he had only been young then, just turned nine. It seemed a lifetime ago: a time when he had thought that Mum's illness was just an ordinary sort of illness and that she would soon get well again; a time before he had discovered the existence of Eidolon; a time before he had got to know a talking cat, and a selkie called Silver; a time before he had seen real-life monsters, a war, or anyone die right in front of his eyes.

He hadn't really had any idea what the Minstrels were then: he'd thought vaguely when his parents suggested the outing that they might be going to a castle where people were all dressed up in medieval costumes playing instruments – because that's what minstrels were, wandering musicians out of history books – and he had been quite looking forward to seeing some for himself; especially if one of them had a sword, and there might be a fight. So when they had parked in a lay-by in a country lane and climbed over a stile into a field where there were nothing but a few grim-looking grey stones in a circle, he had been rather disappointed.

They had had their picnic sitting in the middle of the stones, and his parents had given him his birthday presents there: a new cricket bat signed by some of the country's best players, and an anthology of poetry. He had hit some pebbles all around the field for a while with the bat, but he hadn't been very interested in the poetry book, even though it had a funny picture on the cover. And then his mother had walked around the circle, touching each stone she passed. 'Come here,' she had called to Ben and he had left the grasshopper he had caught and run over to where she stood with her hands pressed up against the lichen-patched granite. 'Touch this and tell me what you feel.'

And he had put his hands where hers had been, and nearly been knocked off his feet by a sudden surge of electricity. Little hairs had stood on end all down his spine.

His mother had smiled and taken his hand away. Then she dropped him one of her long, slow winks. 'That's what they call a piezoelectric shock,' she said softly to him. 'They say the crystals in the rock can conduct a current. But I know where that energy really comes from.'

And for a few weeks after that she had seemed a lot more like herself: more radiant, more alive, and complaining less of aches and pains. But Ben had been scared by the stone he had touched. It had given him nightmares for months. The idea of coming back to that place in the dead of night was not a good one. Perhaps they should wait until it was light?

But just as he opened his mouth to suggest this to Iggy, the little cat became suddenly animated, shook himself vigorously and vanished into the hedge to their left.

'Iggy?'

But he didn't reappear again, and there was nothing for it but to follow. As he did so, the rain stopped quite abruptly and the moon slid out from her cover of cloud and shone a path across the road for him. And all at once, there was the lay-by, and there was the stile, silvery-grey in the moonlight, just waiting for him to climb over it. So he did.

There, in front of him was an ancient circle: nine standing stones, none as large as the Aldstane, but in a perfect ring, as if frozen in the middle of a dance. Perhaps, he thought, they *had* been minstrels playing a jig, and someone had cast a spell on them, turning them to granite. Perhaps they were in there still, trapped and aware, but unable to do anything about their predicament.

In the middle of the stone circle stood Ignatius Sorvo Coromandel; and now he did not look like the rain-soaked, rat-like creature who had run along the road ahead of Ben. Now he looked tall and proud, and his tail was a flag. His ears were pricked and his eyes were as large and round as saucers in the moonlight. He looked the very icon of a cat; proud and solitary.

When Ben got within earshot, Iggy said triumphantly, 'You see? I did it! I found them!' And he rubbed his head excitedly against Ben's leg. His purr rumbled in the night. 'I could feel the stones,' he said, in awe. 'They *called* to me.'

Ben had no idea what that meant, but he stroked Iggy's wet little head anyway. 'Well done, Ig. You really are the Wanderer. You managed to navigate your way here without a single visible star in the sky.'

Iggy puffed out his chest. 'Ain't I the cat's whiskers?' he chuckled. And then, finding this suddenly excruciatingly funny, he took to his feet and hurled himself around and around the stones, a little furry ball of energy.

Ben got dizzy just watching him. Suddenly he said, 'You're running widdershins. Shouldn't you be running around the circle in the other direction? Clockwise, I mean.'

Iggy came to an abrupt halt and stared at him, whiskers bristling. 'What?'

Ben felt uncomfortable. He wasn't quite sure why he'd said that: the word 'widdershins' had just come into his head. 'It's something to do with bad luck, and witches,' he said, rather lamely.

'We don't have clocks in Eidolon,' Iggy replied, giving Ben

a look. Then he backed away from the stones as if they might bite him.

'So now what do we do?' Ben asked, to break the awkward silence.

The little cat shrugged. 'I don't know. One of them must lead into Eidolon. But which one?'

'We could try them one at a time,' Ben suggested, and took a step forward.

'No!' Iggy's claws dug sharply into his leg.

'Ow!'

'Remember what I told you about the wild roads,' the little cat said severely. 'They run between the two worlds, this world and Eidolon, and some are new and some are as old as time itself. Some will take you to the Secret Country and set you down in a pleasant woodland glade. But nowadays some will drop you into a bottomless ocean or the depths of a volcano; and some will whirl you into Eidolon's history, centuries past. It depends how frequently they've been used, and by whom. Cats used to keep them all open and safe; but there are not as many of us in the Shadow World as there once were.'

Ben's heart sank. 'Then how are we going to get into Eidolon?'

Iggy looked away. 'I don't know.'

'But I thought you knew! You brought us here, after all!'

'I know only that there is supposed to be a wild road amongst the Minstrels by which the Secret Country can be gained. But I don't know which of the nine is the right one. I was hoping, maybe . . .' He paused.

'Maybe what?'

'Maybe you'd know.'

Ben laughed bitterly. 'Not much chance of that!'

'But you're her son, a Prince of Eidolon. Whereas I am only the Wanderer. That must mean something.'

So far in his adventures between two worlds, Ben thought, that fact hadn't seemed to make much difference. 'Couldn't you, you know, sniff out the right one? Cats have a good sense of smell, or so I'm told.'

'What did you *think* I was doing when I ran around the circle? One thing I can tell you, though. There's a familiar smell here. Someone I know has visited the stones, and recently. I just can't quite put my paw on who it is.'

Ben frowned. 'Not Uncle Aleister? Perhaps he came back to Eidolon from here once he'd pulled up the Aldstane.'

Iggy paced over to the stones and walked about a bit, inhaling deeply. 'No,' he said at last, 'though there is a faint whiff of something I can't quite identify. But the most recent smell is female. No doubt about it.'

'Grizelda?'

Iggy snorted. 'You think I don't know the smell of an ogre when I find one? Most insulting. I can see you have no faith in my professional abilities at all.'

'Sorry, Ig. I didn't mean it like that.'

Silence fell, and clouds drifted across the moon. Ben stared gloomily at the stones. They were all different shapes and sizes. None of them looked like the Aldstane, though that might not be much of a clue.

In the distant woods an owl hooted, and then there came a tiny high-pitched shriek. Iggy's ears pricked up, all his ancient cat hunting instincts alert. Someone had caught a small rodent. Ben, having (for the most part) human ears, did not hear the dying vole; but the sound of the owl dislodged something in his memory.

'The Owl and the Pussycat!' he yelled suddenly.

Ignatius Sorvo Coromandel stared at him. 'I do hope that's not the beginning of a terrible joke,' he said, whiskers bristling.

Ben laughed aloud and started to run across the field. 'It's a poem!' he cried joyously, and now Iggy knew his friend must be going quite mad, because poetry had never been something in which Ben had ever shown the slightest interest.

Ben had come to a standstill in front of one of the larger stones and was gazing at it intently. Iggy slunk across through the wet grass.

'It's this one. I'm sure of it.'

'Oh, just like that you think you can tell the difference?'

'Mum was touching this stone and she called to me, and when I touched it it gave me such a shock that I dropped the book I was holding and it fell open on "The Owl and the Pussycat". Just there.' Ben pointed to a patch of bare earth on the other side of the stone. 'Funny what you remember.'

'You didn't tell me you'd been here before,' Iggy said in an accusatory tone. 'You didn't really need me at all.' And his tail drooped sadly.

'Oh, Ig, I always need you. I couldn't have found it in the

dark. And I wouldn't have wanted to come on my own.' He picked up the little cat. 'Shall we try it?'

The amber eyes regarded him steadily. 'Are you absolutely sure?'

Ben reached a hand out towards the stone, not quite touching it. Slowly, the hairs on the back of his neck started to rise, but he wasn't sure whether it was because he was afraid, or because it was the stone that had caused the reaction.

'Hold tight, Iggy,' he said, and his voice was shaking. 'Here we go.'

CHAPTER EIGHT
A Wild Road

Cradling Iggy against his chest, Ben stepped *into* the stone and suddenly there was no night or moon or wet field, but a blur of shapes, a flicker of light and shade. He would never get used to the sensation of being caught up in the power of a wild road. It was sort of exhilarating, and sort of scary, like a fairground ride that might run out of control. The first time he had stepped into the Aldstane he had not known what to expect, and it had all been over so quickly he hadn't had much chance to think about it. After that when he had entered the wild road he had experienced a second of dread and then the step into the void, but at least he had known where he would end up. This time was different.

Colours rushed at him. Shades of grey – the night colours of Bixbury's countryside – gave way first to golds and reds, then an astonishing blast of blue, as if an ocean were flashing past; until at last the hues paled and ran together in an extraordinary whirl. The wind of the wild road whipped at his face as if it would rip his eyelids off. It battered him so hard that his waterproof flapped as loudly as a ship's sail in a storm. He tumbled over and over, his feet kicking out into space. What had happened to the little cat he did not know: his arms had been thrown wide by the power of the wind, ripping Iggy from his grasp. There was nothing Ben could do about it. He cried out, but the very sound was torn away from him, and he was suddenly very frightened indeed.

To fall through a wild road between worlds was scary enough even when you knew where you were likely to end up, and that a friend was with you. But to fall alone into the unknown was terrifying.

And then, with sudden brutal force, he hit something very solid and everything went quiet.

Ben lay there stunned for several moments, not sure whether or not he was alive or just dreaming that he was. He moved his limbs carefully, but nothing seemed to be broken. Then he sat up and looked to see where he'd landed.

It was like nowhere he had ever seen in his life. He was on a wide, white beach, in the middle of a circle just like the Minstrels in his own world. Except that this was not a stone circle but one made of wood: ancient, black, seeping wood, stark against the white sand. On one side of the circle lay an expanse of pale blue sea. When he turned around all he could see was a vast stretch of sandy dunes sown with strange-looking plants and a grass which was so grey it was almost as white as the sand. There was no strong colour anywhere except for the wooden circle. It was eerie and serene: like finding yourself in a faded photograph.

Ben got to his feet and shaded his eyes, for the lightness of everything was blazing. He closed his right eye, and at once spotted something he had not seen the first time of looking. A tiny weatherbeaten shack amongst the dunes, surrounded by a broken fence and rambling weeds. The upturned hull of a rowing boat lay in what had once been a garden. And on it sat a small dark figure.

It was Ignatius Sorvo Coromandel.

'Iggy!'

Ben had never been so glad in all his life to see his friend. He started running up the beach, his feet slipping and sliding in the shifting sand. He had no idea where in the two worlds he was; all he knew was that wherever he was would be a better place with a cat by his side.

'Ssh!' The little cat jumped down off the boat and ran to him, his paws barely making an indentation in the sand. 'There's someone in there.' He indicated the shack. 'I saw a face at the window.'

'Perhaps we should just leave,' Ben suggested nervously.

'I thought,' Iggy said, 'that whoever it was looked more frightened of me than I was of it.'

'I'm not surprised. It's a bit weird here.'

'Stay here. I'll go and have another look.' Iggy ran back, wriggled through the broken-down fence, jumped up on to the boat and then on to the narrow windowsill. He pressed his nose against the glass, then emitted a wail and promptly fell off.

'What? What is it?'

Ben ran into the remains of the little garden. Vines, columbines and some other plant with long, spidery runners had taken possession of it now and seemed to be slowly dragging everything in it down into the sand. Ben had the unpleasant thought that he might be next if he stayed there too long.

'Them. It's them,' Iggy whispered, hiding behind Ben's legs. His ears were flat against his skull. 'Two . . . people. Old people.'

'Not monsters of any sort? They haven't got – well, wings or horns or . . . big teeth or anything?'

'They look just like people from your world. You know . . . ordinary.'

Trying to appear braver than he felt, Ben walked up to the house, trying not to step on too many of the spidery plants. He looked in at the darkened window, his heart hammering.

A pair of watery grey eyes peered back at him. They blinked. Then another face appeared.

'Oh, my!' Ben exclaimed.

Without another thought, he ran to the front door. It opened with a creak, but easily. From the gloom inside two elderly people gazed back at him, holding hands as if in fear for their lives.

'Mr and Mrs Thomas!'

'Maud, it's . . . I can hardly believe it . . . it's young Benjamin Arnold, from next door.'

'Ben?' The voice was quavery. 'That nice little boy? Who broke our garage window with his football?'

'Yes, dear. I'm sure he didn't mean to.'

'I didn't—' Ben started.

'I saw you!'

'I mean, I didn't mean to.'

'That's all in the past, dear. He helped us mend it. And brought you some flowers.'

The old woman chuckled. 'That he picked from our garden.'

Ben felt himself redden. He hadn't realised she'd seen that. It had seemed like a nice idea at the time.

'What's he doing here?' Maud asked.

'I don't know. What are you doing here, Ben? And, um, this may sound like an odd sort of question, but, um, exactly where *is* "here"?'

Ben didn't really know what to say. 'I'm not sure, Mr Thomas. It's certainly not Bixbury.' He gave a little laugh. 'How did you get here?'

The old couple exchanged a glance. 'It's a bit hard to explain,' Henry Thomas started.

'Nonsense,' said his wife. 'It was that awful woman.'

'Mrs Bagshott?' Ben asked with a sudden flare of instinct.

Maud Thomas regarded him suspiciously. 'You know her, then?'

'She's the one who bought your house, isn't she? She keeps coming round to see Dad.'

'Bought our house! Hah! That's what she's been saying, is it? Despicable old witch.'

Something fell like ice into the bottom of Ben's stomach. The Bag-o'-Bones was a witch. A *real* witch. Of course she was. How could he have been so stupid? And he had left Ellie and Alice to her mercies.

'Now, now, dear, be reasonable,' said Mr Thomas. 'You don't *know* she's a witch.'

His wife turned a furious gaze upon him. 'Of course she's a witch! Do you think anything less than magic would have got me out of that house?' Her face started to crumple. 'I was born in that house. I've lived there all my life. And I want to go home.' She began to sob.

Henry Thomas took her in his arms. 'There, there, dear. Of course you shall go home.' He looked at Ben despairingly. 'Ben's here to take us home, aren't you, Ben?'

Ben hesitated. What could he say? If he started to explain the situation, it would take as long as getting them back through the wild road. And he could hardly leave them here. All he had to do was work out which of the nine stumps in the wooden henge on the beach was the one that led back to Bixbury. After that, they would have to fend for themselves, he reckoned, while he went in search of his mother. (Though what they were going to do about the Bag-o'-Bones was another matter.)

'Yes, of course,' he said, trying not to worry about it all at once. 'Let's get out of here first of all.'

Just as he finished saying 'all', the door slammed shut behind him. A freak gust of wind. Surely.

He caught hold of the doorhandle and twisted it. Nothing. He pulled; but it was stuck tight. Alarmed now, Ben ran to the window. And rather wished he hadn't, for it was the stuff of nightmares.

The entire garden was writhing. All over it, the spidery plants were on the move, snaking across the ground, binding the door and window shut.

'Oh dear,' said Mr Thomas over his shoulder. 'That's what happened to us, too.'

'The plants must have retreated in order to let you in,' said Mrs Thomas.

'Great,' said Ben, unable to stop himself. 'You might have told me.'

He looked desperately for the little cat, who had been right behind him.

'Iggy!'

There was no sign of him, and no one responded to his cry. Ben stared and stared through a window crowded with jostling vines. For one, long, horrible moment, Ben thought he detected a scrap of black-and-brown fur moving beneath a mound of twisting runners in the middle of the garden, but it turned out to be only a dead leaf. And then the vines had covered the glass, and he could see nothing at all, inside or out.

Behind him there was a click, then a bloom of light.

'Henry's always on at me to give up,' said Maud Thomas, holding up a cigarette lighter, 'but there are times I'm jolly glad

I didn't. Being trapped here is bad enough; but being here in the dark . . .' She shuddered. Bustling about the tiny room, she managed to find a candle in an ornate golden holder. It seemed an incongruously pretty thing to be lying around in such a hovel, but Ben took it from her gratefully. He walked around the shack, peering at the walls in the vain hope of finding a way out.

Mr Thomas laughed bitterly. 'No chance of that, I fear,' he said. 'We've been here, well, I don't know how long . . .'

'Ages,' said Mrs Thomas. 'Weeks, perhaps.'

Ben looked aghast. 'Weeks?' he echoed. 'But how have you survived? I mean, there's nothing here, nothing to eat, no water. Nothing.'

'It's very odd,' said Mr Thomas, 'but you know, we just haven't been hungry at all.'

'At first I thought that was just because we were too frightened to want to do anything as ordinary as eat; but it's more than that,' said his wife. 'Magic, Henry. It must be: I know you say you don't believe in it, but what other explanation can there be?'

'I've been giving it a great deal of thought,' Mr Thomas said, in what was meant to sound a scientific, rational kind of way. 'And I've come to the conclusion we're in a place out of time. A sort of limbo. Suspended animation.'

'You're in Eidolon,' said Ben. 'It's the world that was created when the big comet struck the Earth and split it in half. This is the half which contains all the magic and the dinosaurs and stuff. It's the Shadow World. My mum's the Queen here, but she's at war, and I need to find her.'

Mr Thomas gave his wife a knowing look. Then he tapped the side of his forehead. 'Poor lad.'

'Did you bump your head, dear?' Mrs Thomas asked solicitously.

Ben cursed himself. It did all sound a bit mad when you said it like that. But really, not that much madder than saying Mrs Bagshott was a witch. It was all part and parcel of the same thing. But he really didn't feel like explaining it any more.

'Perhaps we could burn the door down,' he said instead, looking at Mrs Thomas's cigarette lighter.

She put it hastily into her handbag and snapped the clasp shut. 'Ooh, I don't think that's a good idea, dear. You'll remember what happened the year your barbecue got out of hand.'

Ben did. He and his friend Adam had decided to build a barbecue at the bottom of the garden and cook some sausages on it. Unfortunately, they hadn't taken into account the direction of the wind or the nearness of the fence, or the fact that Mr Thomas's prized garden shed was on the other side of it. There had been a fire engine and lots of embarrassment.

'Well, we have to do something. I'm not just going to sit around here for weeks waiting for old Bag-o'-Bones to turn up!'

'Who?' Mr Thomas frowned.

Mrs Thomas gave a wheeze of laughter. 'Oh, very good. Yes, she is a bony old crone, isn't she?'

Which surprised Ben a little. 'Yes,' he said. 'I thought it was only me who saw her like that. Dad seems to think she's rather attractive.'

'So did I,' Mr Thomas said quietly. 'She seemed a lovely

lady when she came calling that day. I invited her in for a cup of tea. How I wish I hadn't.'

His wife grimaced. 'You always were susceptible to a pretty face; but really, Henry, she must have put a spell on you because she's a frightful-looking creature: all teeth and claws and rats'-nest hair.'

Caught in the impossible position of having either to admit to finding teeth and claws and rats'-nest hair attractive, or accepting the possibility that the woman really was a witch, Mr Thomas had the grace to look shamefaced.

Ben, meanwhile, got down on his hands and knees and started prodding the floor. He got under the rickety old table in the middle of the room and felt around. There was an old carpet, rotted away to hardly anything, and a few unidentifiable objects that he really didn't want to examine too closely (they felt like bones beneath his fingers). He crawled further and came up against a wall; turned and bumped into Mr Thomas's legs. 'Sorry!'

The old couple watched him, bemused.

'What are you doing, Ben?' Mr Thomas asked at last.

'Looking for a trapdoor,' Ben said matter-of-factly. 'I bet an old shack like this will have a smugglers' tunnel, down to the sea.' Then he remembered that he was in Eidolon, and they probably didn't have smugglers here. But it was something to do, so he kept on looking.

And then, suddenly, as if the house was obliging him, he found it. Grabbing the candle, he showed the old couple excitedly. 'Look!'

There was a rusty iron ring in the floor. Sand had gathered around the great square flagstone into which it was set.

Mr Thomas looked at his wife. 'I'm sure that wasn't there before,' he said uncertainly.

'Well, it's clearly here now,' she retorted briskly, and got down on her knees to help Ben clear the sand away.

Together, they hauled at the ring. Stone grated upon stone; and then it came free and they found themselves looking down into a deep, dark hole. Chill air drifted up out of it, bearing a scent of salt, seaweed and dead things. The candle guttered, and went out.

CHAPTER NINE

Stealing Alice

The rain was lashing against the window so hard that Ellie barely heard the doorbell. Who could it be, so late? Perhaps Ben had changed his mind and been unable to climb back in. She pressed her nose to the glass to peer out; but the roof of the porch obscured her view. All she could see was a long black coat flapping in the wind, and then someone – Dad – had opened the door and the figure was inside the house.

She crept to the door of her room and opened it as silently as she could, only to hear a familiar voice in the hall below.

'Poor Clive, you look exhausted. And no wonder, when you've been managing so well, all on your own. You poor soul . . .'

'Yes, well, it's not always easy . . .'

The voices began to move away into the living room. Ellie strained her ears to catch: 'so difficult, yes, I know how it is . . . single-parent family . . . such difficult children . . .'

Difficult children! I'll give her 'difficult', Ellie thought fiercely, balling her fists. She changed from her pyjamas back into her jeans and sweatshirt, thrust her feet angrily into a pair of baseball boots and ran down the stairs as quietly as she could. On the threshold of the living room, she paused to listen.

'You put your feet up there, Clive dear,' Mrs Bagshott said soothingly, 'and I'll make you a good stiff drink. That'll relax you nicely.'

Ellie poked her head around the door, just in time to see Bag-o'-Bones heading into the kitchen with a bottle in her hand. It didn't look much like any of the bottles they had in the drinks cupboard (all of which Ellie had secretly sampled one night when left to babysit, and had made herself thoroughly sick in the process). She stepped into the room. Her father was reclined on the sofa with his feet up on a brightly coloured leather pouffe. In the other corner of the room, Boneless Bob sat coiled up on the floor in front of the television, flicking listlessly from channel to channel. Seeing Ellie, he ran a hand through his crest of red hair and flicked his tongue at her in a peculiarly repulsive way. Ugh! Ellie glared at him. Did he really think she would fancy a creep like him? Not in a million years. Not when there were handsome young Horse Lords in another world, or anything even remotely warm-blooded in this one. She tossed her head, dismissing him.

'Dad,' she started, 'if you're tired, why don't you go to bed? I'm sure Mrs Bagshott would understand.'

Mr Arnold turned his head slowly, as if surfacing from a dream. He looked at his daughter and a puzzled expression crossed his face, as if he didn't recognise her and had no idea what she could be doing here.

But before he could form a word, Mrs Bagshott was back with a glass of foaming green stuff which looked, Ellie thought, rather revoltingly like a glassful of Fairy Liquid. This she handed to Mr Arnold. 'Drink that, Clive dear,' she cooed. 'It'll really take you out of yourself.'

Clive Arnold took the glass wordlessly and tipped it towards his lips.

'No!'

For no reason that Ellie could put a name to, she knew it was imperative that her father not drink whatever it was that Mrs Bagshott had prepared for him. She shot across the room, hand out to snatch the glass. But Boneless Bob was quicker. In a blur of motion, he had slithered out from his corner by the television and, before she knew it, Ellie was sprawling headlong over his outflung leg and crashing headfirst into the sofa. Mr Arnold spilled some of the green stuff down his shirt, but an awful lot of it had gone down his throat. He coughed and spluttered, and the glass flew out of his hand. It landed on the Chinese rug, the one with the border of pretty flowers that Ellie's mother particularly loved because, she said, it reminded her of the spring meadows of her home. Nobody at the time had realised she meant the meadows of Eidolon; for although they didn't really know much about their mother's past, the idea that she might be referring to an entirely other world would never have crossed their minds.

As it touched the silk of the rug, the liquid sizzled. Ellie stared at it in horrified fascination. Then it burnt right through the fabric, and down into the floorboards. Within seconds, it had made a number of tiny holes right down into the cellar. Which was sort of interesting, because until that moment Ellie had never before realised the house *had* a cellar. She turned back to see what terrible effect the stuff had had on her father, but he had his eyes closed and was snoring loudly.

'Badness me,' said Bag-o'-Bones with a malicious gleam in her eye. 'I would never have imagined that Isadora would spawn such a clumsy daughter.'

'I am not clumsy!' Ellie cried, leaping to her feet. 'It was your horrible son. He tripped me up on purpose!'

'Robert would never do such a thing, would you, dear?'

But Boneless Bob just sniggered and flicked the remote at the TV. The channels jumped and came to rest on a station showing a film in which a hideous black dinosaur with a hooded figure on its back was flapping its way across a mournful-looking landscape in which three small figures cowered out of sight behind a bush.

'How curious,' said Mrs Bagshott, squinting at the television as if she wasn't used to focusing on such a strange object. 'Isn't that Corinthius flying across the Great Mere? Though I don't recognise the rider. How did they ever get cameras into Eidolon?'

'Nah,' said her son. 'Nothing like. Your eyes don't work too well over here, Ma. That's not a pterosaur, that's from *The Lord of the Rings*, that is.'

Ellie stared at them. 'Eidolon?'

Mrs Bagshott's hand flew to her mouth in a show of shock. 'Badness me, how indiscreet I can be. Did I say Eidolon?' She smiled, and as she did so the spell she had been using to beguile Clive Arnold wore right away, and Ellie saw her as she really was: Maggota, Witch of the First Order. Her face was a crescent moon of bone: a great hooked nose and curved chin, a Hallowe'en pumpkin grin. Maggots writhed in her hair; rotten meat hung in scraps between her fangs. Ellie screamed.

Bag-o'-Bones snapped her fingers and her original guise resumed itself. The full spell worked only on those without a touch of the Secret Country, so Ellie could still sense the real horror behind the mask; but at least now she could breathe when she looked at the woman, even though her knees were still shaking.

'I wouldn't want you to die of fear, dearie,' Mrs Bagshott said. 'At least, not just yet. Where's your brother?'

'He's . . . out,' Ellie said, as resolutely as she could manage.

'Out? How very . . . unlikely, on a night like this. And his mangy cat, too, I suppose?'

Ellie nodded.

'No matter. You're either lying, in which case I shall find out soon enough; or you're not, and I shall find *them* soon enough. Now, go and get your little sister and we'll be off, there's a good girl.'

'My s-sister?' Ellie stammered.

'The bay-bee,' Bag-o'-Bones spelt out, thrusting her face at the girl.

'Alisssss,' hissed Boneless Bob, and just for a moment Ellie thought she glimpsed a forked tongue flickering out of his mouth.

That did it. Ellie hated snakes, and she hated Robert Bagshott, and no one was taking Baby Alice anywhere. She drew herself up to her full height (five foot two) and took a deep breath.

'Get out of this house! Get out and never set foot in it again!'

Bag-o'-Bones laughed. 'What a brave little creature it is. And how very stupid. We were invited in, dearie: and once you've invited a witch over your threshold, you're in her power and there's really nothing you can do about it. Tut, tut.' And she tapped Ellie on the shoulder with a long, scarlet-painted nail, which looked, if you stared at it hard enough (and Ellie did), like a bony talon dipped in blood. 'Didn't your dear mother teach you anything about magic?' She shook her head sadly. 'She never *was* the most attentive student when it came to spellcraft, our Isadora.'

'You know my mother?' Ellie regarded the Bag-o'-Bones with loathing, although she was surprised to find that the revelation that the wretched woman was a witch was really no surprise to her at all.

'My dear, I was Isadora's magic tutor. For years and years and years. Until we had – how shall I put it? – a little falling-out.' She gave Ellie her ghastly grin, revealing gums filled with flies' eggs and centipedes. 'She had no sense of the practicalities of life. No realpolitik at all.'

Ellie frowned.

'Oh dear, is that a word they haven't taught you at school yet? Such ignorance, such naivety. Education standards really are quite woeful in this world. It won't be long before we witches can fly back in and reclaim what is rightfully ours. Practical politics, child. But she wouldn't play the game: wouldn't give and take. She could have had a legion of witches at her command, with a little forethought, a little . . . compromise. Instead of giving my proposal the sensible consideration it deserved, she stamped her pretty little foot and got all hoity-toity with me. Had me thrown out on my ear. Me, Maggota Magnifica, oldest witch of the First Order! Listened to her brother, she did, little fool. Everyone knew he was in league with the Dog-Headed One even then. Everyone but her. It's really no wonder Isadora's lost her realm!'

'Lost?' Ellie cried.

'As good as. That silly dog-headed creature's strutting about like a wolf around a sheep-fold. He's got trolls and ogres, ghouls and goblins at his command. Soon he'll have the dinosaurs and dragons, too. And what's she got? A Wildwood stag, who has long puffed himself up with his own ancient grandeur and wants Eidolon all for himself; a few measly fairies and a rogue dragon or two.'

'And the centaurs,' Ellie added in a low voice.

'Neither horse nor man: a hybrid confusion and no use to anyone.'

'And a minotaur.'

Maggota exchanged a glance with Boneless Bob, who shrugged. 'I thought he was held fast in the castle dungeons?'

Ellie raised an eyebrow. 'I see you don't know everything,' she said triumphantly.

'Be that as it may, your mother's reign will soon be over and mine shall begin!'

'Yours?'

'They are all so blind,' Maggota smiled blithely. 'They do not see what's truly precious or what's truly possible. It's a shame I am as old as I am now. Older than the hills, than the seas, than the mountains. How I would have loved to be Queen of Eidolon in my prime. Queen Magnifica. Even the name is perfect; such an improvement on Queen Isadora. I was such a beauty then. Or rather, I was maintaining the illusion of beauty just beautifully.'

She stretched out a bony hand and regarded it solemnly. It flickered and for a moment Ellie saw it as it really was: a collection of dry bones and sinews stitched with ribbons of ancient skin. Then Mrs Bagshott's hand was back in sight, complete with its long, red nails.

'It's all your wretched mother's fault!' she spat suddenly at Ellie. 'If she hadn't upped and left the Shadow World for that – that useless worm over there –' she pointed at the snoring form of Clive Arnold '– I wouldn't have lost the power to hold it all together. Such a drain on our resources, stupid Isadora. She never understood her place in the scheme of things, the well of magic that springs from her. She is the source.' She paused, cast a glance towards the ceiling. 'For now. But I shall have my revenge. Now: are you going to fetch your sister, or am I going to do it?'

And she treated Ellie to her best, unmasked smile.

Maggots spilled from between her teeth and fell squirming on to the carpet. Ellie imagined the maggots falling from the witch's mouth on to her baby sister's face.

'I'll get her,' she said.

She went slowly up the stairs, trying desperately to think what on Earth she might do. Her father was clearly going to be of no help: he was comatose on the sofa, drugged by the horrid green drink. How could she save herself and Alice? Could she crawl on to the roof with the baby in her arms? Could she shin down the drainpipe like Ben? Could she summon help? She did not know the minotaur's real name; so that was no good. The Nemesis would be useless out of water. She knew the dragon Xarkanadûshak only as Zark, and try as she might to rack her brains, she could not remember the true name of his wife either. How she wished now she'd paid more attention. She thought of the handsome Horse Lord, Darius. How she would love to see him now, have him carry her and Alice on his glossy brown back off into the night. But Darius was too short a name to be his true name; and he had given it too easily. Tears pricked Ellie's eyes. Princess of Eidolon, indeed! What was the use of being a princess if you were powerless and alone?

By the time she entered the baby's room, tears were streaming down her face. In the cot, Alice stirred and waved her fists. Ellie leant in over the bars and touched her cheek. 'I'm sorry, Alice, I just don't know what to do.'

Alice regarded her older sister steadily with her wild green eyes.

'Ellie cry,' she said. 'Don't cry, Ellie.'

Ellie blinked and tried to smile. Most of the time Alice was a very unremarkable baby: but sometimes she could surprise you.

'Come on. We'd better go with her before she puts a spell on us and I'll try to think of something on the way.'

Alice gurgled something unintelligible and Ellie picked her up, wrapped a warm blanket around her and turned to leave.

A dark figure filled the doorway.

For a wild moment Ellie thought that help had somehow, miraculously come. But it was Bag-o'-Bones.

'You seemed to be taking a rather long time, dearie,' she said. 'I thought I'd come and . . . help.'

She leant in over the baby, but instead of cowering away and wailing her head off like any normal child at such a horrible sight Alice laughed. 'Witch!' she said delightedly. 'Witch!'

Maggota's eyebrows flew skywards. 'Great pits of lizards!' she exclaimed, taking a swift step backwards. 'What a discerning child. Remarkable . . . quite remarkable.' The witch rubbed her bony hands together, but despite her words she looked rather discomfited. 'Come along then, let's be away.'

'Away where?'

'Infinity Beach, dearie. For the time being. I have a little place there where I like to keep my precious things. I think you'll like it.'

CHAPTER TEN

The Centaurs

The minotaur shaded his eyes. 'There is a disturbance on the hill.'

Isadora followed his gaze, but all she could see was that some of the trees were moving more than the light summer breeze allowed for. 'What do you see?' she asked after a while.

'I think . . .' He paused. He was not sure what he had seen; or whether he believed his eyes at all. For a moment, it had appeared that a flock of birds had circled the woods there, then sailed across the sun. A flock of huge, ugly birds, like the biggest herons in any world. He shook his head. Ridiculous.

Darius scanned the area. 'I can see nothing out of the ordinary,' he admitted at last.

Isadora sighed. 'Where will Cernunnos go first, do you think?'

The centaur turned his sharp brown eyes upon her. 'I fear, my lady, he will go to my people. He will try to persuade them to his side.'

The Queen looked shocked. 'But the centaurs are my most important allies. Without their support I am lost. But you; you are their lord . . .' She left the rest unspoken.

'He knows that. He will try to turn them against me; against you. He will promise them swift, decisive action against the Dodman; he will call them to war.'

Isadora looked dismayed. 'He cannot do that! A few brave centaurs against the army the Dodman is gathering? They will be massacred.'

'They are impatient, my lady. They want to do something, anything.'

'But we must go there! We must stop them!'

The tendons stood out in the young Horse Lord's neck. He knelt suddenly at the Queen's feet.

Isadora regarded him with consternation. 'Really, Darius, there is no need for that. You have proved your loyalty time and again.'

Despite his concerns, the centaur smiled. 'I just thought, my lady, that we would be likely to go faster if you were to get on my back.'

Isadora coloured. 'Forgive me, Darius: I am still a little

distracted. You are right, of course.' And she gathered her skirt and climbed on.

They plunged through the sun-dappled woods, the small folk watching them curiously as they went. They had already seen the stag-headed man pass this way, at equal speed, and his face had been terrible to look upon, twisted into a furious contortion.

'What is happening?' one young female gnome asked timorously, watching them go. 'I have never seen the Lord of the Wildwood in such a hurry; and then the Queen gallops by on a centaur, followed by a hulking great minotaur! Something is going on!'

'Nothing good, Toadflax,' declared her neighbour, shaking his head. 'Nothing good ever comes of such rushing about.'

'Are they leaving us?' Toadflax asked, her eyes large with fear. She looked to where her children were playing, riding a pair of black-spotted frogs around a sunlit pool. 'I cannot bear to live under such a cloud of fear. My poor babies have known little else all their lives, and just as it seemed a little of our long-lost magic might be coming back too.' And she called her children to her side. Remarkably, despite their fine game with the frogs, they came running at once: for gnome offspring are somewhat more obedient than human children. She sighed. 'Maybe it would be better for all of us if Cernunnos and his precious Queen did up and go away and leave us all in peace!'

'Toadflax! Stop your mouth: you don't know what you are saying!'

One of the fairies who had been sitting in the tree

overhanging the pool now flew down from his perch, his wings twitching angrily. 'If they leave us, they leave us to the mercy of the Dodman, and he is a monster. He won't rest until he's rooted out every bit of magic in Eidolon and trampled it to bits. And that means you and me and every creature in this Wildwood.'

Toadflax glared at him. 'That's what *you* say. I'm exhausted by it all. All I want is for all the unpleasantness to end so that we can live in peace.'

'That won't happen until the Dodman has been well and truly defeated and the Queen takes back her throne,' the fairy declared flatly. 'Believe me. I've lost two brothers, an aunt and three cousins to the Dog-Headed One. Do you know what he did to them?'

The gnome-woman shook her head unsurely. 'No . . .' Another of the fairies intervened. 'For goodness' sake, Catchfoot, don't frighten the children with your horrid tales!'

Catchfoot pushed him away. 'People need to know,' he declared furiously. 'The goblins caught them and took them to the Dodman. And what did he do? Why, he bit their heads off. That's what he did!'

There were gasps of horror: the children immediately began to cry.

'Yes!' Catchfoot went on, making his point triumphantly. 'He bit their heads off and drank their blood. Drained their magic. They say it makes him stronger. And you –' he turned to Toadflax, who had gone an odd shade of green, much paler than her usual colour, '– want to give up Eidolon to him! Well,

I won't stay here and listen to such cowardly, treasonous talk. I'm going to follow Cernunnos and see what he's up to and what we can do to help bring down the Dodman!'

And with that he soared off into the blue, followed by several of the other fairies, all muttering about the distressing lack of backbone owned by so many of the Queen's Wildwood subjects.

Toadflax stared around, but no one would meet her eye. 'Well, what can I do?' she complained. 'I'm just a poor gnome trying to raise my children on my own. It's not easy trying to stretch an acorn stew to last three days, and no one to bring me worms or anything good to eke it out.'

But one of the other gnomes tutted angrily. 'That's all very well, but you have to ask yourself what happened to your husband, Toadflax. What happened to old Crowfeather, eh?'

Toadflax squared her shoulders. 'I don't want to talk about that in front of the children. As far as they're concerned, he's travelling.'

One of the other gnomes guffawed. 'That's a long road,' it said sardonically. 'One he's *never* coming back from.'

Toadflax's lips set themselves in a hard, straight line. 'I'll thank you to keep your remarks to yourself, Oakum,' she said, marching her children past him.

Oakum and the other gnomes watched them go. 'What *did* happen to Crowfeather?' one of them asked curiously.

'He got trod on,' Oakum replied unceremoniously. 'By something very, very big. Something that had no business being in these parts at all.'

'A dragon?'

Oakum rolled his eyes. 'No, not a dragon.'

'A troll?'

'Well, I believe a troll was involved, but we're used to them around here, great lumbering brutes.'

'A blinking great dinosaur,' Oakum said, lowering his voice. 'A vast monster of a thing. What chance did he stand against that? What chance do any of us stand when they come crashing through the Wildwood?'

On and on they galloped, the centaur with the Queen on his back, her hands knotted in his mane. The minotaur thundered behind them, his hooves pounding into the forest floor. They passed through stands of oak, ash, elm and hartsfoot, through bramble and bracken and furze; past thorny brakes and tumbling streams where the ground grew steeper and boulder-strewn. Stones skittered away beneath Darius's feet; Isadora ducked to avoid the branches of the gnarled and spiky trees which clung to the sides of precipitous ravines. The minotaur simply blundered through them. And still there was no sign of the Horned Man.

'Are you sure he has gone to the centaurs?' the Queen cried, exhausted and a little frightened by the speed of their pursuit. It seemed impossible that anyone could have run faster than Darius, even the Lord of the Wildwood himself. He had, however, been in a fury.

'Quite sure, my lady. His track is clear.'

The minotaur lagged behind them now: he was too big a

creature to keep up with the fleet centaur, but they could hear his rough progress behind them. They plunged into a rocky dell and at last even the centaur had to slow to pick his path more carefully without throwing off his precious cargo. Then the ground rose again and they reached the cover of the tower-ing sapin trees which ringed the centaurs' domain. And at last there he was, Cernunnos, his antlered head bright against the dark foliage, his arms thrown wide as he made some dramatic point. All around him centaurs had gathered – bay and black, grey and white, dappled and painted, every hue of coat you could find on a horse in our world, and a few (lilac, red and striped as vividly as any zebra) that you would not. His voice rang off the trunks of the trees, rebounded from the boulders and echoed from the cliff-walls. His audience listened raptly to his every word. No one even noticed the arrival of the two newcomers as the Lord of the Wildwood roared, 'And so we must wait no longer in the shadows, cowering like mice as the hawk circles above us, ready to stoop to the kill: we must take the war to the Dodman. Aye, and we must do it now!'

Cheers split the air. Some centaurs waved their fists; others their shortbows.

Darius turned to the Queen. 'We have come too late,' he said despairingly, 'though I went as fast as I could.'

'None could have been fleeter,' Isadora assured him. 'But perhaps they will listen to me.'

She slipped from the young Horse Lord's back and walked quickly into the circle of centaurs, her head held high, her heart hammering.

'Centaurs!' she cried, and every eye turned towards her.

Some fell to their knees and bowed their heads. Others shouted, 'War! For the Queen. We ride!'

'No!' She spread her hands. 'Now is *not* the time to face the Dodman and his hordes. You are too few, though full of courage. He has arrayed an army of monsters; and he will have more—'

'Exactly!' Cernunnos stormed. 'We must strike him now. Before he can summon more to his side. Before he can further use the Book.' He gave Queen Isadora a hard and significant look, and she knew from that look with a sinking heart that he had told them of her folly.

She rallied herself quickly. 'I say no. There has already been too much blood shed in this conflict; and I will not have my centaurs cut down in my name for the sake of needless action, needless glory. I have brought your own Lord Darius with me. Hear what he has to say.'

Darius stepped to her side. He surveyed his centaurs, and saw from the set of their faces that they would be hard to sway. 'Now is not the time,' he said simply. 'Our forces are few and feeble in the face of the Dodman's might. Besides,' and he cast a cool look upon Cernunnos, 'what would you do, swim the moat to the castle and batter uselessly upon its gate for him to let you in? Or stand forlorn on the lakeshore and tempt him out to slaughter you where you stand fetlock-deep in its waves? Then will the waters of Corbenic run red: with your blood, all spilled in vain. I say we bide our time and seek a strategic advantage. I have spoken. I hope you have heard me.'

A stillness fell over the circle as if the centaurs were deep in thought: which they were.

When they made no immediate answer, the Lord of the Wildwood tossed his antlers impatiently. 'The Dodman has gathered his forces in the eaves of the forest on the far side of Corbenic. That is where we will take them; by night and by stealth. We can damage his army cruelly in this manner; for we know the secret ways through the forest and they do not. They will not expect an attack now: let us take our advantage while we have it. I do not want to spend more of my days hiding in a hole, afraid to venture out, while he summons ever more terrible allies to his side. I say we strike, and strike now!'

Hooves began to stamp the ground; tails flicked the air.

Darius held up his hand. 'Wait!' he cried. 'We centaurs are few and growing fewer by the season. How many foals were born to us this spring?'

There was some muttering in the herd. Then someone called out, 'Twenty-three.'

'Twenty-three youngsters this year. Twenty-eight the season before. I remember when there were seventy foals in a season: one hundred, more. Shall we reduce our stock still further, and for no good reason?' Darius looked steadfastly around the gathering; but several of his centaurs would not meet his eye.

'Shall you dwindle fearfully into the darkness?' Cernunnos asked contemptuously. 'Or will you set an example for your youngsters and go out and fight while you have a chance?'

'Against the wishes of your Queen,' Darius reminded them sternly.

One of the older centaurs, his mane streaked with grey, his beard falling white upon his deep brown chest, stepped forward. He dipped his head respectfully to Isadora. 'My lady. We are your subjects, this is true, and our blood is your blood to spill as you command. If you say we are not to fight, then I for one will stand by your word.'

The Lord of the Wildwood glared furiously at the speaker. 'You are old, Mentius,' he said dismissively. 'You are wise to know your limitations. Those with more vigorous blood in their veins will join with me to win back the Lady's realm for her, whether she wishes it or not.' And he strode out of the circle without looking back to see if they followed him, almost colliding with the vast dark shape of the minotaur as he did so. The two great figures regarded one another wordlessly, then the stag-headed man pushed the minotaur out of his way and stormed past him.

The herd of centaurs milled uncertainly. Then with a cry a dozen or more of the younger stallions galloped after Cernunnos. They were followed by others, and more again. At last, only a handful were left, and some of those gazed waveringly after their departed friends.

'What has happened here?' cried the minotaur.

'Ah,' sighed the Queen. 'They are going to fight the Dodman, though I begged that they did not go.'

'Do not despair, my lady.' The minotaur's monstrous face was thoughtful. 'Maybe the time is right and he will succeed. Maybe there *is* an advantage to be seized.'

The Queen nodded. 'I cannot believe it, but perhaps that is

because I feel so weak in myself.' She sighed. 'If he fails, the Dodman's army will come after us, knowing we are vulnerable. We must gather those folk who will follow us, Darius, and find a place of greater safety.'

The minotaur gazed after the retreating centaurs, his eyes wistful. He had been imprisoned by the Dodman for a long time, cooped up in a tiny cell. He had scores to settle and a lot of unused energy to expend.

'I am going with them!' he announced a moment later.

Isadora stared at him in dismay. 'But . . . I do not want you to.' In the short time she had known the bull-headed man she had come to be fond of him, despite his grim and bloodthirsty reputation.

He bobbed his horned head impatiently. 'I know, I know. But they will need all the help they can get. And what better to fight a monster than with another monster?' His huge black eyes gleamed with anticipation. His massive hoofed feet pawed the ground.

Tears welled in the Queen's eyes. 'But, we need you . . .'

'To help round up the little folk?' The minotaur snorted. 'Do you think they will willingly come to me?' He laughed as her face fell. 'You know the truth of it, my lady.' He took her fingers in his, and they vanished inside those huge brown hands. 'We shall bring you a great victory!' He turned to the Horse Lord. 'I know I will leave her safe with you, Lord Darius.'

The centaur regarded him angrily. 'Go, then. Go and die with the rest of them.'

'Ha! You wish you could come with us rather than nurse-maiding the little folk!' the minotaur cried, stung by his comrade's remark. Then he turned and galloped after the centaurs.

Isadora and Darius watched him go, and now the centaur looked more sad than angry.

'There was nothing I could do to stop him,' Isadora said quietly. 'He has his own strong will: it does not answer to mine.'

The Horse Lord nodded. He touched her on the shoulder, then swiftly went amongst the remaining centaurs, dividing them into two groups. The first would lead the young centaurs and their mothers to the labyrinth of caves above the forest, where they might watch and wait. The rest he collected about him. 'Tonight we will carry the small folk of the Wildwood, the old and the injured,' he told them. 'The Queen has two dragons at her command: they will spy out our way and guard our backs. The rest must follow on foot as best they can. None can remain safely in the Wildwood.'

The centaurs bore this news with grim expressions, and went about their business swiftly and matter-of-factly, making their farewells, gathering small necessities, strapping on bows and swords and panniers of food.

Darius watched them, and though he appeared impassive, inwardly he was grieving. He had been raised in the Wildwood. He had never left its safety for more than a day; and neither had most of the creatures in this domain. 'Where will *we* go, my lady?' he asked after a while.

The Queen looked at him long and steadily. Then she spread her hands.

'I do not know.'

The Dodman balanced the Book of Naming carefully on the ground, just out of Cynthia's reach. She was a spiteful little thing, unpredictable too. He didn't want to risk her destroying such a precious item. He patted her cage absent-mindedly, then sat down on it, facing the Book.

Its thick vellum pages stirred in the breeze, showing him an illustration of a troll here, a nymph there; then a whole array of other creatures. The images flickered unhelpfully and he glared at the ridiculous jumble of letters that accompanied them. He blamed his inability to use the Book on his lack of magic; but beyond that, he had never learnt to read. It had never seemed a very useful skill; even if anyone had shown enough interest in his future to teach him.

They were on the shore of the great lake opposite Dodman Castle. He needed a bit of space for this. The last time he'd tried it, several goblins had got badly squashed and ended up having to be eaten for supper. The taste had been revolting. Filthy little beasts never washed.

'Call the next one!' he commanded Cynthia.

She cast a furious gaze up at him. 'You promise you'll let me out when we've done this?'

'Of course.'

'Show me your hands and say it again.'

The Dodman gave her his best dog-smile, which was very,

very wide and shiny. Then he stretched his paws out in front of him. 'I promise,' he said, without, this time, crossing his fingers.

'And you'll give me my Sphynx back?'

'Of course, my dear.'

'All right, then,' Cynthia said, watching him with narrowed eyes. She did not trust him (and quite rightly) but what choice did she have? 'Turn over three pages from there. That's the tyrannosaur, Tyrant Megathighs III: that one there.'

The Dodman gazed at the picture of the most fearsome dinosaur in Eidolon. Despite its ridiculous name, it really was the most satisfactory monster!

As she read the page carefully, the dog-headed man's smile turned inward and private. Crossed fingers! What a silly superstition. As if not being able to cross his fingers made the slightest difference. Foolish girl.

'Are you quite sure you want that one? He's very dangerous,' she said at last.

'Oh yes,' he nodded quickly. 'Bring him to me. He's just what I need.'

CHAPTER ELEVEN

Infinity Beach

Ellie was just a little disappointed that Mrs Bagshott ushered them into a quite normal-looking car rather than on to a broomstick; though she drove it without touching the steering wheel once, instead staring very hard at the road ahead and muttering instructions at bends and junctions so that the car would lurch suddenly sideways, throwing everyone this way and that. But Baby Alice did not once cry: she just watched everything the witch did with fascination. Clive Arnold snored in the back seat, with Boneless Bob: it wouldn't do, Maggota declared, for him to raise a hue and cry when he woke up and found his family missing.

They went straight across the roundabout on the outskirts of Bixbury, churning up the winter marigolds the council gardeners had so carefully planted the week before, and Alice laughed and clapped her hands.

Even in the dark, in the rain, with no headlights, Ellie knew this wasn't the way to Aldstane Park. 'Where are we going?' she demanded again.

But the Bag-o'-Bones had her attention fixed on the road ahead and it was Boneless Bob who said with a horrible hissing giggle, 'You'll see soon enough!'

Ten minutes later they pulled into a lay-by on a deserted country lane.

'Out you get!' cried Maggota.

Ellie stepped gingerly out of the car, trying to avoid the huge muddy puddles that were everywhere, in the hope of keeping her pink baseball boots clean. It was a vain hope. Within seconds the boots were soaked through. She had no idea where they were, and when they climbed the stile and jumped down into the soggy field on the other side, she was still none the wiser. All she could see through the dark and driving rain was a circle of stones which looked very ancient and broken-down and forbidding.

'But this isn't the Aldstane!' she cried.

'How remarkably observant the child is. Not the Aldstane, no. Not one ancient stone, but nine: a place of much greater power. My chosen road, of course: it keeps the riff-raff out. Not a place for the uninitiated, or the unconscious.' And she cast a look back at where her son (who was evidently a lot stronger than his weedy frame suggested) was dragging Clive Arnold unceremoniously through the mud and wet grass.

Ellie shivered. Her first and only trip into Eidolon had been quite scary enough. She glanced down at the baby, but Alice's wide green eyes were fixed on the stones. She gurgled. She smiled. And then she pointed at one of them.

Moments later, the witch walked up to the very same stone. How strange, Ellie thought. How did she know? Baby Alice could really take you by surprise on occasion. She wasn't like a baby at all sometimes. In fact, Ellie reflected, there were times when she looked positively ancient.

As if she knew Ellie's thoughts, Alice transferred her gaze from the stone to her elder sister. 'Don't worry, Ellie,' she said, and pulled her hair.

'Ow!'

'Get your carcass over here,' the witch snarled. 'And pay attention: once you're in the grip of the wild road, keep your eyes fixed on a single point or you'll get dizzy. And hold the baby tight. Now, in you go!' And she shoved Ellie into the stone.

'Hold on, Alice,' Ellie started to say, but the wild road had her and suddenly she was tumbling over and over and over. Colours rushed at her till she felt sick. She couldn't find a single point to focus on; instead her head whirled around and around till her neck was sore and her skull felt as if it might burst. The wind was so strong that it closed her nostrils tight against her face and stuffed itself into her mouth. She couldn't breathe . . .

She came to lying face down in sand, with cold water

lapping about her feet, soaking through her baseball boots and jeans. She had no idea where she was; who she was, even. She lay there, stunned, trying to think. She recalled at last the witch; the stones; falling through the wild road. Then she remembered Alice. For a moment the awful thought that she might have crushed the baby beneath her in the fall occurred to her. She staggered upright, but there was no sign of her sister. No sign at all.

Ellie turned around and around. Her eyes weren't working very well: and that detail alone convinced her that she had landed in the Secret Country. She squinted and after a while could make out a circle of what appeared to be stumps of wood sticking out of the sea, a long white beach, a wide grey ocean and an expanse of sand dunes. A chilly wind had followed her out of the wild road. But, it dawned upon her horribly, Alice had not.

She cried her sister's name, but her wail of distress slipped forlornly away into the empty air, and there came no response. All she could hear was sea and wind.

Then there was a splash, and there amidst the circle of wood was her father, sitting upright with the water around his waist, still fast asleep. He had a long red-and-white scarf wrapped tightly around him. The scarf stirred. It raised its head and flicked its tongue at her. The expression in its eyes reminded her of something. Someone.

It was Boneless Bob!

Ellie shrieked.

Before she had time to consider this bizarre transformation, there was a whirl of colour and the witch appeared, perfectly composed, apart from the fact that her maggoty hair was standing on end, hovering just above the surface of the waves.

'Badness me!' Maggota declared. 'It's high water. I really must remember to consult my tide tables next time.' She glided to dry land and scanned her surroundings. Her eyes came to rest on a small wooden cabin amongst the dunes. Weeds had pushed their way through the sand and swarmed over its old fence, covering its garden and the shack itself. She frowned.

Ellie couldn't quite make out what the witch was looking at, but she had the distinct and eerie feeling that there was someone over there, looking at her.

'Alice?' she cried again.

Maggota's head swivelled, like an owl's, without her body moving an inch. 'What?' She stared at Ellie's empty arms. 'Where's the baby?'

A tearful lump got stuck in Ellie's throat. 'I . . . I don't know,' she stammered at last.

The witch's eyes flashed dangerously. 'Don't know? What do you mean, you don't know?'

'I've . . . lost her.'

'Lost her? Preposterous! I saw you both go in together, and there's only one place she can be. Here. That's where the road leads. Here. Infinity Beach.' She stamped across to where Ellie stood, her eyes switching back and forth as if to catch Ellie out in some deception. As if she might have her baby sister cunningly hidden about her person.

Then she turned suddenly and stared at the sea.

'Oh no!' Ellie wailed. She dashed into the water and fell to her knees in the circle of stumps without a thought, for once, of ruining her favourite jeans, her baseball boots or her make-up. She felt around wildly beneath the surface of the incoming tide, and when that yielded no result, took a deep breath and stuck her head under the water. Nothing. Nothing but her father's legs, his trousers flapping gently with the movement of the sea; and Boneless Bob's bobbing tail. Gasping, she emerged. Seawater ran down her face, mixing with her tears. And her mascara.

The witch flew above her, shading her eyes. 'Bob!' she cried.

'Yes, Mother?'

'Search for the baby.'

The snake regarded her. Then it looked at the ocean. Its bright orange crest rose and fell. It didn't look happy. 'It'ss sso big—'

He had no chance to say anything else, for Maggota had him by the throat. (Snakes do have throats, though they're hard to distinguish from the rest of their thin, slippery bodies.) 'My darling boy, you're so lazy,' she said, staring him in the eye. 'Now stop complaining and do what Mother says.'

Boneless Bob flicked his tongue once, in what was either assent or insult, and slithered into the water.

'If she's in there, he'll find her,' she declared, satisfied. 'He's quite a marvel, my boy.'

Ellie stared miserably at the encroaching sea. What if Alice drowned and it was all her fault? What would Mum say? She felt like the worst daughter in the world.

'Stop feeling sorry for yourself!' Maggota snapped. 'Feel sorry for *me*! Now all my plans are awry and it's all your fault. You people are such a nuisance.' She glared at Ellie, then at her unconscious father, and sighed. 'Such a waste of my magic.' She muttered something and Clive Arnold came dripping out of the sea. He rose into the air till he was over the witch's head. Then he dripped on that, too.

'Ugh!' she cried, and sent him roaring up the beach towards the ramshackle cabin.

'Come along,' she said to Ellie. 'We have a little visit to pay.'

CHAPTER TWELVE
Third-time Unlucky

With a final look back at Mr and Mrs Thomas, Ben lowered himself through the trapdoor and landed with a thump: it was further down than he'd expected.

Mrs Thomas peered down at him. She had relit the candle. 'Here,' she said, handing it down to him (it was quite a stretch for both of them), 'if you're going to look for a way out you might need this.'

Ben took it gratefully. It *was* awfully dark. He looked around. The tunnel he was in was long and narrow. Just at the edge of the candle's light it looked as if it went around a corner. The walls were hard and sandy. There was an old wooden box pushed against one side. He went to investigate it.

Fine Old Bermuda Rum, it read. It was empty.

Bermuda? Wasn't that in his world? Ben's geography was a bit hazy, he had to admit, but he could have sworn that was the case.

Just beyond the box was a door. Ben examined it. It seemed to be made of metal, and when he pushed it it didn't budge, though he could find no handle or lock on it anywhere. High up there was a small spyhole covered by a brass lid. Ben put the candle down and fetched the crate to stand on. Then he opened the spyhole and peered in. It was very dark inside the room behind the door, but if he held the candle steady he could see –

– treasure!

It was piled high from floor to ceiling. He could make out the glint of gold coins and vessels and bars in higgledy-piggledy piles, statues, boxes of jewels and precious stones, paintings, including a rather ugly one of a man holding his head and screaming; and something vast made out of loads of bright snakeskin.

'Wow!' breathed Ben.

He was beginning to enjoy himself now: he felt like an explorer finding a pharaoh's tomb.

The candle's flame shuddered suddenly. Ben's heart thumped. Just for a moment he thought he had seen something in the storeroom move . . .

He jumped down off the crate, but luckily the candle didn't

go out. He listened. Was something breathing in there, or was it just the distant sound of the sea he could hear?

With a flourish of her hand and some words Ellie couldn't quite make out, Maggota banished the weeds which had swarmed up all over the shack, barring the door, which now swung open. Inside, Ellie could see something moving, but it was too large to be Alice.

Then someone appeared at the door.

Ellie cried out in surprise. It was Mrs Thomas, their neighbour.

The old woman's eyes went round at the sight of Mr Arnold, who had, she was sure, been floating in the air a moment before, and was now propped upright against the cabin, for all the world as if he'd sat down to take in the view; except that his eyes were firmly closed. Puzzled, she glanced at Ellie, who was soaking wet, her hair hanging in rats' tails over her shoulders. Then her gaze settled upon the witch. 'Oh, no you don't,' she said, barring the door with her arms spread wide. 'We made that mistake once before, welcoming you across our threshold. Well, you're not coming in this time.'

Mr Thomas appeared behind her. He stared in horror at the apparition at the door. 'Is that what she looked like last time?' he whispered to his wife.

'To me, dear, yes.'

Mr Thomas shook his head sadly. 'I really must get my glasses changed.'

Maggota laughed. 'Do you really think you can keep me

out?' She pressed one bony finger against Mrs Thomas's capacious chest.

Maud Thomas stood her ground. 'Henry,' she said. 'There's something you need to do.'

'What's that, dear?'

'Remember the garage window.'

Mr Thomas frowned. 'The one that was broken by—'

Mrs Thomas shot him a furious look over her shoulder. 'Yes, dear. You remember how difficult it was to *shut it.*'

Comprehension dawned slowly on Henry Thomas's face. He faded out of sight into the darkness of the interior. Moments later, there came a muffled thud.

'Let me in,' said the witch, pressing harder. 'Or you will regret it.'

At last, Maud Thomas stood aside.

The tunnel had got very narrow beyond the door. It had curved around a corner and sloped down and down, and Ben now found himself having to shuffle along in a crouch. The sand underfoot was compacted as hard as concrete. There was a line of what looked like limpet shells clinging to the walls at about knee height. The tunnel took another turn and suddenly Ben could see light.

He grinned and started to run towards it (though running was rather hard when almost doubled over). After a moment, he realised his feet were getting wet; and as he ran, water was beginning to splash up his legs. In fact, the closer he got to the source of the light, the more water there seemed to be.

A moment later, he was wading, and it was becoming quite hard to move forward. He realised the sea was pouring into the tunnel.

Never mind, Ben thought, *at least I'll be out of here soon.*

By the time he reached the end of the tunnel, the water was up to his waist, and rising all the time. The light from the outside world was so brilliant that Ben couldn't see a thing. He dropped the candleholder and it vanished at once in a tumble of water. Rather than stop to find it, he reached out blindly with both hands and moved forward.

And ran smack into something immovable. It was a huge iron grille.

Behind him, in the distance, there came an indistinct thud.

Gosh, thought Ben, shaking the grille as hard as he could. *Wouldn't it be awful if the trapdoor closed and no one could get it open again?*

Inside the shack, Ellie stared around. 'You haven't seen a baby anywhere, have you?' she asked the Thomases. 'My little sister, Alice?'

They exchanged a curious look. 'No . . .' Mrs Thomas said slowly. 'Not a baby.'

They didn't seem anywhere near as surprised to see her as she was to see them, Ellie thought.

The witch dragged the snoring body of Clive Arnold into the shack and closed the door behind her. She sniffed the air. 'The baby's not here,' she told Ellie sharply. She sniffed again. 'But someone else is.'

Mr Thomas sat down hard on the floor and stared at her defiantly.

'Someone else? There's no one here but me and Maud, and now you and—' He gestured at Ellie. He had never known her name; but then, she'd never broken one of his windows.

'Ellie,' Ellie said.

The witch waved her hands impatiently. 'Enough of all this nonsense! You – up!' And she levitated Henry Thomas and left him hanging in the air. Then she flicked back the carpet. 'Someone's been here and moved the stone.'

She snapped her fingers and the huge slab hovered above the hole. She sniffed again. 'Boy!' she declared triumphantly. 'The perfectly lovely scent of boy!' And she grinned from ear to ear: an unnerving sight. 'How very, very convenient.'

Ellie looked fearfully at Mrs Thomas. 'Ben?' she mouthed silently.

Mrs Thomas gave a single, tiny nod.

'Ah,' Maggota sighed, without turning. 'Ben. Yes, Benjamin Arnold. Excellent. Just where I want him. Well, he can await my pleasure down there in the dark, while I decide which one of you to kill first.'

'*Kill?* Ellie shrieked.

The witch regarded her askance. 'Well, my dear, you're not much use to me. No magic to speak of and you even managed to lose the baby in a wild road. Extraordinarily incompetent. And as for these two useless creatures –' she indicated the Thomases '– if they'd had the sense to behave themselves I might have let them live. But I happen to have a couple of potions that are an eye or two short, so they'll come in very handy for the store cupboard.' She turned to regard Mr Arnold. 'I have other plans for your father.' She lifted his chin with one spiky fingernail, but Clive Arnold, having no conception of the danger he was in, just kept snoring and snoring.

Ben ran back up the tunnel: but it wasn't long before he realised that the trapdoor – his only means of escape – really was closed. He was about to call out for the Thomases to open it, but above him he heard the unmistakable tones of Bag-o'-Bones, and then someone shrieked. For a moment he thought it was Ellie; but that was ridiculous. Even so, he dragged the crate over and stood on it, but he could only graze the stone above with the very tips of his fingers. He stood there, feeling useless, trying to think what to do.

Then someone called his name.

It floated through the close tunnel air like the answer to a wish. It was a light, musical voice with just a touch of the sea about it. It came from the end of the tunnel. Ben knew that voice. It made him shiver; not with fear, but with delight. Despite his fear of water (he was a useless swimmer) he jumped off the crate and started to wade towards it. He passed the strongroom door, and as he did so, there was an enormous thump and the door bulged. Ben started. If there was something in there, it was trying to get out; and if it could make a metal door bulge like that, it was something very big indeed.

'Ben!'

The voice came again, closer now. He kicked out and

started to swim. Or rather, he started to push himself along with one hand against each wall. The current was strong against him as the tide rushed in to fill the tunnel. There came a particularly strong surge and Ben lost his grip on the walls and was tumbled over and over until he had no idea which way was up or down, nor which way back or forward.

Oh no, he thought, sinking fast. *Third-time unlucky.* (For he had nearly drowned in Eidolon twice already.) Then he banged up against something hard. He reached out and grabbed at it and found that it was the iron grille. The water roared and pushed at him, smacking his face into the grating.

'Ow!' he cried, forgetting that it is not a good idea to open your mouth underwater.

The sea rushed in, choking him. After that, it was all a bit of a blur. He opened his eyes and thought he saw a seal looking back at him. And then something caught him round the waist and hauled with terrific force, and the grating disappeared and suddenly he was in the air and coughing up water.

Someone was laughing: a tinkling sound like a stream running over pebbles, and he stared and there was Silver: or rather, there was Silver's head, drying in the air, her pale hair merging with her mottled sealskin where her body was still immersed. Then who had hold of him? He turned around and found himself face to face with a giant squid. It was the nautilus: Nemesis – and in one of his other tentacles he held the broken grille.

Ben grinned and grinned. He could not help it, no matter how awful things were: seeing Silver always made him happy.

'Silver! Nem—' He managed to stop himself saying the nautilus's true name just in time. 'Nice to see you,' he finished lamely.

The selkie swam over and climbed on to the nautilus as if they were the best of friends (which perhaps they were now) and hugged Ben with flippers that gradually became arms as they dried in the chilly sea air.

'Thank you. Thank you so much!' Ben cried, hugging her back.

'Well, don't bother thanking *me*,' growled an irritated voice from higher up. 'After all, it was only me who had the wit to summon them.'

Perched on top of the nautilus's head was a small black-and-brown cat.

'Oh, Iggy! You're so clever!'

Ignatius Sorvo Coromandel gleamed with appreciation. 'Job well done,' he congratulated himself.

Ben remembered the voices in the shack. 'Well, not quite—' he started, but Silver held a hand to his mouth.

'Stop, Ben,' she said. 'There's something else. It's . . . it's . . .' And she burst into tears.

Ben stared at her in dismay. Then he stared at Iggy, who pretended to wash his face. 'What is it? Tell me!'

'Your sssissster.'

Ben stared around. In another of the giant squid's free tentacles something red and white writhed. It was a snake, quite a big snake, with an ugly orange crest, which it now waved at Ben.

So it *had* been Ellie he had heard scream.

'Tell me what's happened to Ellie,' he demanded, glaring at the horrid snake, which oddly reminded him of someone.

The snake's tongue flickered slyly. 'Well, that I don't know. She's with my mother, who is, I am sssure, taking great care of her.'

'Your mother?'

'Ah, yesss,' said the snake. 'I forget. You haven't had the honour to encounter Mother and me in our Eidolon forms.' And it grinned at Ben in such a way that he was suddenly struck by its likeness to his horrible new neighbour, Bob. 'Mrs Bagssshot; otherwise known as Maggota, Witch of the First Order.'

'Oh no,' Ben groaned. 'You mean the Bag-o'-Bones has got Ellie?'

'Show ressspect!' the snake hissed. 'Or she will make you.'

'It's Alice,' Silver sobbed, unable to bear the suspense any longer. 'She's lost. In the sea. We think she's—' She couldn't say the word.

'Drowned for sure,' said Boneless Bob cheerfully. 'The baby. Your other sister – the one who thinks she's too cool to give me the time of day – dropped her in the ocean as she came out of the wild road. That's what I reckon.'

'Drowned? Alice?' Ben stared at the snake aghast.

'We looked for her,' Iggy said softly. 'Silver and the nautilus looked in the sea; and I've sniffed all around before the tide came rushing in. There's no sign of her at all. I'm so sorry, Ben.' And he climbed down from his perch, negotiating Nemesis's strange face (carefully avoiding that cruel beak of a mouth, which might bite you in two by mistake, or on purpose), and nestled against his friend.

Ben closed his eyes. He thought about Alice and her ways of surprising you with odd words. How she pinched your nose if you got too close and then laughed and laughed and laughed. How she seemed to see things no one else could see. How at home she had seemed in the Secret Country.

It was all too much. He had come here to find his mother and tell her that her evil brother had escaped from prison, and on a dinosaur, too; and now he would have to take her the worst news of all. He was too stricken even to cry.

CHAPTER THIRTEEN

The Darkest Hour

All the rest of that day, Isadora and the Horse Lord Darius and his centaurs gathered about them the denizens of the Wildwood. There was a lot of weeping and wailing from the female gnomes at the thought of leaving their safe forest nooks, which had lately been spruced up with hope and optimism, with the return of the Queen and her magic to their realm. There was confusion amongst the flying creatures: for could they not conceal themselves better than the rest and ride out whatever storm should come their way? But worst, there was despair from the dryads, who had never before in their long, long lives been forced to abandoned their trees. Some opted to stay behind and take their chances; but most had already borne too much in the war against the Dodman to want to risk direct attack. Sprites and fairies, nymphs and satyrs, all had lost friends and relatives in the dog-headed man's quest to eradicate magic from Eidolon. They had heard terrible tales of what he had already done; or had seen such horrors for themselves. All had heard of the army he was gathering, of the monsters he daily summoned to swell the ranks. Things had been bad enough when their opponents had comprised just a few bad trolls, the spectral hounds, Old Creepie and a band of wicked goblins: but now it was rumoured that dinosaurs and dragons were coming to his side: and surely even their returned Queen and their beloved Wildwood could not protect them from such foes.

It was a sorrowful procession which wound its way along the well-trodden woodland paths that night. Even the moon hid her face, leaving them in the pitch-dark. Her withdrawal left the pair of dragons who flew as sentries through the night sky above as invisible as bats in a cave. It was the wood-sprites who led the way through the forest, their pale green light making everything eerie. Branches became witches' fingers, roosting birds demons crouched ready to spring, woodland pools sucking mires which might swallow them all before dawn.

The Queen walked slowly at the head of the refugees, with Darius at her side. A small host of gnome-children had tangled themselves in his mane and were trying to sleep. Their parents sat solemn and silent amongst their hastily-gathered bundles, attempting to accustom themselves to the odd sway of his move-ment and trying not to think about everything and everyone they had left behind. Above them, fairies wove and dived, flitting bright shapes in the dark canopy, whilst the dryads drifted alongside, heads down, weeping silently. No one spoke. Someone had tried to start a rousing chorus of 'Woodland Creatures Free' some while back, but had at once been shushed into silence by half a hundred others. Even the sound of a twig breaking underfoot set everyone on edge, gazing fearfully into the shadows in case it had betrayed their presence to the enemy.

So when the silence was broken by the sudden crash of something large breaking through the undergrowth and the sound of stertorous breathing behind them in the night, panic reigned.

The fairies and sprites vanished into the night; dryads found the arms of a welcoming tree and slipped inside; gnome-children wailed in distress. Grim-faced, the centaurs drew their bows and shortswords and formed a protective barrier around the Queen.

Everyone waited in the thick darkness, not knowing what to expect. Then a huge figure burst through the trees. It was the minotaur. One of his great bull horns had been cloven in two: blood washed his face. One arm hung useless at his side. He was weaponless. When he saw the guard with their swords drawn, his eyes rolled up white and he bellowed.

Centaurs and small folk cried out in fear: he was a terrifying sight – a monster looking for more blood to spill.

Darius let fall his sword and came forward, hands spread to pacify. 'Minotaur, calm yourself. It is I, Darius. No harm will come to you here. Fear not.'

The bull-headed man staggered and fell sideways, exhausted. Isadora broke through the rank of guards and knelt beside him. She brushed the bloodied forelock out of eyes that stared wildly and did not focus.

'Hush, now, hush,' she said over and over. 'You are amongst friends now.'

Gradually, feeling her gentle hands upon him, the minotaur began to calm.

'Tell us what has happened,' Darius said softly.

The bull-headed man gazed up at him with haunted eyes. 'Dead,' he said in a voice that was barely above a whisper. 'All dead.'

'All?' the Queen echoed in horror.

The gnomes whom Darius carried in his mane and on his back began to wail.

'The centaurs?' Darius asked, dreading the answer.

'Every one . . .' The minotaur coughed, and blood spattered on to the ground. 'We did not stand a chance . . . they tore us to pieces . . . We were too few . . .'

At close quarters now it was plain to see where something with terrible claws had raked his side.

'He . . . the Dodman has . . . many monsters . . .'

'Dinosaurs?' the Queen asked in fear, but he did not answer her, only groaned and groaned, both from physical pain and the horror of his memories.

'And Cernunnos? Where is the Lord of the Wildwood?' Darius prompted gently.

The minotaur closed his eyes in pain. 'Lost. I saw him fall.'

The Horse Lord and his Queen stared at one another in shock. Around them, the Wildwood folk close enough to hear the terrible news began to weep. Word spread as fast as a forest fire. The fairies and wood-sprites hovered over the heads of the gathered crowd, many of the sprites showing the pale red glow that is their tell-tale sign of fear.

'We are all that are left,' one of the old centaurs said to a companion. They stared at one another, thinking of all those who had left to fight – sons, and nephews, daughters and cousins.

The minotaur turned his ravaged head. 'There was nothing I could do,' he started, as if accused. 'I—'

Isadora stroked his cheek. 'Hush, now,' she said. 'Do not distress yourself further.'

'They were all dead . . . and there were so many . . . I fled . . . I should have died with them . . .'

And with a look of terrible anguish on his face, the minotaur gazed at her. 'Tell the Princess . . . Eleanor . . . I fought bravely.' Then the great black eyes lost their focus, and he exhaled his last breath.

The Queen bowed her head and wept. The Horse Lord gently closed the staring eyes. 'Poor fellow,' he said softly. 'He has seen such horrors.' He picked up a handful of leaves from the ground and scattered them upon the minotaur's chest. 'He that has come of Eidolon returns now to Eidolon.' It was what you said when someone died: but no one really knew where the bull-headed man had come from. He had come to them as a mystery, and died a mystery.

'We should bury him,' Isadora said, gazing miserably at the noble creature.

'There is no time—'

And even as Darius said this there was a flash of fire in the night sky and when they stared upwards they saw for the briefest moment a dragon beset by flying creatures. Then another dragon came roaring through the trees.

It was Xarkanadûshak, the dragon Ben had saved in the Other World. He hovered above them, beating his wings furiously. Blood poured from a dozen small wounds. Smoke trailed from his nostrils. His snout was charred and soot had gathered between the scales on his face. He looked exhausted.

'Run!' Zark cried. 'Run for your lives! We will hold them as long as we can!'

And he gave a huge flap of his long, leathery wings and soared up through the canopy into the night sky, screaming defiance at the creatures attacking the second dragon. With a mighty effort, he hurled himself amongst them, slashing with his claws and shooting fire from his roaring mouth. The moon drifted out from her cover of clouds and at last they could see that the flying creatures were a flight of pterodactyls, with wickedly long, sharp beaks and terrible claws. Even though they were much smaller than the dragons they attacked, there were very many of them. One took the full brunt of Zark's fury and came plummeting down, trailing smoke and flames. They saw it crash into the trees away to the south; and then watched in despair as the trees there caught fire and burned like torches into the night sky, illuminating the horrors above.

'We must away!' Darius cried.

'But I know these dragons well,' Isadora replied, staring up at the aerial battle taking place above them. 'It is Zark and Ishtar, his wife, and they have done me fine service. I cannot just desert them as they fight for their lives.'

'There is nothing you can do,' the Horse Lord replied; and indeed it seemed what he said was true.

Ishtar was tiring visibly, and seemed to have run out of fire. She turned and tried to fly away from her attackers, but they were too fast. Evading Xarkanadûshak with terrifying swift aerobatics, the pterodactyls sped after their wounded opponent, stabbing at her and swiping her with their claws like malicious crows mobbing a hawk. Three of them landed on her back and began to hammer at her head and neck with their vile beaks.

Zark threw off the pterodactyls which beset him and rocketed in to rescue his mate, but it was too late. Her wings drooped suddenly and she began to spin, slowly, very slowly, like an autumn leaf spiralling down from a tree. One by one the dinosaur birds peeled away to watch her fall. Zark stooped like a kestrel, his wings tucked close to his body, his neck stretched out in a hard, sharp line of desperation. But all his efforts were in vain. Ishtar crashed into the trees at appalling speed. Even at a distance, they could hear the way great branches were ripped apart by the impact of something huge and inert carrying everything in its path down to the hard, hard ground. Xarkanadûshak followed, howling his despair, his wings and feet pummelling the air in an attempt to break his own plunging fall; they saw the way he yawed sharply left, then right, to avoid the hazards of his path. Then he dived through the trees, disappearing into the darkness of the canopy close to the place where his mate had fallen.

Seconds later, there came a terrible keening cry, and then there was a silence which was more terrible still.

Isadora's eyes welled with tears. 'Oh, no,' she mouthed. 'I must go to them.' And she began to gather her skirts to run.

Darius caught her by the arm and pulled her back. 'You must save yourself, my lady; your duty is with these folk, who will not leave without you.'

Overhead, the pterodactyls wheeled and shrieked their triumph as if to illustrate his words. Mutely, Isadora stared back into the dark where the dragons had fallen, disbelief and misery etched on her face. When she turned back to the Horse Lord her eyes seemed like black, glittering holes in the whiteness of her face. She looked as if she had aged a hundred years in as many seconds.

'Such sacrifice shall not be in vain,' she declared, bitterly. 'The Dodman must be made to pay for the blood he has spilt this day.'

'He shall,' Darius averred grimly. 'Oh, he shall.' And he retrieved his sword and ran a thumb down the sharp blade as if applying it to the dog-headed one's throat. He sheathed it angrily, then dipped a shoulder to his Queen. 'Get on, my lady: we must make speed.'

The gnomes who rode upon Darius rearranged themselves and their belongings swiftly to make space for her. When she was safely on his back, Darius gave a signal and his centaurs kicked up their heels and followed him, their riders holding tightly to mane and tail and each other so as not to fall off. The fairies and wood-sprites flew above them, keeping noticeably closer now, not daring to fly high amongst the trees with such frightening predators aloft.

Along the ancient forest pathways they ran, dodging between the trunks of spruce and sapin, larch and oak, and beside them the dryads ran like shadows of the trees themselves, fleet and silent.

Gradually, they began to hear the unmistakable sounds of pursuit. At first, it was the baying of the Gabriel Hounds which carried most clearly through the night air; then came a thundering which boomed and thrummed, making the ground tremble and shudder. Trees cried out and came crashing down, as if blundered into by something huge.

'Hold tight!' cried Darius and broke into a gallop.

The Queen knotted her hands in his thick black mane and held on grimly, and the gnomes and gnome-children clung on to her. Between the uprights of trunks they ran, between thickets and over rocks and hummocks; and wherever they passed, new creatures joined their flight in panic, knowing nothing but that something terrible was about to happen, and was coming their way. Overhead, the ghost-dogs howled and streamed and the flock of ancient birds glided, their black eyes glinting, their gaze malevolently trained on the ground below, their wicked beaks (bloodied now) eager for new prey.

They sped along, joltingly fast, led by the fiery red trails of the terrified wood-sprites who shot through the darkness like fireworks. Isadora gradually became aware that the spaces between trees were becoming wider; that the forest was beginning to thin out. Soon she could even glimpse through the gaps a wide and featureless terrain beyond – a great open tract of moorland.

'Darius!' she cried above the pounding of his hooves. 'We have almost reached the Black Heath!'

The Horse Lord had bent all his concentration on the ground immediately before his feet, rather than gaze around, and break their necks in a stumble. This was unwelcome news. With a lurch, he pulled up, signalling for the rest of his centaurs to do likewise. 'If we ride out on to the heath, in full sight of the enemy, we are lost.'

'We must disperse,' Isadora said bravely. 'They cannot chase us all at once, and I fear it is me they most want to capture, or . . .' she swallowed, 'to kill.'

There was a brief silence. Then one of the older centaurs concurred with a toss of his head. His flanks were heaving: salty foam speckled his dark hide. 'There are caves in the hills to the north of here. I know them well, for I was raised in this region. I can lead some of our folk in that direction. No – nothing very . . . big can enter there.'

He avoided saying the word.

'Good,' nodded Darius. 'Take as many with you as you can.'

'Go with them,' the Queen told her nymphs and dryads. 'There is no cover for you out there,' and she gestured out to the heath.

Swiftly, the gnomes on Darius's back were transferred to another. A gnome-child dropped its doll of twigs and howled mightily, but there was no time to retrieve it, and their parting took place under the pall of this small but painful loss.

'You fairies and sprites,' Isadora called, 'can you fly a trail to the south and distract their attention as best you can? You will find a wide marshland there with a great river running through it. They cannot cross the river, for it is too swift; and the marshland is treacherous. Stay in the air; but beware those flying monsters.'

'We are quicker than they,' a fairy cried contemptuously. 'If we cannot outfly them we deserve to fail!'

'If we can, we shall lead them *into* the mere,' another declared boldly.

'And watch them perish!' a wood-sprite finished, its red light washed through with pale green as a small measure of its courage returned.

'Then go!' cried the Queen, 'with my love. Do what you can, but save yourselves.'

And with that, the larger part of their gathering split away into two, the centaurs taking to their heels and heading north; the flying creatures to the south; while the Queen and her Horse Lord and a small brigade of centaur-guards headed straight on to the farthest extent of the Wildwood – farther than any of them (save Isadora) had ever travelled before; and then out into the scrubland where forest gave way to scattered trees and then petered out altogether into a welter of thorn and bramble, then gorse; then nothing at all but bleak, bleak moor.

'Once we are in the open, I will give them clear sight of us,' Darius proposed breathlessly, 'and when they give chase we will cut back and bury ourselves once more amongst the trees. Once we have split their forces and sown confusion, we too should make for the caves.'

'I trust to your good judgement, Darius,' the Queen replied, though the idea of fleeing out on to the empty moor filled her with dread.

Through the ferns and bracken they ploughed like ships breasting a rough sea, then out on to the moonlit moors. For creatures born of the Wildwood this was a grim and eerie place, with not a tree in sight; just tumbles of rock and bare earth, as if the world here had had its skin stripped back.

Above, the pterodactyls screamed in excitement. Two of them peeled away from the rest and headed back over the woods, no doubt to carry word of their sighting, and soon the crashing noises of pursuit came closer and closer. For a little while the sound was muffled by the forest; then the roaring and howling became suddenly sharp and imminent, and when Isadora turned at the sudden change in note, she saw the enemy clearly defined by the silver light of the moon.

The sight was so terrible that she could not suppress her cry of horror.

The Horse Lord wheeled around. 'By all that is sacred!' he gasped, and the other centaurs stopped in their flight and stared where he stared.

On the edge of the moor, towering above the thorn and scrub, the Dodman sat upon his mount. He balanced high on its shoulders, held in place by a contraption of straps and harnesses, and in his dog-hands he carried a long, many-tailed whip weighted with spikes, with which he beat the creature that carried him mercilessly.

Twenty feet and more in height was this monster. It stood, slightly hunched, its huge legs bent as if ready to leap, its smaller arms caught up to its chest, claws curled. Its vast head swung slowly left then right; and even at a distance they could see how the moonlight rendered its massive reptilian eyes a flat and deadly silver. Then it opened its mouth and roared, showing teeth as long as swords and twice as sharp.

'He has a tyrannosaur,' Darius breathed in dismay. 'He has used the Book.'

Now other figures emerged from the Wildwood, dinosaurs both large and small. Some were similar to the tyrannosaur, but smaller and with long, wicked faces, crouched as if waiting for a starting pistol to fire, when they would hurl themselves across that empty space like the wind. Others were huge, lumbering beasts which trod bushes and thorn trees underfoot as if they were grass. Hordes of goblins clung to their backs, chattering and waving their swords. A triceratops bellowed, its great rhinoceros-horns savaging the air.

'Oh, my heaven,' cried the Queen. 'It was already too late for Cernunnos and the brave centaurs: the Dodman had summoned these monsters.'

'It may be too late for us, too,' the Horse Lord said flatly. 'A tyrannosaur can run almost as fast as a centaur; and over a short distance the velociraptors can outrun us easily.' He turned to his comrades. 'Scatter!' he commanded them. 'Fan out and double back when they have committed themselves to the chase. If you evade them, make for the caves and we will find you there.'

'Go with blessing, my brave centaurs!' cried Isadora, and they bowed and ran.

'Now, my lady, if you have any magic left to you I hope you will use it in our cause,' said Darius, gritting his teeth. 'For there is only so much that a strong heart and four legs can achieve against such odds.'

Then he kicked up his heels and carried her on a breakneck path between heath and scrub, across streams and through mire and bog. Isadora focused hard. It had been a very long time since she had studied spellcraft under the tuition of Maggota Magnifica of the First Order of Witches, and since then the world had lost a lot of its magic. For a while she managed to maintain a weak invisibility spell: but it was hard to hold on to a galloping centaur and keep all her mind on it, so every few seconds it would disperse and they would reveal their position again. The Gabriel Hounds came flying out between the feet of the dinosaurs, their noses full of scent: no spell of invisibility was going to fox them. Next, she attempted sowing spells of confusion in her wake, sending some of the pursuers in one direction and some in another, but still the Dodman, fixed in his purpose, drove his terrible mount onward.

Darius cut this way and that; but he could not shake his pursuers. There was no chance to double back towards the forest, and so on he went, and on.

At last, his breath labouring and his flanks salt-streaked and heaving, Darius climbed a steep and rocky hill, topped by a rock in the shape of a raptor's head. 'If you have the power to summon a dragon, my Queen, now is the time to do it. Here at Eagle Tor is where we must make our stand, for I can run no more.'

In a fluster, Isadora could barely remember the name of a single one. She bent her mind upon the dragons she had called to her, dragons who had arrogantly shown her their back, or cruel words, before flying away again, refusing their aid. Would such a creature be compelled by a summoning? She did not think so. At last, and reluctant, she cried:

'Xarkanadûshak!'

They waited, their heartbeats fast and loud in their ears, watching the dark sky. But all they saw was the pterodactyls gathering above, eyes glinting in anticipation. No dragon came.

It was not long before the tor was ringed around with dinosaurs, with spectral hounds and goblins and trolls; a dark tide surrounding their little island of rock. The Dodman rode towards them, stately on his giant tyrannosaur, his long white dog-teeth flashing with triumph.

Darius drew his sword. 'I am sorry, my lady, that it has come to this,' he said. 'It has been my honour to serve you.' And he stepped in front of her to meet the monstrous army ascending the tor towards them.

CHAPTER FOURTEEN

Mummu-Tiamat

'Stay back out of sight,' Ben warned Silver. He squeezed her hand, then let it go, feeling awkward. 'I want to make sure you're safe. You never know what a witch might be capable of.'

The selkie shivered.

'What about me?' growled Ignatius Sorvo Coromandel. 'Don't you want me to be kept safe?'

Ben thought about this. 'Well, you can stay with Nemesis, too, if you like.'

Iggy curled his lip. 'I don't fancy my chances if he decides to go for a swim.'

'Well, I can't carry you *and* the snake,' Ben said crossly.

'What do you want with that horrible thing?'

'You'll see.'

In the end, Iggy balanced himself awkwardly on Ben's shoulder. 'There,' he purred into Ben's left ear. 'Isn't that better?'

It wasn't, but Ben nodded. Then he gathered all his courage, turned to face the shack and shouted, 'Mrs Bagshott! Come out of there and let my sister and my friends go free!'

A face appeared at the window of the shack, looking deeply surprised. There was a flurry of movement, then the door opened, and there stood Mrs Bagshott in all her Eidolon glory: bones, maggots and all. Ben couldn't help but stare.

'Robert!' she cried; then uttered something Ben could not make out, which made the red-and-white serpent coil itself desperately around Ben's wrist.

'Ugh!' said Ben, who wasn't very keen on any sort of snake, let alone one that in the Other World was his horrible neighbour's horrible son. He held Boneless Bob at arm's length, and shouted again. 'Let them all go or the snake gets it!'

The sea was beginning to lap at the broken old fence surrounding the shack now; the strangling vines in what had once been its garden floated on the surface of the water like seaweed.

'Put Robert down or I shall pull out your sister's teeth, one by one!'

'If you harm one hair of Ellie's head, I shall kill your familiar.' Ben was in no mood to trifle. 'I hold you responsible for what has happened to my baby sister.' And he gave the bit of Boneless Bob directly below his orange frill a hard squeeze.

Bob made a horrible squawking sound.

Maggota's hands flew in the air, weaving some sort of spell. Whatever it was came flying at Ben, but before it could reach him something dark and swift leapt through the air in front of him, caught it and came to rest on the fencepost. It was Ignatius Sorvo Coromandel; and in his mouth he held an ugly batlike thing, which flapped and flapped as Iggy's teeth closed on its wings. It had mad red eyes and leathery feathers and when it opened its mouth to protest, it showed two nasty-looking fangs. Iggy bit down sharply and the thing went limp. Disgusted, he threw it into the water, where it floated like a black plastic bag.

'Yuk! Vampire chicken,' he declared, spitting feathers after it.

Ben grinned at his friend, balancing neatly on the fence. 'Thanks, Ig.' He waved Boneless Bob in the air. 'You'll have to do better than that.'

The witch disappeared inside. When she returned a moment later, it was with Ellie in her bony clutches. 'Perhaps I'll start on her eyes,' she cackled. 'Since they don't work very well here anyway.'

'Ben!' Ellie shrieked. 'Don't let her hurt me!' Her mascara had run so much that she looked like an anorexic panda.

Ben firmed his jaw. He held the dangling snake out and gave it a hard shake.

'What do I care about a ridiculous snake?' Maggota cried. 'It means nothing to me. Go ahead: do your worst!'

'Don't take any notice of her,' Iggy said softly. 'It's her familiar: she can't do without it.'

It was a terrible risk, but the loss of Alice had made him reckless. 'Last chance!' Ben cried, squeezing till Boneless Bob's long forked tongue shot out and waved around as if it were an entirely separate snake of its own.

Maggota's eyes bored into him. He could feel the intensity of her gaze like maggots crawling on his face. Something moved on his nose. Ugh! Maggots *were* crawling on his face! He very nearly dropped Boneless Bob then; but instead his start of horror made his fist close even tighter and Bob lolled suddenly limp.

Abruptly, the maggots vanished. So did the vampire chicken.

Ben stared at Iggy.

'Is he dead?' Iggy enquired curiously.

Ben examined the snake. It was a bit hard to tell. 'Not sure,' he whispered.

'Never mind,' Iggy said cheerfully. 'Everyone knows that witches are nothing without their familiars. It's where they store their magic. If a familiar dies or falls unconscious, they can't do much at all.'

And indeed, when Ben looked back at the shack again, Mrs Bagshott was holding on to the doorframe with one hand and Ellie with the other; but now it seemed as if she was holding on to them for support. She looked suddenly old: not just ordinary old, like Mr and Mrs Thomas, but OLD; like a withered tree, or like the fallen Aldstane.

He was about to press home his advantage and demand the release of her captives when suddenly the ground in front of the shack started to shake. Iggy took one look at it, then leapt from the fencepost back on to Ben's shoulder and teetered there with his claws digging through Ben's so-called waterproof (which was now wet through). Ben didn't even think to complain: he was rooted to the spot. Earth and sea began to push upwards, like a slow eruption; then there was a mighty roar and a head emerged from the ground.

It was huge and golden and covered in scales.

It was a dragon.

Ben gasped.

It rammed upwards and freed its shoulders and stones and water began to tumble down into the hole it created for its huge body with every writhing effort it made to break free. It shook its head, and chunks of sand and rock splashed down into the incoming tide. Its eyes, as big as dustbin lids and an unearthly shade of green, blinked rapidly, as if it was not used to daylight. It turned its head and looked at Ben.

Then it opened its vast mouth and treated him to an array of teeth. A rumble filled the air. Ben felt it first in his breastbone, then it travelled all the way down till he felt his knees go to jelly. Was he about to be roasted? Or just have his head bitten off? He remembered his first encounter with Xarkanadûshak and how he'd been a bit worried even then about being barbecued: but this dragon was at least three times the size of Zark and looked a lot more annoyed. If this thing decided to roast him it wouldn't just be a barbecue: it'd be Armageddon!

The shock of seeing it meant that it took him several moments to realise it was speaking. To him.

'Thank you,' it said. 'I take it it's you who broke her spell.' It glanced at the limp snake Ben held in his fist. 'Since you appeared to have killed her traitor worm.'

'Well, actually,' said Ben, 'I'm not sure it's—'

The dragon didn't let him finish. It leant in closer to get a better look at him and its eyes whirled like Catherine Wheels. Ben felt his head going all loose and dreamy. He almost dropped Boneless Bob.

'Well, well,' the dragon said at last. 'A prince of Eidolon. That's an unusual thing to find.'

Ben stood there stunned, not knowing what to say. At last he stuttered, 'D-did she summon you here? The witch, I mean.'

The dragon snorted. It puffed out its chest. 'No one can summon *me*. *I* was here before the world began.'

Ben couldn't make much sense of that. 'Then how did you get trapped down there?'

'Greed,' the dragon replied simply. It opened its mouth wider, showing all its teeth. Apparently, it was amused. 'Always the curse of our kind. We do so love pretty things.' It swept a wing in an expansive gesture. 'Infinity Beach. Most beautiful place in Eidolon; and the most remote. I made it mine. I chased the dinosaurs out of it and made it my home. Mine, all mine. This beach, those dunes, everything, apart from that ugly little house the witch made to hide her comings and goings.'

'And the Minstrels?' Ben asked.

The dragon wrinkled its brow. 'The Minstrels?'

'I mean, the wooden circle . . .' Ben pointed to the almost-submerged stumps.

'Ah, those. No the fairy folk put those there. They used to dance around them and leave me little offerings. To persuade me not to steal their children, I suppose. Though what would I want with a fairy child? Too small even for a titbit: one bite and they're gone. No, it was the gold they brought me I treasured: gold and jewels, precious stones . . .' Its whirling eyes went misty. 'Gems and rare objects, golden fleeces, magic swords, antique statues, pharaohs' death-masks – ah, they travelled far and wide to keep me in a good temper.' It sighed, remembering. 'Good times then: better times than these. Proper respect shown. I could breathe fire back then, fire that could singe the hair off a ghost-hound at a hundred paces. Mmmm, roast dog . . . that was a treat.'

'Can't you now?' Ben asked, feeling faintly relieved.

'The witch took my fire. While I was sleeping.' The dragon turned one of its remarkable eyes upon Maggota, who quailed.

'How did she do that?'

'You are too full of questions, Prince of Eidolon.' The dragon shifted its vast bulk, sending ripples across the sea in all directions. There was the sound of earth moving and stones falling, and then its tail came free, sending the walls of the flimsy shack tumbling around the ears of those inside it. Someone shrieked.

Alerted by the familiar sound of fear, the dragon whipped around. First it eyed the Thomases, then seemed to dismiss them; *then* it focused on Clive Arnold, who had just sat up, yawning and rubbing his eyes.

'Goodness me,' he said, 'I must have fallen asleep on the sofa.' He squinted around. 'What's happened to the house?' he asked in confusion. 'And what's that horrible-looking thing?'

The 'horrible-looking thing' shook its golden head furiously and peeled its lips away from its teeth as if in preparation to eat him head first in a single swallow.

Ellie planted herself firmly in front of her father. 'You leave my dad alone,' she told the dragon fiercely.

'*Dad?*' Ben goggled. Was his father here too?

The dragon stared and stared at Ellie. Its eyes flared with interest. It regarded her first with one side of its head then the other. 'Another of the royal blood. How curious. What's your name, young beauty?'

Ellie smiled tremulously. She had been quite afraid of the monster till that moment, despite her bravado. Now it seemed rather charming.

'I'm Eleanor Arnold,' she said, 'Princess of Eidolon. Who are you?'

Maggota chuckled. 'Bless the child. How are the mighty fallen! She doesn't know who you are, O Great One. Times really have changed in the Shadow World.'

The dragon shifted its weight again so that its huge golden head overhung the witch. Its shadow fell across her. 'Yes, you managed to keep me imprisoned for a long time, didn't you, old woman? Did you think I would wither in this treasure-tomb?'

'It was your own fault, foolish worm.' Maggota grimaced. 'Had you forgotten how stupid it is to invite a witch over your threshold?'

'I was blinded by the gifts you brought me,' the dragon growled. 'Gold was always something that tricked my wits. I have learnt a hard lesson in my long confinement. But you, what have you learnt, crone? The treasure you have stashed away for your glorious future is floating away on the tide –' and indeed, dozens of lighter items, like paintings and robes, were bobbing up and down in the water '– or sucked down into the earth where such lifeless things belong. What good will your hoard do you now, old woman, with your familiar dead and your magic gone and a hungry dragon ready to bite off your head?'

At this, the serpent in Ben's hands gave a sudden convulsion. Boneless Bob was not dead after all.

'Ma!' he squawked, and even as he spoke the witch seemed to grow in strength and stature.

Maggota shot a spiteful look at the dragon. 'Not finished yet, Mummu-Tiamat. There – that's a surprise for you, isn't it? I spent a long time searching for your name.'

Mummu-Tiamat shook out its wings. 'You may well know my name, crone. Such things do not concern the Old Ones. In the ancient times everyone knew the name of the Mother of Dragons. Do not think it gives you any power over me. It was only a trick that caught me unawares. But now I shall exact my revenge.' It turned to Ben.

'Tell me, Prince of Eidolon, shall I eat the worm first, or its mother?'

Ben was a bit taken aback by the question. He wasn't sure he wanted to see anyone eaten. 'Um . . .'

Mummu-Tiamat laughed, and all around the sea stirred with her amusement. 'If you're going to survive very long in the Shadow World, young man, you're going to have to be ready to make many more difficult decisions than that.'

Ben held out the snake. 'Here,' he said. 'Take it. I don't want it.'

'No!' the witch shrieked. Something bright and spinning zigzagged through the air like a ball of lightning. The dragon swatted it boredly away. It fell into the water by Ben's feet with a monstrous sizzle. A huge cloud of vapour mushroomed into the air.

'No!' Maggota cried again, and this time her tone was plaintive rather than challenging. 'Don't kill my son. He's all I've got.'

'Ah,' murmured Mummu-Tiamat, 'how touching. You're trying to appeal to my maternal senses, witch, but it won't do you any good. Don't you know that half the time we dragons eat our young?' And the dragon gave her a ghastly grin. 'Anyway, I've changed my mind. I'm going to eat you both!'

The Mother of Dragons reared up and grabbed Maggota, one of her great clawed hands encircling the bony witch's waist.

'Wait!' shrieked the witch. 'Don't eat me. What good am I to you dead?'

'What good are you to me alive?'

'I could give you back Infinity Beach.'

'Pah! You have made it loathsome to me: I never want to see it again.'

'I could restore your fire.'

The dragon's eyes gleamed. She looked thoughtful. 'Ah. Now that *would* be good. For me. But to extract a favour just for myself seems a little, how shall I put this? Selfish.'

The witch looked crafty. 'I know something the Boy wants to know.'

Ben stared at her. 'You know where Alice is?'

Maggota stared back. 'Maybe.' Though she didn't.

'Don't kill her,' Ben implored Mummu-Tiamat.

'Don't listen to the dragon!' Ellie shouted. 'The witch knows nothing!'

Maggota shot Ellie a look of pure venom. 'Oh, don't I? I happen to know the Dodman's true na—'

'His true name?' Ben interrupted. He stared at the witch, then at the dragon, hope dawning in his eyes. 'That could save the world!'

Maggota laughed, though it pained her to do so, so tightly clutched was she. 'How naïve the Boy is! How foolish!'

Mummu-Tiamat squeezed her till she choked. 'You will be respectful to the Prince of Eidolon, crone. He saved me and I owe him a gift for that. So you are going to tell me what he wishes to know, and that will be my gift to him.'

'Ow!' Maggota squawked. 'Prince or no prince, he should know it's most rude to interrupt his elders. What I was going to say is that I know something about the Dodman which would be very useful to him.'

'And what would that be?' The dragon's eyes whirled.

'You must think I am stupid, to give away all my secrets so easily.'

Mummu-Tiamat growled. 'Give me back my fire, or I shall know you to be a lying and powerless creature.'

'All right, all right.' The witch said something strange, which sounded like *takat l'hisht*, and Boneless Bob twisted suddenly in Ben's hand. His eyes bulged till it looked as if they would pop out of his head. Then a little wisp of smoke emerged from the serpent's mouth, followed by the tiniest red flame, and smoke and flame fled across the space between snake and dragon and disappeared inside Mummu-Tiamat's open mouth. For a moment, the extraordinary green eyes whirled faster than ever; then a golden light appeared in them. At last, the dragon turned a beatific smile upon the company. She took a deep breath and directed a huge sheet of fire at the incoming sea.

There was a whooshing sound.

Then Ben yelped. 'Ow! The water's boiling!' He bolted towards the remains of the shack and the safety of dry land.

But he found when he got there that no one was looking at him. They were all staring at the sea. Or rather, where the sea had been. There was now nothing but scorched sand all the way back to the wooden circle; inside which a very cross-looking giant squid and a rapidly drying selkie had been left beached.

But of Alice there was no sign at all.

Maggota regarded the dragon steadily. 'I have given you your fire back, isn't that enough for now?'

The dragon rumbled. It shook its golden head. 'I still owe the Prince of Eidolon a gift.'

'Please,' said Ben. 'I don't mean to interrupt, but can I say something?'

The dragon and witch looked at him.

'Mummu-Tiamat, if you would be so good, I'd like you to carry me across Eidolon to find my mother.'

'And that is to be my gift to you?'

'Well . . .' Ben hesitated, torn between the absolute truth and the need for a very small lie. He blushed. He was hopeless at lying. 'I was going to ask you for something else, when we get there.'

The dragon's eyes flared and for an awful moment Ben thought she was going to get angry and let loose her new fire. She gave him her cat-smile. 'Ask me the thing you wish when we arrive, and I will consider it. But I promise nothing.'

'OK,' said Ben in a small voice. Then he braced himself. 'Now for you, Mrs Bagshott –' Ben gave a meaningful glance at the red-and-white snake in his hand '– Ellie and I will keep Bob safe, if you will, please, search for my sister Alice. Wherever she may be. And when you find her . . . her . . .' He couldn't finish the sentence.

Maggota fixed him with her gimlet eyes. 'Her body, do you mean, Boy?'

Ben nodded miserably. 'Bring her back to me,' he finished almost on a whisper.

Mr Arnold sat up straighter and squinted into the light. 'Eh, what? Ben, is that you? And what do you mean by "finding Alice's body"?'

141

Ellie began to cry. 'We've lost Alice,' she sobbed.

'Lost?'

But Ellie could say no more.

The witch watched all this with some satisfaction. Then she said to Ben, 'Boy, tell the dragon to put me down and I will do what you say. I, too, have an interest in your sister Alice. But if you harm my son, I shall know it at once and I shall find you, wherever you are, in the twinkling of an eye. I am not so stupid as to store all my magic in one familiar, whatever you may think.'

Ben thought about this. Then he said, 'Mummu-Tiamat, would you please release your captive?'

'Is that the boon you wish me to grant you, Prince Ben?'

Ben blushed. 'Er, no, actually. It's just a request.'

The dragon's eyes went round and round as if she was carefully considering whether she might still manage to eat the witch, and thus put an end to her troublemaking for all time, or whether she should honour the young prince and let Maggota go. In the end, she uncurled her claws one by one by one and set the crone down on the scorched sand. Then she bent her huge head very close to the witch's ear. 'But if I ever see you again,' she hissed, still keeping her final claw firmly in place, 'Maggota Medusa Magnifica, you are toast.' Her long lips curled into a catlike smile. 'You see,' she whispered, 'I know your true name, too.'

The witch looked shaken by this, but she bowed her head, and turned to leave.

'And, er, Mrs Bagshott?'

Maggota turned back.

'Do you think you could take my dad and Mr and Mrs Thomas back to Bixbury?'

Maggota regarded Ben askance. 'You'd trust me with that task?' Her eyes narrowed. 'You are so very like Isadora. You believe there is good in everyone. I'm not sure that's wise in my case but –' before he could interrupt her again '– but I will do this thing; and then I will look for Alice.'

'And you will bring her to me?'

'Dead or alive.'

Ben swallowed. 'I am going to my mother.'

The witch cackled. 'I hope not, Boy. I have a fairly good idea of where she will be. But I will find you. And my son.' And she gave him a horrible wink.

Ellie came to Ben's side. 'Wherever you're going, I'm going with you,' she said staunchly. 'Only, don't make me fly on that thing.'

Ben gave her a wobbly grin. He knew his sister was terrified of heights. 'You can go with Silver and the nautilus.'

Ellie regarded the giant squid dubiously, remembering the battle on the lake. 'I'll probably get seasick,' she said. Then she wiped her eyes fiercely with the back of her hand, smearing what little was left of her mascara over her face. 'But I'm sure Silver will look after me.'

'Mummu-Tiamat and I will be flying overhead,' Ben promised.

'And what about me?' Iggy jumped down off the burned fence and stepped gingerly across the hot sand. He rubbed his head against Ben's legs. A purr like a rusty old machine starting up filled the air. 'I can navigate for you.'

Mummu-Tiamat snorted, and a little puff of smoke rose from one of her nostrils.

Iggy glared at the dragon. 'I hope that was a hiccup and not a snigger,' he growled, puffing himself up to his full (not very large) size. 'I'm known as the Wanderer, you know.'

CHAPTER FIFTEEN
The Dark Mere

The first time Ben had flown on a dragon's back had been when he was helping Xarkanadûshak to escape back to the Secret Country. He remembered how terrified he had been as they skimmed over the rooftops of Bixbury. It had been weird to see such familiar landmarks as his school and the football fields, the church and the supermarket car park from such a vantage point; let alone while he was trying to hang on to Zark's neck and not plummet to his death.

But flying on the back of Mummu-Tiamat was quite a different affair. It was a bit like suddenly finding yourself sitting in a comfortable open-topped limousine after bumping precariously along on a scooter. The Mother of Dragons was massively wide, and she flew with such smooth and powerful grace, her neck stretched out like a swan's in flight, that he soon found there was no need to be afraid of falling off. He had made a rudimentary bag out of his waterproof and stuffed Boneless Bob into it. The snake had immediately dived down a sleeve and had not re-emerged. Ben had tied the strings which fastened the hood around one of Mummu-Tiamat's scales for good measure. He had made a promise to the witch to keep her horrid familiar safe, and he intended to keep his word.

He turned around to see how Ignatius Sorvo Coromandel was faring, and found that the little black-and-brown cat was curled up in the wide space between the dragon's great shoulder blades, fast asleep. In fact, if you listened very hard, you could just make out his snores between wingbeats. Ben grinned. He was glad someone was untroubled enough to sleep. For himself, he did not think he would ever sleep soundly again. Leaving his father had been difficult. Worse, now he had time to think about it.

Mr Arnold, free at last of the witch's sleeping potion and the strange glamour she had cast over him, had not been in the best of tempers. And that had been before he realised that Alice was missing.

'I blame you for this!' he berated Ellie first of all; but then she had burst into tears again, and when Ben had bravely suggested that maybe if he had taken Ellie and Alice with him to Eidolon, then they would both have been all right, Mr Arnold had exploded.

'It's this place that's the problem! None of this would have happened if you'd stayed in Bixbury, and now you're all coming home with me!'

'I have to find Mum,' Ben said stolidly.

His father went red in the face. 'Your mother's a grown woman: she can take care of herself. But Alice is just a baby. Whatever were you thinking of?'

Ben wanted to point out that in fact if it hadn't been for his father meeting his mother and keeping her away from her realm, things wouldn't have got out of hand in Eidolon and none of this would have happened. But then he realised that if that had been the case then he, Ellie and Alice would never have been born; and again, none of this would have happened. Which was very confusing. So in the end he stared at his feet and said nothing at all, and thought instead about his mother being 'a grown woman'. Did that mean she'd sprouted up out of the ground, like a plant? He was a bit hazy on the details of human reproduction (since on the day it was taught at school he and Adam had been sitting at the back of the biology class, secretly letting the frogs out of their tank before they were dissected, and he hadn't been paying attention). Anyway, his mother wasn't technically human, if she came from another world, was she? And since he was half Eidolonish (if there was such a word) then perhaps *he* wasn't fully human, either. Cheered, slightly, by this thought, he managed a weak smile.

'I'm sure Alice will turn up, Dad,' he said. Curiously, when he said this he suddenly felt it to be true, though he couldn't explain it to himself, or anyone else.

And it was at this point that Clive Arnold's fury revealed itself to be not true anger but terrible anxiety, for his face crumpled.

Maud Thomas put an arm around him. 'Now, now, Clive,' she soothed. 'Tears won't bring her back. Let's go home and wait for her, and let Ben and Ellie do what they have to do here.' She turned to the witch. 'Come along, Mrs Maggot, or whatever you're called, and take us back to Bixbury. What we need's a nice, strong cup of tea.'

Maggota gave Mrs Thomas her most untrustworthy smile. 'Oh, I could rustle one of those up for you in a jiffy.'

Mr Arnold had braced his shoulders and given her a hard stare. 'I shan't be drinking anything *you* offer me in a long time,' he said.

And then he had hugged both Ben and Ellie so hard Ben thought his ribs would break.

Already, all this seemed like days ago, rather than a couple of hours. Being on a dragon's back changed your perspective on things. Ben had seen that Infinity Beach didn't really live up to its name: for eventually the vast stretch of white sand and dunes became a long spit of land sticking out into the sea, then an archipelago of islands, and then, finally, vanished altogether into wide blue ocean. Below them, at first a little way behind, Nemesis had ploughed through the waves with Ellie sitting on top of his head and Silver, sleek in her seal form, swimming beside them. But as the dragon's powerful flight lengthened the distance between them, the nautilus had dived so that it could propel itself beneath the surface in its usual fashion. All except for the one long tentacle which it used to hold Ellie up out of the water, where she hung, as if by magic, above the tops of the waves, shrieking with a mixture of terror and excitement.

The longer they flew, the further behind lagged the nautilus, the selkie and his sister. Soon he couldn't see them at all. Iggy was fast asleep, the Mother of Dragons had her mind concentrated on flying – for the first time in who knew how many years? – and Ben felt suddenly as if he were all alone. Clouds scudded past him through the blue, blue sky, below lay the blue, blue sea, and the sun winking off Mummu-Tiamat's golden scales offered the only other speck of colour he could see. All he could hear were the rhythmic beat of the dragon's wings and the little cat's snores, when the wind of their passage did not blow them away.

Everything seemed so serene. It was as if time itself had stopped and they moved through a space between worlds, a space in which there was no Dodman, no lost realm of magic; no war. In a way, Ben had never felt so calm. It was as if all worries, all fears, all problems had been suspended. It was impossible to believe, seeing all this comforting, quiet blue around him, that Alice could be lost. Even so, somewhere in the back of his mind the burden of the knowledge that he would have to tell his mother about her loss weighed as heavy as lead, immense and terrible and too much for him to bear. He had no idea of what he would say to her. So he tried not to think about it at all.

For a little while, he slept. And as he slept, he dreamt. He dreamt he was in another world where the colours were different from this one, where the cold air tumbled around him in turbulent blasts bringing all sorts of different smells with it. He was flying – not as he flew in the dreams he sometimes had at home, like Batman or Superman, or like James Bond with a jet-pack – but on the back of some great creature which was not a dragon. How he knew this, he did not know, but the knowledge was deep inside him and he felt both powerful and proud, and not like his usual self at all. When he woke up, he was smiling.

'I don't know what you've got to be so pleased about,' said Ignatius Sorvo Coromandel. 'It's freezing up here.'

And indeed the little cat did look half-frozen in the moonlight, with the night-wind whipping the fur back from his face and flattening his ears and whiskers. Ben found himself shivering, just from looking at Iggy. The next minute, Iggy was shivering too.

'Where are we?'

Iggy shrugged. 'How should I know?'

'So much for being the Wanderer.'

'It's dark.'

'There are stars.'

And there were. They shone brightly all around, and Ben seemed to be a lot closer to them than he had ever been before. He stared at them, but couldn't quite make sense of what he was seeing. He was used to finding Orion's bright belt of three stars and working out the constellations from the position of that. But try as he might, he couldn't see Orion at all. At last, by twisting right around on the dragon's back, he located three stars in a line, but they were pointing in the wrong direction. He stared. He frowned.

'Hang on,' he said. 'Why's Orion back to front?'

'Orion?'

Ben pointed out the belt of stars to Iggy. 'In my world they slant the other way, and you see that bright one there? That's Betelgeuse. And that other one's Bellatrix. Except they're in the wrong place.'

Iggy snorted. 'How can they be in the wrong place? They're in the sky, aren't they?'

'No, no, I mean they're inside-out, or something . . .'

Iggy rolled his eyes. 'Are you sure you're properly awake? Anyway, that's not whatever you called it. It's the minotaur. The three stars in a line are his sword.'

None of this made any sense to Ben. He got as far as wondering whether Eidolon lay on the reverse side of the universe, and that idea hurt his head so much he decided not to try to puzzle it out. Instead, he said, 'Why are we up so high?'

The little cat gave his raspy laugh. 'Oh, you'd rather we ploughed into Cloudbeard, would you?'

And when Ben looked down, there indeed was a range of snow-capped mountains right beneath them and the moonlight was frosting the snow with its glittering silver light. 'Wow,' said Ben, impressed. 'Wasn't that the mountain your dad climbed?'

Iggy nodded proudly. 'And now I'm flying over it. Which means,' he said, puffing out his chest, 'that no cat has ever been as high up in Eidolon as me!'

It was getting hard to breathe, each breath feeling like cold needles in the chest. Ben's nose hair froze, which made Iggy laugh; then his whiskers froze, which served him right. At last, the dragon began to descend into the warmer air on the other side of the mountains, and the rim of the sun showed in a thin gold-red band in the distance.

'But what about Nemesis?' Ben said suddenly. 'I mean, he can hardly swim over the mountains, can he? What will they do?'

Mummu-Tiamat turned her golden head. 'The sea will take them further south of here. We will meet at the edge of the Dark Mere.'

It was the first thing she had said since they left Infinity Beach, but she didn't seem inclined to speak further. Her eyes gleamed and whirled at the pleasure of finding the air beneath her wings; then she stretched out her neck and sideslipped swiftly, her scales like a coat of fire in the dawn light.

The Dark Mere was just as grim a place as Ben had expected it to be. Even in the light of a new day, its deep waters seemed as black as ink. Beyond it and a stretch of marshy mudlands, lay the sea. Mummu-Tiamat landed on a rise of higher land overlooking the coast and immediately settled down to sleep, without a word to her two passengers. No birds sang, and nothing stirred, except the wind in the reeds.

Ignatius Sorvo Coromandel wrapped his tail around himself and hunched down next to Ben.

'Don't you want to get off and stretch your legs?' Ben asked. It was the sort of thing his father tended to say after a long car journey.

Iggy gave him a pitying look. 'Here? You must be joking. There's quicksand and bogs and if those don't get you, there are some pretty nasty things in the water. You've got frogs and leeches in your world: here we've got frog-leeches – they'll jump the height of a goblin and fasten on you and suck your blood till they pop.'

Ben grimaced. Perhaps he'd wait till they were somewhere safer before he went to the loo.

So they waited as Mummu-Tiamat snored and Iggy rolled over on his back to let the sun warm his belly-fur; and Ben thought about the Secret Country, about its strangeness and its perils, about its beauty and its amazing (and sometimes horrid) creatures. He thought about wood-sprites and fairies, vampire chickens and frog-leeches, goblins and gnomes, nymphs and dryads; about Darius the Horse Lord and Cernunnos with his stag's head. He thought about the mino-taur and the nautilus, and about flying – on Zark, and then on the Mother of Dragons. He thought about magic, too, and the evidence for it he had seen. He tried to imagine what would happen if the Dodman used the dinosaurs to destroy the forces that stood against him and what Eidolon would be like with-out any magic left in it. No dragons would fly or breathe fire; no fairies or sprites would survive; the trees would wither without the care of their nymphs, the wild roads would fail. He would be stuck here forever. And so would Ellie. He had never felt poorly in the Secret Country, but it made Ellie ill. He remembered how ill his mother had been at home, in a magicless world. It was clear that without magic she could not survive.

A dread like a cold hand wrapped itself around him, and he knew then that he would do anything he could to save her. But what could he do? He was just a boy, and she needed an army.

He hunched his knees up to his chest and stared out to sea. *Come on*, he willed silently. *Hurry up, Nemesis.* But he didn't voice his thoughts in case he summoned the squid and ended up drowning Ellie by mistake.

The sun rose ever higher in the sky. Some birds flew above them, and then veered sharply away when they saw the dragon. Ben watched them disappear with a vague disappointment. It would have been nice to see another living thing close to.

'Sprites,' said Iggy, his eyes narrowed as he focused on the vanishing specks. Ben hadn't even known he was awake. 'They're being remarkably antisocial.'

Ben shaded his eyes. 'And what are those, over there?'

Iggy turned to look at where his friend was pointing. Three small figures were silhouetted against the pale sky. 'Fairies,' he said at last. 'They're a long way from home.' He sat up, his brow furrowed, his whiskers drawn down. 'I wonder what's up.'

'Probably deserted. Cowards, the lot of them. No backbone. Or rather, such small crunchy little backbones. Sssssss.'

Boneless Bob had poked his head out of the waterproof-bag and was grinning widely. 'She has no chance, you know, your mother,' he said, regarding Ben with his chilly eyes. 'I've seen what's she's up against, the monsters the Dodman's gathering.'

Ben stared at the red-and-white snake with intense dislike. 'I know he has a dinosaur,' he said at last, hoping this would shut Boneless Bob up.

'Ssssssss!' the serpent hissed, and by the way it convulsed, Ben realised it was laughing. At him. 'A dinosaur. Ssssss! The boy knows nothing. He has *many* dinosaurs, the Dog-Headed One, large and small, those that run on the ground, and those that fly in the air. And what does Isadora have? Fairies and man-horses!'

Now it fairly whipped from side to side in mirth. Ben felt like throttling the horrid thing there and then, but he had made a promise. Iggy had not. With a single vicious pounce, he had pinned the snake to the dragon's back. With infinite care, he took its head between his jaws.

'You see,' he said indistinctly around Boneless Bob's skull, 'I'm just a cat. I haven't been going around making bargains with witches about keeping you safe, and my friend here can't be held to account for my actions. Quite fancy a chunk of snake for my lunch. I hear it tastes a lot like chicken.'

The snake stopped wriggling abruptly. It tried to say something.

'Let him up,' Ben said wearily. 'He's vile and wicked, but you mustn't eat him. Yet.'

Reluctantly, Iggy released the familiar.

'I was only passing on information,' Boneless Bob whined.

'I'd rather you didn't say anything else,' Ben declared

grimly, and stuffed the serpent roughly back into the make-shift sack.

No one said anything more, for at that moment the dragon stirred and shook her wings. 'Stop playing games on my back!' she admonished them. 'The squid has arrived.'

Mummu-Tiamat's eyes were better than Ben's. He squinted hard into the light but for a long time all he could see was sea. At last he made out a wash of white water, and then a shape; and suddenly there was the nautilus, waving all his tentacles, with Ellie and Silver sitting on his head. As Ben watched, the selkie took Ellie by the hand and they jumped together into the sea.

Ben was impressed by the selkie's persuasive powers: it took a lot for Ellie to agree to get her hair or make-up wet. Let alone her precious clothes.

'We're coming with you,' Silver declared before Ben could say anything. The long walk up from the sea had changed her completely into her human form, but Ben could see how down on the mudflats the trail of her flippers gave way to footprints. 'Nemesis is tired, but if you need him, he will find a way to come to you.'

'Does he speak?' Ben was curious.

Silver shook her head. 'I just knew what he meant.' She turned to the Mother of Dragons. 'Mummu-Tiamat, Great One,' she said, bowing reverently, 'would you be so good as to carry me and the Princess Eleanor as well to the Wild-wood?'

The Mother of Dragons showed her long row of teeth. 'It is good to see that proper respect has not completely deserted this world in my absence.' And she dipped a wing to enable Ellie and Silver to climb on to her back.

Ellie kept her eyes shut the whole way.

As they approached the Wildwood, the dragon's wingbeats slowed. She took a sharp intake of breath, then slewed sideways.

'What, what is it?' Ben cried, staring back at the dark canopy she had just flown away from.

'Are you sure your mother is in the Wildwood, Prince of Eidolon?'

'Yes. She was with Cernunnos and Darius, the Horse Lord.'

The dragon said nothing. She swung her head to regard him. 'I hope for your sake she was not there recently.'

'What have you seen, Mummu-Tiamat? Tell me! Show me!'

Something in the tone of Ben's voice seemed to arrest the dragon. 'Are you sure you wish to know?'

Ben felt hollow with anxiety. 'Yes. I must.'

Slowly, the dragon yawed around and glided back towards the forest. What he saw there made Ben gape in dismay. All around, trees had been burned and smashed. Charred trunks and blackened foliage lay scattered as if something vast and deliberately destructive had laid waste to the Wildwood. Smoke still rose from a dozen small fires. The smell was acrid and unpleasant.

Ellie opened her eyes. She squinted at the wreckage below. 'Oh no.' She reached for her brother's hand, squeezed it. 'Oh, Ben, it's awful.'

'What happened here?' Silver cried.

Mummu-Tiamat made no reply, but the eye that Ben could see as she made her spiralling descent had darkened ominously.

The devastation became clearer the closer they got. Some trees had been uprooted, others torn apart, their exposed flesh in shocking contrast to their burned bark. The ground was churned up. Here and there, dead things lay unburied and uncared for – families of gnomes overcome by smoke and fumes, wood-sprites limp on the branches where they had expired; a dryad who had stayed with her tree and burned inside it. Ellie's hands flew to her mouth. Ben's eyes felt raw, and not just from the smoke.

The Mother of Dragons drew in her wings and glided to a halt in a clearing where fallen trees lay scattered in all directions. The undergrowth here had been burned to the ground, saplings lay black and flattened as if by vast feet.

Mummu-Tiamat looked around. 'The burning was caused by dragon's fire,' she said, her nostrils flaring.

'But why would any dragon do this?' Ben was horrified.

'I do not know. I do not think we should stay here. Let me take you away from here.'

Ben shook his head. 'No. I must find my mother.'

Iggy jumped down from the dragon's back. 'I will go and see what I can see,' he told them. He picked his way gingerly amongst the debris, sniffing here and there. Then he scrambled up over a fallen log and disappeared into the forest beyond. They all watched him go anxiously. Silver started to shiver. Ben put an arm around her and they all sat silently waiting for the little cat's return.

They did not have long to wait. Ignatius Sorvo Coromandel came running back into the clearing some minutes later as if he was being chased by demons.

'Something terrible has happened here,' he gasped. 'A battle . . . a massacre. There are dead centaurs and . . .' He could not finish.

'And what?' Ben's face was ashen, his green eye stark with dread.

'And the body of a dragon.'

CHAPTER SIXTEEN

Xarkanadûshak

The Mother of Dragons gently lifted the burned corpse out from the litter of charred wood and detritus which covered it and laid it on open ground. It was a smallish dragon, maybe a third of Mummu-Tiamat's size. Great gouges rent its flanks, and one of its wings lay at an impossible angle. Its eyes were closed: carrion birds had not been able to penetrate the scaled lids, though it looked as if something had tried to.

Ben fell to his knees beside it. 'Oh, Zark. Oh, no . . .'

His hand was shaking as he reached out to touch it. He remembered how he had found the little dragon dying of neglect and lack of magic in the garden of a stately home in the

Other World. He remembered how sad it had been; and how hungry. How it had resigned itself to dying alone and far from home, far from its wife and kits. He stroked the blackened hide and his hand came away covered in soot. Where he had touched them, the scales showed a dull bluish-purple, the colour of a bruise. Ben frowned. He rubbed away more of the char and again, the hues revealed were indigo and a dull grey-gold. It could not be Xarkanadûshak, for his scales were the colour of flame. For a moment, Ben felt an absurd, happy wash of relief. Then Mummu-Tiamat blew upon the poor dead face and soot drifted up into the Wildwood air.

Ben's heart jumped and thudded. He knew this dragon. But it was the Mother of Dragons who named her: 'Ah, my lady Ishtar,' she breathed. 'A terrible end for one so lovely.'

It was Xarkanadûshak's wife. And now Ben felt terrible guilt for his moment of relief.

Ellie remembered how Ishtar had swooped down out of the sky over the lake to save her from the clutches of the Dodman's evil goblins. Queen Isadora had sat astride her: together, they had made an impressively regal sight as they screamed through the air. She might be dead if not for Ishtar's courage; and what reward had the beautiful dragon had for her bravery and skill? Here she was, destroyed by Eidolon's horrid war, as dead as a spent coal. Ellie bent her head and her tears dripped with a little patter, like rain, onto the charred earth.

Ben remembered his father getting on to Ishtar's back, and how he had climbed on to Zark; how they had flown home together, side by side. It had been the first time his father had experienced for himself the magic of the Secret Country. He could not quite believe such a powerful, noble creature could have been reduced to this grim pile of smouldering scales.

'Goodbye, Lady of Battles,' Ben whispered.

Mummu-Tiamat touched his shoulder with her claw. 'Come away,' she said. 'I must consign her to our ancestors.'

From a safe distance Ben and Ellie and Silver and Iggy watched silently as the Mother of Dragons gathered her wind. Even Boneless Bob seemed struck dumb by the enormity of the occasion. Then Mummu-Tiamat gave forth a great blast of dragon-fire so bright they had to shield their eyes. When they looked back again, the fire had engulfed Ishtar's body and the flames were roaring away in brilliant shades of blue and gold and purple, as if the very essence of the fallen dragon, her magic and her grace, was burning before their eyes. Then, as swiftly as it had burned, the fire died away, leaving behind just a small pile of ash to be dispersed by the breeze.

The after-image of the fire burned on Ben's retinas in bright zigzags of light. So when something came charging and roaring through the forest towards them, he could not for some time make out what it was. All he knew was that Silver and Ellie fled screaming, and Iggy jumped up on to his shoulder, trembling. The Mother of Dragons reared up on her hind legs and flapped her wings in warning at the intruder, but even this awesome display did not deter him.

'Where is she?' a voice bellowed. It was a voice Ben knew, though it was distorted by rage and grief. 'Where is my wife? What have you done with her?'

It was Xarkanadûshak. He stood on the edge of the clearing with his flanks heaving and his eyes glowing and whirling. His mouth was charred and he was missing scales all over his body. One of his forelegs hung useless in front of him. In the claws of the other he held a straggle of withered flowers. Even the sight of Mummu-Tiamat towering above them all seemed to have no effect on his fury; all his attention was focused on the clutter of branches and burned wood where Ishtar's body had lain.

He rushed at the woodpile, casting aside the battered asphodels and lilies he carried, and dug through the debris with his one good arm. Then he turned and faced the silent watchers.

'Where is she?' he roared again.

'She is fire upon the wind, magic upon the air; spirit in the clouds,' Mummu-Tiamat said softly.

Zark looked bewildered, as if the words had no meaning for him. Ben stepped forward. 'Zark, it's me—'

He said no more, for the little dragon broke suddenly into a charge, his neck stretched out, his cheeks bulging as he gathered his wind.

'Get down!' cried the Mother of Dragons and pushed Ben aside.

But the fire Zark released against her was a ragged, pathetic thing: a lick of flame that might roast a fly, but nothing bigger. It caught Mummu-Tiamat on the chest and fizzled out in a second. Zark had used everything he had trying to light Ishtar's funeral pyre, and now he fell to the ground, hollowed out and breathing heavily.

'Oh, Zark!' Ellie was at his side now. She stroked his cheek and her tears fell upon him, leaving streaks in the soot and blood that covered his hide.

Iggy leapt down from Ben's shoulder and butted his head against the little dragon's rough scales. Ben followed behind, not sure what to do or say.

'I'm so sorry, Zark. About Ishtar. We all are,' he managed at last.

Xarkanadûshak raised his head. He looked Ben in the eye. 'She died for your mother. But it was for nothing. Now I will die, too.' And he hunched down as if waiting for death to take him.

'But what about your kits?' Ellie said softly. 'If you die, what will they do without you?'

But Zark just closed his eyes. 'Go away.'

'We won't leave you,' Ben said firmly. 'Not like this.'

A growl built in Zark's throat. He swung his head at Ben. 'I wish you'd let me die in the Other World, Prince of Eidolon,' he rasped. 'Go away! If you hadn't saved me I would never have owed you anything. Ishtar would be alive. I wish you and your family dead. As dead as she is.'

Ben was shocked. He looked from Zark's mad, swirling eye to the calm face of the Mother of Dragons.

She pushed him aside with a wing. 'Leave him. It is not Xarkanadûshak who speaks but his sorrow. There is little respite from that for him, for his world is a different place without Ishtar in it, and dragons have long memories.' Then she leant over Zark and breathed upon him. This time, it was not fire that issued from her great mouth but a pale golden vapour which wrapped itself around him like a veil. The great swirling eyes lost their focus and slowly closed. His shuddering body gradually relaxed and finally his head fell sideways and hit the ground with a thump.

Ben stared in horror. 'You've killed him!'

'Isn't death what he wished for?' the Mother of Dragons asked gently.

'Yes, but . . . He didn't mean it.'

'Are you so sure?'

Ben didn't know the answer to that. He felt miserable to the core. 'I hate this . . .' he said at last. 'This war. All this death. It isn't . . . it isn't right.' He couldn't find the words to say exactly what he meant. The remains of the centaurs had horrified him: their brave bodies struck down and trampled underfoot by the Dodman's monstrous army, their gleaming hides muddy and crushed, their limbs contorted, their swords broken or stolen as booty. But at least he hadn't known any of them personally. To see Ishtar dead, and now Zark . . . Tears gathered and he gulped them back.

Mummu-Tiamat tossed her head. 'There have always been wars: there will always be wars, in your world as in ours. When reason fails, violence triumphs, and there is no reason here. For myself, I do not like to see my dragons caught up in such pointless conflicts. We are so much longer-lived than others: the death of a dragon reverberates down the ages.'

Ben stared at her, feeling bleaker than ever. He had, of course, been going to ask for her aid in bringing the dragons to fight for his mother against the Dodman; and that was to have been her gift to him for freeing her from the witch's cave. But now that he had seen one noble dragon brought to a futile death and another driven mad with despair, he knew he could never ask for such a sacrifice to be made. He hung his head. And that was when he saw Xarkanadûshak move. Just a little twitch of the ear, as if he were trying to dislodge a fly that had landed on him; but it was enough.

'He's not dead!' Ben cried joyously.

'Of course not. Did you really think after all I have said that I would take his life?' Mummu-Tiamat asked curiously. 'He will sleep, for a long time, and that will ease his pain a little. I cannot afford to lose my dragons so easily, young man. Each of them is precious to me: for each of them is my child.'

'Goodness,' said Ellie, flustered by this extraordinary announcement. 'How many children have you had? You've kept your figure very well, I must say.'

Everyone burst out laughing. Ellie went red. It was the sort of thing people said, in the Other World. Then she sneezed and sneezed and sneezed.

'I think she's a bit allergic to Eidolon,' Ben confided to Mummu-Tiamat.

'Allergic?' The dragon regarded him quizzically.

'It makes her ill.'

'Ah. Perhaps she should not be here, then.'

Which was a perfectly logical thing to say. Ben sighed. 'There's a prophecy, you see. And it's about us – me and Ellie and my little sister Alice, who's missing.' And he told the Mother of Dragons the prophecy:

'Two worlds come together
Two hearts beat as one
When times are at their darkest
Then shall true strength be shown
One plus one is two
And those two shall make three
Three children from two worlds
Will keep Eidolon free.
Three children from two worlds
Three to save the day
One with beauty's spell to tame
One bravely to bring flame
And one with the power to name.'

'I see,' said Mummu-Tiamat slowly. Her eyes whirled with colour. 'Well, I hate to say it, but people are always making up songs and verses in Eidolon when they don't have enough to keep them occupied. Even dragons do it from time to time. There are some fine dragon lays I could recite to you, but they would take several days. There are prophecies by the cartload in this world, Prince of Eidolon; but none of them mean any-thing.'

She tried to say it kindly, but Ben's face fell. The Mother of Dragons saw that he had been putting his fragile hopes in the childish verse, and that now those hopes were dashed. She put a wing around his shoulder.

'Never mind the foolish prophecy for now,' she said to Ben. 'Let us see if we can find your mother. You two –' this to Silver and Ellie '– stay here where I can find you. We'll be back shortly.'

Ben and Iggy climbed quietly on to the big dragon's back and found themselves a vantage point at her right shoulder where they could watch the Wildwood pass by below. Mummu-Tiamat took off with a great beating of wings and soared into the still and silent air.

It was still and silent, they soon discovered, because nothing was alive in the Wildwood at all; or if it were, it was hiding. They passed over scene after scene of devastation, until Ben's eyes had grown round and hot with misery. Iggy turned his face away and buried his head in Ben's armpit. Down below were dead centaurs, dead fairies, dead gnomes, dead sprites, dead dryads, dead goblins, dead nymphs, dead trees; and once, even, a huge dead troll pinned beneath a burned and fallen tree.

But of Queen Isadora there was no sign.

'What do you think happened here?' Ellie asked. She peered around a burned tree trunk at the devastation.

Silver shook her head. 'Don't ask me,' she said. 'I'm only a selkie. I don't understand any of it. All I understand is blue seas and sunny reefs and where to find the best rabbitfish. All this –' she gestured around, shivering, '– all this destruction is beyond me.'

Ellie (who rarely did what she was told) had wandered further into the forest, squinting hard. Curiosity was one of her vices (along with vanity and picking on her little brother) and she didn't take well to being told what to do by a dragon who clearly thought more of Ben than her. But even a short way beyond the glade, she found herself rather wishing she had stayed put. Something in the trees above rustled, and Ellie's heart beat wildly.

'Was that you, Silver?' she asked, though she knew it was not; and the sound of her own voice was not as comforting as she had hoped it would be.

'I'm right behind you,' the selkie said. 'I didn't hear any— oh! What's that? Over there . . .'

'Where?' Ellie spun around and almost cannoned into her. 'What have you seen?'

But Silver couldn't speak. She was gazing down at something lying on the ground and her face was twisted into an unrecognisable expression.

Ellie made her way to the selkie's side and stared at the huge dark shape on the forest floor. Her eyes wouldn't focus properly: she couldn't make out what it was. She was just about to ask Silver and reveal just how hopeless her eyesight really was in Eidolon when she managed to make out a horn, and then a muzzle. 'Oh . . .' She bent down, squinting hard, then recoiled, both hands flying to her mouth. 'Oh, no!'

At once tears flooded her eyes. Surely nothing could kill something so big and fierce . . . surely he was only asleep. But she knew at once that he wasn't.

She remembered fire-fairies flying in a glowing golden heart around his head. 'I am in the service of the Princess Eleanor,' he had said. 'And no other.' And now here he was: the minotaur, stone dead, stretched out on the hard, cold ground where he could do service to no one other than the ants and the beetles. Tears came with a vengeance. 'He was m-my friend!' she wept. 'And I n-never g-got to know him properly. It's such a w-waste!'

Silver put an arm around her. 'Come away,' she said quietly. 'This is all too horrible. Let's go back and wait by Zark.'

And they stumbled back through the broken vegetation to the clearing where the Mother of Dragons had left them.

The selkie slumped down beside the hulk of the sleeping Xarkanadûshak and rested her chin on her knees. 'This is like one of those nightmares in which I'm swimming through horrible black suck-weed which is trying to pull me down to the seabed and eat me,' she said after a long silence which had been broken only by Ellie's sobbing. 'And that at any moment I'll break free of it and swim up into sunlight. But this isn't a nightmare, is it? It's real. It's war.'

Ellie nodded and gulped. She wiped her eyes with the bottom of her sweatshirt. Without any make-up left on it, her face looked pale and vulnerable. 'I've only ever come across wars in history books; and the teachers made it all so boring, so none of it seemed real. But people die, really die . . . And for what?' She'd never thought about war before in any serious way. It was a hard and horrible lesson to be learning at first hand.

'My grandfather told tales of a great war in Eidolon,' said the selkie after a moment. 'An uprising against the Queen of the time by a goblin chief who decided it was time there was a King. I never really paid much attention to them, either: it all seemed violent and ridiculous to me. I mean, what's the point of killing anyone just to be King? You're still you, and nothing has changed except that you've done horrible things and made the world a worse place just to live in a castle and have people afraid of you.'

Ellie nodded slowly. 'But this is different, isn't it? The Dodman doesn't just want to be King: he wants to destroy all the magic, too.'

'And then what will be left?' said Silver angrily. 'He doesn't even know what magic is. I believe every creature in Eidolon has some magic: it's why we don't do well in your world. So if he destroys too much of the magic he'll make Eidolon like your world.'

'Thank you,' sniffed Ellie. 'It's not that bad.' She gave a huge sneeze. 'And at least it doesn't make me ill.'

'It makes *me* ill,' said the selkie. 'When your uncle and the Dodman captured me and brought me through the wild road, I thought I was going to die.'

'But it didn't seem to make him ill,' mused Ellie, rubbing her eyes. 'He and Awful Uncle Aleister were coming back and forth all the time.'

'I don't know what he is,' Silver said darkly. 'Perhaps he's not from Eidolon at all.'

'Well, he's not from *my* world! We don't have giant monsters with ugly great dogs' heads walking around as if they own the place.'

The selkie shrugged. 'He has to be stopped. But I don't know how. All this death and destruction, it can't be the way. That's *his* way.'

They sat in silence for a time, pondering this; and thinking about Zark and Ishtar and the poor, dead minotaur. Nothing stirred in the Wildwood. No birds sang. No sprites flitted through the canopy above them. It was as if every creature who had ever lived here had either fled or been slaughtered.

'If only we knew what the Dodman was or where he had come from,' Ellie said at last. 'That might give us some clue as to how to stop him.'

'No one knows,' the selkie replied gloomily. 'I heard he just sort of appeared. At the castle.'

The waterproof bag twitched. Then Boneless Bob's forked tongue flicked suddenly through the narrow opening where Ellie had knotted the sleeves to keep him in.

'I think he's trying to say something,' Silver said. She reached out and loosened the knot a little, just enough for the familiar to poke his head out.

'My mother knows,' he hissed.

'Your mother knows what?'

'She knows the Dog-Headed One's true nature.'

'Whatever *that* means,' Ellie snorted, regarding Bob with loathing. 'What *does* it mean?'

The orange crest flicked and furled as if the snake was tucking its secrets away. 'You'll have to ask her that,' it said complacently.

Ellie and Silver exchanged glances. 'I don't want to ask that old bag anything,' Ellie said viciously. And she stuffed the snake back down into the sack and tied the sleeves tighter.

'I hope they won't be too long,' Silver said, glancing around. 'I never really liked the Wildwood. It always seemed so dark and

dreary and closed in, even at the best of times. But now . . .'
She shuddered. 'It feels, well, haunted.'

'I keep thinking I can hear something,' Ellie confided. 'But
I think it's only Zark breathing; or the trees moving.'

Silver listened intently, her pale hair tucked behind the pink
shells of her ears. 'No,' she whispered after a moment, 'I can
hear something, too.'

They listened together. At first it really did sound like distant branches moving against one another; but it seemed to be
coming closer. Twigs cracked as if someone was treading on
them.

Ellie clutched the selkie's hand. 'Whatever shall we do?'

Silver jutted her chin at the sleeping dragon. 'Hide behind
him.'

They crept to the other side of Xarkanadûshak and peered
anxiously over the great scaly hump of his back. At first they
could see nothing at all, nothing but broken trees and smashed
undergrowth. Then a bush on the edge of the clearing moved.

Ellie stifled a cry. 'What if it's the Dodman?' she whispered.
She certainly didn't want to find herself back in those dungeons. This time he might make good his threat to cut off her
ear; or worse.

'It can't be the Dodman. Why would he be creeping around
here all alone? He's got a great big army and a load of monsters
at his command. Besides, he's a coward: he wouldn't be taking
any risks.'

It could be one of those other monsters, Ellie wanted to say;
but she didn't dare open her mouth because she could feel

another sneeze building up. It started as a tickle at the back of her nose, as if a bee was tiptoeing around in there; then it swelled up as if the bee had become the size of a small kitten. She pinched her nostrils shut. It was coming, it was coming . . .

'*Achooooo!*'

The noise rang across the clearing, bouncing off the tree trunks like a ricocheting bullet. Whatever it was that had been approaching stopped dead. A heavy silence fell. Silver rolled her eyes.

Then, very slowly, a figure emerged into the glade.

Ellie's eyes widened. 'Oh!' she cried, and her cheeks went very red.

Silver watched in amazement as her friend got to her feet, threw her arms around the figure and hugged it tight.

When Ellie stepped back again, a bit embarrassed by her own forwardness, her jumper was stained red. She stared at it as if she couldn't imagine how she'd got blood on it; then she stared at the newcomer. 'Oh, Darius, you're hurt!'

This was something of an understatement. The centaur was covered in wounds. His handsome face bore a great slash, as if from a blade, or a claw, and the blood from it had dried like a mask. His body was covered in cuts and his fingers were red to the knuckle, the nails broken and bleeding, as if he had lost every weapon but fought on with his bare hands.

'Princess Eleanor . . .' He could not meet her eyes.

'What happened? Where's my mother?'

His reply was barely a whisper: his throat was raw from screaming at the enemy. 'He has taken her.'

'What?' Ellie was sure she had misheard.

The centaur swallowed the great lump that had risen in his throat. 'The Dodman has her,' he said, more distinctly.

Ellie stared at him in disbelief. 'No! Neither you nor Cernunnos would allow such a thing to happen, you'd die first—'

'The Lord of the Wildwood is dead, as is the minotaur and most of my centaurs,' Darius said flatly. 'I took the Queen and the other Wildwood folk to find a place of greater safety but . . .' He swallowed again, remembering, and closed his eyes. 'What could we do against dinosaurs? He has so many of them, all different kinds, on the air, on the ground. They even killed Ishtar . . .

'We split our forces, such as they were. The Queen and I fled out across the heath. We had planned to draw them out then double back and evade them, but they were too fast.' He bowed his head. 'We took a stand on Eagle Tor and there Isadora called for Zark to take us off; but he didn't answer her call. Perhaps he is dead, too.'

'He's not dead. He's over there.' Ellie gestured behind her.

Darius frowned. 'Well, he resisted her summons. Maybe he was unconscious.'

'Or out of his mind. He was very upset about Ishtar.' She caught his hand. 'But, oh, Darius: tell me what happened to Mum. Is she okay? Is she still alive?' Her breath caught in her throat.

The Horse Lord swallowed. 'I . . . I don't know. They surrounded us. I did all I could, except die. I should have died.

Believe me, Princess Eleanor, I wished to. To have let him take the Queen without giving up my soul is the greatest shame to me. I killed I don't know how many . . . goblins mainly, two velociraptors. I wounded another, bigger dinosaur, but then he sent in a triceratops and my sword broke against its monstrous horns. I fought on without my blade, but they were savage. The great beast which the Dodman rode simply plucked us up. They took Isadora away from me and cast me away, like rubbish . . .' His voice broke and he wiped a hand fiercely across his damaged face. '"Go back and tell them that I have their Queen," the Dog-Headed One sneered. "Tell them how mighty I am become, and that there is nothing left to them now but despair." He left me alive to carry that message to the surviving folk of the Wildwood. But until I found you, I had yet to see another living soul.'

Ellie went pale. 'Oh, Mum—' she started, and could say no more. She closed her eyes, swaying. Little black stars danced on the inside of her eyelids. *Don't be stupid*, she told herself sternly. *It's only silly women in old novels who faint at bad news. Pull yourself together.*

She blinked and tried to focus on Darius as if he might make the feelings of despair and dizziness evaporate; but although she could only see him through a blur she could tell that he was watching her intently with tears in his dark brown eyes, and that just made her feel worse.

'Oh,' she groaned at last, and sat down heavily.

'Now look what you've done,' said Silver severely to the centaur. 'Couldn't you have broken the news more gently?' She ran to Ellie's side and grabbed the girl's hand as if she would comfort her. Then she pinched the web of skin between Ellie's thumb and forefinger hard.

'Ow!' Ellie cried, leaping to her feet in outrage. 'What did you do that for?'

Silver grinned. 'Old selkie trick,' she said. 'If you want to stop yourself transforming back to being a seal for a minute or two. Hurts, doesn't it?'

'Yes,' said Ellie crossly, pulling back her hand. 'Anyway, I'm not a selkie.'

Silver shrugged. 'But it worked, though.' She gazed up into the darkening sky. 'Look: I don't want to be here when night falls. We'd better call Ben and Mummu-Tiamat, let them know there's no point searching the Wildwood for your mother.'

Ellie scowled. There were times when she found Silver very annoying indeed, and she was just about to say so when the selkie hollowed her hands around her mouth and let forth an ear-splitting cry.

It was the sort of cry selkies use to let others of their kind know that they have sighted prey – a fine swarm of rabbitfish, maybe; or a shoal of sea-toads – and it was designed to travel clearly across acres of rolling ocean. In the quiet of the late-afternoon forest it was as sharp as a knife in the back.

Darius stared at Silver in disbelief.

'Good grief,' said Ellie. 'They'll think we're under attack.'

'Did you have a better way of contacting them?' Silver glared at Ellie with her hands on her hips.

'Well, no . . .'

'Well then. Mummu-Tiamat will know what it was, and she'll turn around and come back. Just you wait and see.'

'I'm not sure it was wise to draw such attention to ourselves,' Darius said quietly.

Silver held his gaze, and eventually it was the centaur who looked away. He shook his head wearily then crossed the clearing to where Xarkanadûshak lay, unmoving. There, he went down on one knee beside the dragon and laid a hand gently upon his back. 'What happened to him?' he asked, looking back towards Ellie and Silver. 'When last I saw him . . .' He bowed his head, remembering. When he had last seen Zark it had been as the little dragon dived in desperation through the battle-ravaged canopy in pursuit of his stricken mate. It seemed an age ago, though it was only yesterday.

It was the sense of something in the air above which made Darius look up; then a shadow fell over him.

Silver and Ellie stared skywards expectantly. But it was not the Mother of Dragons who had cast the shadow.

Silver screamed.

It seemed to come out of nowhere, it was so fast and so silent. All Ellie could remember was the sight of herself reflected in one of its shining black eyes, and a long, bony beak; wings that beat the air so hard that her hair stood on end in the backwash, as if she had been standing beneath the rotor-circle of a helicopter.

She saw, as if in slow-motion, Darius charging across the turbulent space between them; but there was nothing he could do. The creature reached out with its wicked claws, dragged Silver off the ground with a determined lurch, and soared skywards again before anyone could stop it. All they could do was to watch its spiky black silhouette flapping leisurely away beyond the trees.

Then it was gone.

CHAPTER SEVENTEEN

Capture

'Put it on!'

'I will not!'

Isadora cast the froth of white muslin and lace in the
Dodman's face. It hung on his muzzle for a few moments, looking distinctly strange, then tumbled in a heap to the floor. They
both gazed at it, with very different emotions.

The dog-headed man was fast losing any patience he had
with Eidolon's Queen. He had thought to woo her, at first,
and had been as gentle as he knew how: sending to the room
in which he had confined her little treats — a necklace of
mermaid scales and phoenix feathers, huge bunches of

deadly nightshade; and finally, a pie made of wood-sprite hearts.

Isadora had torn the necklace apart with an exclamation of anger and had left the poisonous flowers lying where he had left them till they were wilted and withered. Hunger had driven her to cut into the pie. But when she saw what it contained the blood drained from her face. That she should have come to this, the Queen of Eidolon, held captive by a monster in the very castle where as a child she had run and played, and fed upon the tiny hearts of her precious subjects. She sat down on the floor with her head in her hands and wept.

When the Dodman returned, sure to find he had won favour, he found her like this, and when he questioned why, she railed at him in fury, and he did not know what to do or say.

Eventually he picked up the dress from the floor and shook it out. A myriad of moths flew up from the folds of fabric. In the light, their wings sparkled and shone.

'Put it on,' he said again, and now his voice was grim with intent. If she would not bow to gentle persuasion, he would bend her to his will.

Isadora shook her head. 'I will not. It was my mother's and her mother's before her.'

'I know. The Queens of Eidolon always wear this dress to be married in.'

'I didn't.'

The Dodman snapped his claws. 'That? That was not a

marriage. It was an abomination, a miscegenation. Different species cannot marry.'

'Clive and I are not of "different species".'

'Clive! A worm. A mere human.'

'He is not a worm,' Isadora said firmly. 'He is a fine man, the father of my children, and he is my husband whom I love dearly.'

'You cannot love such a creature,' he said dismissively.

'But I do.'

'You have made a foolish error. You went away from here in confusion with your head all in a spin; he took advantage of you on the Other Side, and you forgot who you were and where you were from. But now you are back and you can make amends.' He smiled indulgently, giving her the full benefit of his fine array of dog-teeth. 'Soon the children will be no more and that will erase your error—'

'My children?' Isadora went white. 'What have you done with my children?'

'Nothing. Yet.'

She scanned his dog-face anxiously, but the flat black eyes gave away no clue. 'Where are they?'

That was a good question. Maggota was taking her time. He avoided answering her directly. 'Safe. Quite safe. For now. Wed me and you have the chance to put right all that you have done wrong. Put on the dress and we shall go down together, hand in hand, to be married.'

'Married?' Isadora laughed. 'By some troll or ogre?'

'Aleister will marry us,' he returned smoothly. 'He has the right, as the head of your family.'

'Aleister?' she scoffed. 'He will not do it. He knows I am already married.'

'Oh, I think he will. Now, PUT ON THE DRESS!'

'My brother has no spine, that I know. But I cannot believe that he is evil through and through.'

She took the dress from his claws. It seemed she had little choice but to play his game. At least she would be out of this room, which she had loved so much as a girl, and which now offered only bitter memories. She remembered the last time she had been here, playing out a scene in which the same characters played out similar roles; when the dog-headed man had fallen to his knees before her and pledged his heart, and she had laughed him out of the room: he was just a servant, a witch's drudge. She could not believe his arrogance. After that, she had felt his eyes on her wherever she went: cold eyes, calculating his next move. Then, one by one, everyone she cared about had mysteriously vanished, leaving only her brother Aleister, who was clearly in thrall to the Dodman. One day she heard them plotting to take her throne by marrying her against her will to the dog-headed beast. The next day she had taken a wild road into the Other World and met Clive Arnold. It had been fifteen years before she had returned.

In her absence, enraged by her escape, the Dodman had set about destroying all the magic in her kingdom. By the time she knew the truth of this, she had been rendered so weak and ill by his depredations, and by the difficulty of childbirth – first Ellie, then Ben – that she had felt like lying down and dying, of shame as much as grief. But then along had come Alice, and although that had been the hardest birth of all, it was the one which had filled her with the most hope: one glance at those bright green Eidolon eyes, and she knew that the old prophecy she had once embroidered on a simple cotton sampler held the key to a new future, a future in which Eidolon should be saved.

My children, she thought now. *I pray that you are safe.*

'If you do not put on the dress, I shall be forced to do something very nasty indeed to little Cynthia.'

The Dodman's cruel words cut into her thoughts. Such a threat surely meant that he did not have Ben or Ellie or Alice. This realisation gave her courage.

'If I put it on, you must promise me you will let her out of that horrid cage.'

'Certainly, my love, for she shall be your bridesmaid!'

'Bridesmaid!'

'She won't be happy, of course,' he went on, shaking his head sadly. 'She was intent on being Queen herself.'

Isadora's eyebrows shot up. 'Oh she was, was she? And was that why she brought you the Book?' She laughed. 'Poor silly girl. She trusted you. I dare say you promised her all manner of things.'

She saw the sly grin he tried to conceal, even as she shrugged into the dress.

'Ah, but you lied to her and crossed your fingers even as you promised,' she said, pulling the white muslin down around her. As she did so, her Other World clothes began to disappear. It fitted her perfectly. It was bound to: there was magic woven through every stitch.

The Dodman gave a little growl. He did not like to be found out so easily.

'So why did you not kill her, as you have killed so many others, once you had the Book in your hands?' Isadora mused; and before he could reply, she had her answer. 'Because you cannot read it. There is no magic in you.' She watched his expression darken and knew she was right. 'Such a shame for you that Aleister never persevered with his lessons. How cosy you would have been then, you and the boy you bullied all his life, summoning all the monsters of the world to do away with the rest of us. Do we really threaten you so fearfully, we of the magic?' And she reached out a hand as if to touch him.

The Dodman flinched away from her. Who knew what magic still resided in this Queen, no matter how weak she had become? He found he could not look her in the face, for the sight of her in the dress made him feeble in the legs. Strange sensations danced in his stomach. He braced himself and looked carefully to one side of her.

'You think you are so clever, you and all you magicked ones, because you are of the old stock, the ones who were here first. Well, I must tell you that your time has been and gone. Control is passing out of your hands. My Eidolon will be a different sort of world, a fairer world, in which magic does not confer power over others.'

Isadora snorted her disdain. 'A world in which power is taken by bullying and murder; a world in which power is horribly abused. You just want to destroy magic because you have none, and what you do not have or understand, you hate and fear.'

The Dodman waved his fingers at her as if shooing away a fly. 'What do I care for your moralising, madam? You are my captive, and when we are married I shall be King and your body and realm will be mine. And yes, I hate all things of magic: but not just because I have none myself. I hate them because they are unnatural, vile and sneaking. The world will be a better place without them; and you will be better too. Without the magic in you, you will love me, I know it.'

Isadora shuddered. 'You disgust me, and you always will, magic or no magic.'

He grabbed her by the shoulder then and his cruel dog-claws dug sharply into her flesh.

'I want you to see something before we go down to be wed,' he told her, dragging her out into the corridor. 'And when you have seen it, then you will know you and your kind are defeated, and you will be able to better accept the inevitable changes that are coming upon Eidolon.'

An unearthly shriek split the darkening air.

'What was that?' Ben stared wildly around, almost losing his grip on the dragon's scales in his startlement. Iggy slipped and scrabbled. 'Hey!' he cried. 'Watch out, Sonny Jim!'

The noise seemed to have come from where they had left Ellie and Silver and the sleeping dragon.

The Mother of Dragons made a lazy circle and cast an eye back at the Wildwood. 'A selkie hunting cry,' she said, sounding puzzled. 'How curious.'

Ben realised she had never really seen Silver in her selkie

form, but only as a girl. 'That'll be Silver, then,' he said. 'I wonder why she's calling us.' Something inside him felt tight and cold. 'Can we go back, Mummu-Tiamat? I think something may be wrong.'

The Mother of Dragons gave a great flap of her wings and headed back to the clearing. As they neared the site, Ben could just make out a familiar figure – half-man, half-horse: a centaur. Was it Darius? From high above it was hard to tell; the figure didn't stand like Darius, straight and tall. It looked smaller and less proud. Ben frowned. But the centaurs were their allies, so there could be no danger here, and whoever it was, perhaps he would have news of where his mother might be.

As Mummu-Tiamat came in to land, Ben jumped down, hitting the ground running, just like he had seen commandos do in war films. Unfortunately he hadn't bargained on the fact that he was still moving and the ground was standing still: he hit hard, tripped over his own feet and fell flat on his face. He got up slowly, waiting for Ellie to pour scorn on him in her usual fashion. But his ignominious arrival was met by an ominous silence.

He looked up to find the centaur looking down at him.

'Oh, Darius! What happened to you?'

The Horse Lord's handsome face was haggard. 'I . . . ah . . . it's hard to know where to begin.'

'The beginning's always good,' Iggy suggested helpfully.

'The boy's mother!' a voice boomed. 'Tell us what you know of the boy's mother.'

Darius gazed at the giant dragon with dull eyes. She was the most magnificent creature he had ever seen: a legend made flesh. The very sight of her should have lifted his heart, but it was just too heavy. 'The Dodman has her captive.'

Ben felt the world collapsing around him. He grabbed hold of the centaur's arm. 'What? No! It can't be – neither you nor Cernunnos would allow such a thing.'

'The Lord of the Wildwood is dead,' Darius intoned flatly. He had no wish to discuss the details again, even for Ben's sake, for nothing could change the facts. 'So is the minotaur, and most of my centaurs. We are defeated. And now there is other evil news—'

Ben felt dizzy. 'A-Alice?' he stuttered.

The Horse Lord frowned. 'No, not Alice. Silver.'

'Silver . . .?' Ben spun in a circle. Over by the bulk of Xarkanadûshak's sleeping form he could see his sister in a heap, her hair covering her face. But the selkie was nowhere to be seen. He turned back to the centaur, hardly daring to ask his question.

'A quetzalcoatlus,' Darius said baldly. 'A flying dinosaur. It swooped down and took her. It came out of nowhere. There was nothing we could do.'

'When?' The Mother of Dragons was at once practical. 'How long ago was this? We heard a selkie cry out.'

'That was before she was taken. She was calling for you.'

'Foolish child! It must have heard her and gone to investigate.' Mummu-Tiamat shook her head. 'A shame. She was a pretty girl. Come, Ellie, Ben: we shall resume the search for your mother.'

Ben was aghast at her hard-heartedness. 'But we can't just let the dinosaurs take Silver. We must find her. We must save her!'

'She's gone, Prince of Eidolon. The quetzalcoatlus is probably eating her even as we speak.'

Ben stared at the Mother of Dragons. 'Mummu-Tiamat, I now ask you the favour you owe me for your life. Pursue the dinosaur and help me save my friend.'

The dragon regarded him with one of her heavy-lidded eyes. 'If that is what you wish, Prince of Eidolon. I would have thought you would be more concerned about the fate of your mother.'

Ben felt a sudden pang of guilt. Did he care more about Silver than his mother? It was an impossible question to ponder. 'I am . . . but, well we can't just give Silver up without a fight.'

Mummu-Tiamat sighed. 'As you will. I fear it is a wild lizard chase and already too late.'

Ben started to climb back on the dragon, only to feel something pulling him back. He looked around. It was his sister and her eyes were flashing.

'Ben, the Mother of Dragons is right. We should be trying to save Mum. I'm sorry about Silver, really I am: but surely our mother's more important than a selkie?'

Ben took a deep breath. He loved his mother deeply; but he couldn't explain what he felt for the selkie. What he did know was that he couldn't just stand by and let her be eaten without at least trying to rescue her. He would never be able to live with the thought that he might have saved her.

'Look,' he said, shaking Ellie's hand off, 'it won't take long: they can't be that far ahead and Mummu-Tiamat's faster than any old dinosaur. We'll overtake them, we'll rescue her and we'll be back before you know it. And then we can make a plan for saving Mum from the Dodman.' He couldn't even think about that at the moment: it was too big and too complicated to contemplate, especially with this new emergency on hand. He boosted himself up on to the dragon's back and found the Wanderer already there, waiting for him.

'Well, come on, then!' said Iggy impatiently. 'We're wasting valuable time.'

Ellie didn't know what to do. Part of her couldn't bear the idea of staying behind, in case another monster appeared; part of her needed to do something: anything. And beneath these warring sensations, another part of her yearned for none of this to be happening. She hesitated for just a moment, glancing at the Horse Lord. But Darius said nothing, just stared at the ground as if he wished it would swallow him up. 'I'm coming with you,' she declared fiercely. 'She's my friend as well.'

She handed up the sack containing Boneless Bob to her brother then grabbed a scale with both hands and climbed aboard.

'Princess Eleanor!'

Ellie turned.

The centaur gazed up at her uncertainly, then turned away.

'What? What were you going to say?'

He turned back. 'Don't go,' he said in a low voice.

Ellie blushed. 'Come with us. He can, can't he, Mother of Dragons?'

'We haven't time for this,' Mummu-Tiamat said firmly. She fixed Darius with a glowing eye. 'Stay here and look after my dragon, Lord Centaur. He will wake soon, and he will be grief-stricken and miserable. Take him with you to the rest of the Wildwood folk. They will take care of him. Do this for me. You have failed twice. If you fail a third time you will have me to answer to.'

Darius hung his head.

Despite his shock, Ben felt his heart go out to the centaur. He had taken many wounds: he looked ready to drop. As Mummu-Tiamat gathered her haunches to leap into the air he called out, 'It's not your fault, Darius! We'll get Silver back safely, and Mum too: just you wait and see.'

He only wished he could believe his own words.

CHAPTER EIGHTEEN

To the Rescue

The Dodman dragged Isadora to the top of the battlements and pushed her hard against the jagged crenellations.

'There!' he exclaimed, throwing an arm wide. 'Now do you see? Those who were with me at Eagle Tor were mere skirmishers, no more than a small advance guard. These are the ones who will change the world with me. The ones who will rout all the magic out of Eidolon. Look on my army and despair.'

The Queen stared out into the gathering gloom. On the northern shores of the lake surrounding the castle were gathered thousands of monsters. Isadora had good eyes; green eyes: Eidolon eyes. She could see: goblins and hobgoblins, demons and sabre-toothed tigers; trolls and ogres trussed up in armour. There were allosaurs and triceratops, velociraptors and megaraptors, tyrannosaurs and brontosaurs and stegosaurs. In the air above what had once been forest, banshees howled and trailed their tattered shrouds. Pterosaurs and pterodactyls wheeled like giant bats. Some that flew there *were* giant bats. Vampire bats.

The Wildwood had once extended almost to the shore. But now the trees were stripped bare, the plants beneath them flattened to hard earth. Other trees had been ripped out by their roots: a huge, ramshackle bridge now spanned the lake between the shore and the castle. Campfires burned, sending trails of acrid smoke and the smell of charred meat up into the darkening air. Isadora shuddered. Goodness only knew what those monsters were eating.

Even as she thought this, a great bird flapped slowly overhead. In its claws something struggled.

'Help me!'

The voice was tiny; but it was familiar. Isadora strained her eyes. It was Ben's little selkie friend, Silver, in her girl form.

'No!'

The Queen turned to her captor. 'Help me save her!' she commanded, and her eyes burned bright green.

The Dodman felt his legs tremble. He turned away, fixing his gaze on the prehistoric monster, but his eyes were not as good as Isadora's. All he saw was a small creature struggling helplessly. 'Ah, my fine dinosaur, I see you have found some supper for your friends!' he called to the monstrous beast. 'Feed well, my friend!'

Isadora cried out, 'You cannot be so cruel!' But she knew he could. She dragged her hands free of him, hammered blows down upon his torso. 'I will never marry a monster like you. Never! Save that poor child or I shall not go down with you.'

The dog-headed man shrugged, but he kept his head averted. He had the measure of her magic now: it would not save her; or others. 'My army must be kept fed and happy. And as for you, madam, know that you have no choice in the matter. I shall wed you and become King whether you will or not; and if you must needs be insensible for the ceremony, I am sure that can be arranged.'

The Queen started to cry. Not for herself but for the poor selkie-girl; for her helpless subjects, her helpless world.

The Dodman risked a glance at his sobbing bride. Her eyes were downturned but even so the rising moon made her white form glow ethereally. He could almost see the elf-blood moving in her veins. He looked away quickly.

'I see that at last you understand the despair of the truly defeated,' he said soothingly. 'I will not ask you to dry your eyes and be glad for our nuptials, for the happy are strong, and that would never do.'

Then he caught her fiercely by the wrist and dragged her behind him down the steeply winding stairs, down and down and down to the throne room below.

'Hold tight!'

The Mother of Dragons stretched out her long neck and her great long tail so that she formed a line as straight as an arrow in flight. The wind whistled past Ben's ears. When he looked down, it was to see Iggy's fur plastered so hard against his face that he looked more like a rat than a cat.

Ellie's eyes were squinched hard shut. She was beginning to wish she'd stayed on the ground with the handsome centaur.

Around them, the air darkened and the moon came up. Try as he might, Ben could see nothing of the flying dinosaur who had stolen Silver. 'Faster, Mummu-Tiamat!' he urged, without once thinking this might not be the most respectful way to address the Mother of Dragons.

Mummu-Tiamat made no response. She hurtled through the skies like a jet aircraft. At any moment Ben expected to hear a sonic boom as she broke the sound barrier, but all he could hear was the boom of his blood in his ears. He thought about summoning Silver: would that save her? He imagined her flying through the sky to land beside him, breathless and grinning. But then he imagined her being whipped from the quetzalcoatlus's back and plummeting hundreds of feet to her death. He remembered how he had been summoned by Iggy when the troll was about to eat him: how he had been dragged through thorns and brambles and everything in the path between them, regardless of comfort or possibility. It was just too risky. So instead he shielded his eyes and stared out into the falling night and hoped and hoped.

The Mother of Dragons soared high over the Wildwood, so high that little clouds scudded past them. So high that it was hard to breathe. Ben had never been so high in his life as he had on the back of this magnificent dragon. He had never been in an aeroplane, for his mother had never been well enough to go abroad on holiday. And anyway, they had never had enough money.

Family life, in which illness and lack of money caused problems, seemed a lifetime, an aeon, away. He wished with all his heart that he could return to that time of innocence, when it had all been someone else's responsibility; when the adults in his life had been there to take charge and make decisions, but he knew it was impossible. His mother was a prisoner of her deadliest enemy; and his father was able to do nothing in this magical world. Even his older sister was less effective here. Alice was missing, and now so was Silver. It was too much for a boy of twelve to bear, prince or no prince.

He pushed his thoughts away; his despair, too.

'Can you see anything, Mummu-Tiamat?' he cried into the streaming wind.

'Over there,' came back the dragon's voice. 'Do you see the flickering lights?'

Down below and ahead of them, Ben could make out a great swathe of darkness relieved only by a myriad of orange dots, like a swarm of fire-flies against a black cloth. Beyond this was something wide and gleaming; then a darker lump with what appeared to be a fortress on it. It must be Corbenic Castle and the great lake that surrounded it! But what could the orange lights be? There was only Wildwood on the northern shore.

Mummu-Tiamat gave a titanic flap of her huge wings and dived towards the lake.

Ellie gave a muffled scream, and Iggy dug his claws into Ben's leg. 'She's trying to kill us!' he miaowed.

But Ben's attention had been caught by a figure moving away from the castle across the surface of the lake. From above it looked like a skinny crow carrying a twig for its nest; but within seconds he knew he was seeing the dinosaur that had snatched Silver.

'There she is!' he shrieked. 'Go get her, Mummu-Tiamat!'

The dragon flicked her mighty tail and stooped like a hawk, and now Ben could say nothing at all. The skin of his face rippled and wobbled like a shaken jelly. Ben had once been on a fairground ride that had a similar effect and he hadn't enjoyed the sensation much. What he *had* enjoyed had been seeing his dad step down from the ride swaying and then tip over on top of some poor woman carrying two huge sticks of candyfloss for her children. It had taken ages to disentangle them, the children had thrown tantrums, and his dad's jumper had never been the same again.

Despite everything, Ben couldn't help grinning. They were gaining on the quetzalcoatlus with every beat of the great dragon's wings. They were going to catch it. They were going to save Silver!

The lake skimmed past below at impossible speed. Ben thought if they went any faster his ears would probably come off: a horrible but rather fascinating image. Knowing Eidolon, they'd probably take on a life of their own and go flapping away like butterflies.

He was just imagining this when Mummu-Tiamat pulled

up so fast that Ellie howled and grabbed at him and, because he hadn't been paying proper attention, he lost his balance and slipped sideways. Suddenly he found himself hanging upside-down, watching blurry shapes flee past him. Even as he was falling, he closed his ordinary eye and looked with his Eidolon eye, and suddenly the shapes resolved themselves into forest and campfires and huge creatures moving slowly around. Then there was a terrific pain in his leg and hands around his ankle and between them Iggy and Ellie hauled him upright again.

'You idiot!' said Ellie.

Ben blinked and frowned, disorientated and confused. One minute they had been right behind the flying dinosaur, but now he couldn't see it anywhere. He twisted around and realised that the great dragon had wheeled about in a huge curve and that now they were heading in the opposite direction to which Silver was being taken.

'Mummu-Tiamat! Don't stop – we have to save her!'

The Mother of Dragons flapped her wings implacably, and the distance between them and Silver extended itself with each beat.

'Mummu-Tiamat, go back!'

She made no immediate response. Then: 'Did you see what was down there?' she said at last.

Ben thought about this. It had all been a bit of a blur. He closed his eyes, remembering. 'Monsters,' he said eventually. 'Goblins and trolls and dinosaurs. Hundreds of them.' He swallowed.

'Thousands,' the Mother of Dragons corrected him grimly.

'I thought they were extinct.'

'In your world. Not here. Here they thrive. They breed. Oh, how they breed!' Mummu-Tiamat spat. 'A dragon pair may raise two kits in a hundred years; but those monsters . . . Clutches of eggs in the tens and twenties. Swarms of them, overrunning our ancient ancestral grounds, our sacred territory. They are a plague on the face of Eidolon, and every year there are more advancing: stupid, cunning and greedy and ready to pick a fight at the drop of a scale. No wonder he was able to persuade them to his side. I would hazard he didn't even have to summon half of them; give them the chance of fighting the dragons and they'd volunteer for the sheer pleasure of spilling our blood and taking more of our land.'

Much of this long speech went over Ben's head; so all he really took from it was that dinosaurs and dragons didn't really like one another. It didn't seem anywhere near a good enough reason for turning tail and leaving his friend.

'I don't care about all that. All that matters is Silver. I won't leave her to be killed among monsters!' He felt his eyes fill with tears of frustration, and when the dragon said nothing he screwed his fists up and hammered on her back. 'Turn around, Mummu-Tiamat!' he cried.

The Mother of Dragons sighed. 'I am carrying two children of the royal blood; to one of whom I owe my freedom. The cat and the snake mean little to me . . .'

'Oh, thanks,' snarled Ignatius Sorvo Coromandel. 'I'll remember that the next time you need rescuing from a witch.'

The dragon ignored him, '. . . and there are plenty more

selkies in the sea. But there is only one Prince and Princess of Eidolon . . .'

Actually, Ben corrected her silently, *there are two princesses. Or rather, there were . . .*

'. . . and my duty is to keep you safe, to say nothing of myself—'

'You are a coward!' Ben was beside himself now: he hardly knew what he was saying.

'I am a realist,' Mummu-Tiamat said tightly, keeping her temper with difficulty. 'One dragon, two children and a scruffy little cat are not going to go very far against a thousand hungry dinosaurs.'

Ben took a deep breath. 'The selkie is my friend. She means a lot to me, and she has saved my life not once, but twice.'

'Twice?' The Mother of Dragons thought about this for several long slow wingbeats. Then she began to turn. 'A life-debt is a heavy thing, Prince of Eidolon. If you are set on sacrificing yourself for it, that is your choice. I will drop you on the edge of the forest.'

Ben gulped. 'Alone?'

The dragon flicked an eyelid at him. 'It is your debt, not mine.'

'But what am I supposed to do on my own against an army of dinosaurs?'

'You seem to be a resourceful boy, Prince of Eidolon. I'm sure you'll think of something.' And she soared back towards the Wildwood, getting lower to the gloomy canopy with every flap of her great leathery wings.

Ben fell silent. He couldn't think of anything at all. It was as if his brain had slipped down into his stomach and he was now digesting it bit by bit. The inside of his skull where he believed his brain had once been now felt all shiny and empty and useless. He wasn't even sure he could speak.

There was a warm pressure on his arm. He looked down and found a small black-and-brown paw resting on it.

'I'll come with you,' said Iggy.

'And I will, too,' said Ellie, taking everyone by surprise.

Mummu-Tiamat shook her head sadly. 'If you are really determined to cast your lives away for no good reason, there's nothing I can do to stop you. I hope you rescue your friend. Perhaps we will meet again. In another lifetime.'

She set the three of them down on the ground. They watched as she flapped slowly away.

CHAPTER NINETEEN
The Law Book

All the usual suspects were gathered in the throne room of Dodman Castle. Eight spectral white dogs, known as the Gabriel Hounds, lay tangled up with one another in front of the fireplace, even though no one had been so organised as to light a fire in it for weeks and weeks. They were lazy creatures. Which was why a large band of goblins – including Batface and Bogie, Gutty and Grabbit, Beetle, Brimstone, Barfer and Blaggard – were congregated on the other side of the room: for one of the ghost-dogs' favourite habits was biting goblins. Which they were very good at, despite having ghost-teeth.

The little witch, Cynthia Creepie, had managed to turn over in her wooden cage and now lay on her back, with her carroty hair poking through one end of the cage and her pointy feet out through the bars at the other end. Her father, Aleister – known to the Arnold children as Awful Uncle Aleister – sat on the throne behind her. Absent-mindedly, he had put his feet up on the cage (forgetting that it contained his daughter) and was coming to the conclusion that the Dodman had a point: having your legs stretched out so really was quite comfy. His bald head (on which a delicate crown of silver and crystal was precariously balanced) nodded dreamily over the hands that lay folded in his lap. Really, the nails needed cleaning badly. Hygiene standards in Eidolon had fallen woefully low. Disgusted, he threw the hands across the room, where one of the Gabriel Hounds fell upon them in delight, then stood guarding them, fangs bared, in case any of its fellows fancied stealing such a tasty morsel. The rest of the wood-nymph they had belonged to had been consumed last night by the Dodman, along with a dozen fairies: he seemed to need more every day to keep his strength up.

'Aleister!'

Old Creepie shot upright in panic and the crown tipped dangerously low over one eye, making him appear both furtive and ridiculous.

The Dodman hauled Isadora the length of the chamber, glaring so furiously it looked as if his eyes were on fire. 'Take that off!'

Isadora regarded her brother curiously. 'I wondered what

had become of my crown.' She glanced down at her sleeping niece. 'She must have taken it when she stole the Book.'

Aleister coughed. 'Oh, I'm sure she . . . er . . . only borrowed it.'

The Queen's eyes flashed. 'Just as you are only 'borrowing' my throne, sweet brother?' She reached over and snatched the crown off his head. She turned the delicate web of silver and crystal over and over in her pale hands and then set it firmly on her own head. As she did so, she seemed to grow in stature and power. Old Creepie quailed away from her.

'I . . . er . . . just put it on for safety.'

Isadora laughed. 'Yes, well you can see it wasn't fashioned for the head of any man, fat-headed or –' she turned her fierce green gaze upon the Dodman '– dog-headed. The Crown of Eidolon passes from one Queen to the next. There has never been a King in Eidolon. And there never shall be!'

The Dodman growled suddenly. It was the sort of noise a mad dog makes before it bites. He loomed up over Isadora and raised his hand. Then he swiped the crown from her head and it went flying in a swirl of crystal, smashing into the wall on the other side of the room. After the terrible clatter, a heavy silence fell.

'That is a tradition I mean to break,' he snarled. 'When Aleister marries us you may wear your little trinket, but I shall take your power and *I* shall be King. King Dodman the First. Yes.' And he licked his long black dog-lips as if savouring his victory.

Isadora stared at him scornfully. 'Never.'

Aleister was frowning. 'I hate to say anything, old chap, but—'

The Dodman rounded on him. 'But *what*? Spit it out!'

'I can't officiate, old man. She's . . . er . . . already married. Technically, I mean. She already has a . . . er . . . husband. Don't think she can have another. . .'

The Dodman waved a paw dismissively. 'Counts for nothing. A Queen of Eidolon can't marry a worm of a human. Come on, Aleister: can't you see she's dressed for the occasion?'

'Hah!' cried Isadora. 'This is a nonsense. You, sir, are a monster, and my brother is a fool. I am already wed, and nothing changes that.' And she folded her arms and turned her back on the two of them.

Old Creepie gazed helplessly up at the Dodman and what he saw in that monstrous face made him go pale, then bright red, which wasn't a pretty sight. 'I . . . ah . . . Let me just . . . er . . . go and get the Law Book, old chap. Check the wording and such.' And with this excuse, he slipped swiftly from the throne and sped across the hall remarkably smartly for one having such short, bowed legs.

The Dodman kicked the cage a ringing blow. Cynthia, rudely awakened, snorted and tried to sit up, which resulted in her banging her head hard against the bars. 'Ow!'

'Don't you think you've tortured the poor child enough?' Isadora said over her shoulder. 'Let her out of that cage!'

The Dodman favoured the little witch with his widest smile. 'No, not at all. She shan't come out till our wedding: she's going to be your bridesmaid.'

'Bridesmaid?' Cynthia screeched. 'Whose bridesmaid?'

'Your aunt's, idiot, when she marries me.'

'I've only got one aunt and she's already—' Cynthia's gooseberry-green eyes almost popped out of her head. 'You can't! You promised!'

'Oh, Cynthia.' Isadora turned to regard the little witch pityingly. 'Silly girl, for trusting such a monster.'

'Silly you,' Cynthia retorted. 'For trusting me.'

Isadora nodded. 'Yes, I was foolish indeed. It is not a lesson I shall need to learn twice.'

Her niece pursed her thin lips, wondering what that meant. She didn't get a chance to ask, for at that moment her father returned, bearing a large, grand-looking volume bound in thick red leather. He trotted to the Dodman's side and opened it at the page he'd marked. 'See here,' he said eagerly, turning it and thrusting it at the dog-headed man. 'Here are all the rules concerning royal marriages in Eidolon.' It had entirely slipped his mind that the Dodman could not read. His fingers traced the words: 'The Queen has the right to take to husband whomsoever she chooses – be he elf or troll, giant, selkie or any other creature of her choosing—'

'It doesn't say anything about human worms!' the Dodman sneered.

Aleister wetted his lips and read on: 'Once the Queen has chosen her mate, he shall be her mate for life. Only Death shall part them.'

The Dodman ripped the ancient tome from Old Creepie's hands. Then he flung it down upon the floor and jumped up and down on it. 'That's what I think of your stupid old book and its stupid old laws!'

Aleister looked horrified. 'But, old chap, it's the Law Book. It's sacred. It's what Eidolon was built on.'

'Stuff and nonsense! Who cares about the past? It's the future that matters, and my future shall be glorious!'

There was a brief pause. Then Aleister suggested timidly, 'Perhaps she could make you her chief counsellor, old chap. There's a nice chain of office you could use—'

The Dodman gripped him by the throat. 'Perhaps Isadora could feed your liver to the hounds!' he roared.

The Gabriel Hounds raised their heads from what they'd been occupied with. Who wanted a pair of stringy old wood-nymph hands when there was an entire fat necromancer to be chewed upon?

Aleister looked as if he might faint. 'I . . . er . . . don't think that would be a good idea. Look, old man, it's not my fault that you can't marry Isadora while her husband's still alive.'

'Bravo, Aleister!' Isadora clapped slowly. 'You tell him.'

The Dodman's beady black eyes bored into him. Then he laughed. 'What was it your precious book said again? About Death?'

Aleister retrieved the even more battered volume from the floor, found the page again after a lot of huffing and puffing and read: 'He shall be her mate for life, and only Death shall part them.'

'Only Death shall part them! What a fine ring that has to it. Only Death shall part them.' This he repeated over and over as he strode around in military style, his boots thumping the marble floor in rhythm to the words.

Aleister and Isadora exchanged a worried look. 'You don't think . . .' the Queen whispered; but the dog-headed man turned back sharply. 'You forget that dogs have extremely finely-attuned hearing. Think? Your brother rarely *thinks*, my dear.'

'I do try—'

'Well, don't! I, however, have a brain that works remarkably well: and do you know the solution that this fine organ has offered me?'

They shook their heads.

'It's absurdly simple.' And he clapped his hands as if to applaud his own brilliance. 'I shall have your "husband" brought here.'

He paused to watch Isadora's face.

'And then I shall kill him, and you will know yourself a widow, so there will be no impediment to our marriage.'

Isadora fainted clean away.

CHAPTER TWENTY
Among the Dinosaurs

The eaves of the Wildwood were dark and eerie and what little moonlight there was made Ignatius Sorvo Coromandel's eyes shine like headlamps. Ellie caught hold of Ben. 'Just to make sure I don't trip over and make a noise,' she assured him; but he could feel her heart hammering against his arm.

They walked as quietly as they could into the forest with the Wanderer leading the way. It was preternaturally quiet. No owls hooted; no sprites chattered; no insects chirred. Nothing stirred in the dark canopy of stark branches overhead: not a fairy; not a bird. Through the trees ahead of them they could see flickering orange light.

Ellie screwed up her eyes. 'Is the Wildwood on fire over there?' she asked fearfully.

'Nah.' Iggy's nose twitched. 'Those are cooking fires. Things are being roasted on them.'

Ben wondered what 'things' those might be. Dread settled in the pit of his stomach; and then he started running, towing Ellie behind him, the makeshift sack containing Boneless Bob tucked firmly under his arm. Ignatius Sorvo Coromandel shook his head, then belted after them.

If they had been worried about alerting the Dodman's army to their presence, they needn't have been concerned. The camp was full of noisy hubbub. There were monsters everywhere: a sea of brown and dark green, broken by the occasional glitter of lizard-scales or the magnificent striped coat of a sabre-toothed tiger. Bands of goblins had lit cook-fires, several of which had got out of hand and set fire to trees in which pterodactyls were roosting for the night. There was a great deal of squabbling and squawking about this: and one group of pterodactyls had killed an unfortunate goblin in retaliation and were currently engaged in eating him piece by piece.

'Ugh!' exclaimed Ben. He looked away, distressed by the sight, even though the victim was a hateful goblin.

'What?' said Ellie.

'You don't want to know,' her brother replied fervently.

'Can you see Silver?'

'I sincerely hope not.' Ben searched the rabble in front of them; but there was no sign of her in this quarter of the enemy camp. Which was probably a good thing. Here, there were mainly goblins, a few smaller trolls snoozing in heaps and some enormous, slow-moving creatures stripping the last remaining leaves from a large tree.

Ellie clutched Ben's arm. 'What on Earth are those?'

'Don't worry about them: they won't eat you. The really big one there's a brontosaurus, and the one next to it, with the beak-thing, is an iguanodon. They're herbivores. They don't eat meat.'

Ellie's eyebrows shot up. 'Oh, you mean vegetarian. Like Melissa, in our class. Wow.'

'They must have been driven to the edge of the camp because they've run out of stuff to eat,' said Ben. He paused, staring at them. 'The one we're looking for, the one that took Silver, must be closer to the centre.'

They skirted the edge of the camp, keeping downwind all the time: as Iggy pointed out, he didn't really want to be sniffed out by a horde of hungry goblins and eaten for dessert. An area of huge boulders, which must once have formed the walls of a long-dried-up river, provided them with cover as they made their way closer to the heart of the enemy army, and soon they were seeing all sorts of extraordinary creatures. Satyrs had mock-fights with one another, butting their heads together and locking their goats' horns, watched by a swarm of hungry-looking vampire bats. Beyond these loomed the allosaurs, as tall as the trees against which they lounged on their powerful haunches. One of them opened its mouth to laugh at something its comrade had said and moonlight glinted off its long, serrated teeth. There were armour-plated stegosaurs and triceratops, a sad-looking diplodocus nosing around in the vain hope of something to eat, and a horde of small raiders which Ben did not recognise but which looked rather like miniature tyrannosaurs darting between the feet of the others, stealing whatever food they could lay their little clawed hands on. Some of them wore scraps of fur and bone and hair around their necks.

'I like their necklaces,' Ellie whispered, after one had passed close enough for her to peer at it. 'I've seen things like that at Top Shop. Jungle Chic, they call it.'

Iggy favoured her with a hard stare. 'That's not fashion,' he said scathingly. 'That's our friends.'

Ben closed the eye he thought of as his Earth eye and focused with his Eidolon eye. He recoiled. The little raptors were sporting sprigs of centaur hair, wood-sprite husks, fairy bones, gnome ears. 'They've taken trophies,' he said, disgusted. 'Bits and pieces of the woodland folk they've killed.'

'Oh—' Ellie felt sick. It wasn't all that different to the jewellery she and Cynthia had made with the feathers and bits of fur Uncle Aleister had brought home for them. There were girls in her class still wearing their earrings made out of mermaid scales, their necklaces of unicorn horn. Except then she hadn't known that was what they were. And now that she did, she couldn't bring herself to tell them.

They edged closer. Close enough to hear a pair of allosaurs having an argument.

'I want to go home.'

'Stop whingeing, Ancasta. We can't. We've been over this a thousand times.'

'And you've never given me a good reason for us being here. I mean, look at the company we're keeping – stegosaurs and eoraptors – idiots and thieves. Very noble!' And she folded her arms and glared at him.

'We're here to support the clan-chief. As you know.'

'Well, it's not *my* fault he got summoned, is it? It's not even our war!'

'Be quiet!' The larger of the two allosaurs looked over his shoulder. 'You'll get us into trouble.'

'You're such a wimp, Pertinax. Mother was right. I should never have mated with you.'

'Wow,' Ben whispered. 'This is great: I can understand dinosaur.'

Iggy rolled his eyes. 'They're not speaking "dinosaur", Sonny Jim. They're speaking Eid, like everyone in Eidolon.'

The two allosaurs had moved closer. 'We could just . . . go,' said the female, Ancasta.

Her mate stared at her. 'And leave our comrades in the lurch?'

'They don't want to be here, either. Maximus said so yesterday. No one knew it was going to be like this. They're ready to leave.'

'The Dodman will reward us when he wins.'

'Oh, yes? And how's he going to do that?'

Pertinax looked nonplussed. 'Well, I'm not sure. But that's what they're all saying.'

'That puny dog-headed creature's got nothing I want,' Ancasta said sullenly.

'He could drive the dragons out of the Eastern Quarter. We could move back there, have some babies . . .'

The female tutted. 'He's not going to bother doing that. What's in it for him? Anyway,' she sniffed, 'I'm not sure I *want* babies with you; not unless we can live somewhere really special. Kits need space and light, somewhere to run around in safety.'

Her mate hung his head, looking dejected. Then, as if he had suddenly come up with a winning argument, he looked up, his eyes gleaming. 'He could take back Infinity Beach for us.'

'The stuff of fairy tales,' Ancasta said scornfully. 'It doesn't even exist: it's just some mythical paradise they wave in front of you to make you hate the dragons for stealing it away.'

Ellie's fingers tightened on Ben's arm. 'Infinity Beach. Isn't that—?'

Ben nodded. 'Ssh – look, something's coming.'

Something had caught the allosaurs' attention and they had stopped their bickering. Creatures everywhere were staring up into the dark sky.

'Is it Mummu-Tiamat? Has she come back?' Ellie asked hopefully; but whatever it was was much too small to be the Mother of Dragons. It circled over the army camp, then flapped towards them.

Iggy bristled as moonlight delineated the dark shape. 'It's that horrid bird!' And he started to chatter furiously. 'You should have let me eat it the first time!'

Ben reached out a hand and folded it over his friend's muzzle to keep him quiet. He could still feel the little jaws chattering involuntarily: Iggy was a cat and he hated birds – he couldn't help himself – and in this case, Ben couldn't blame him. It was the Dodman's mynah bird. He remembered how it had turned up one day on their garden gate back home in Bixbury, bearing a nasty message from its master.

The bird hovered for a moment over the gathered troops as if searching for someone in particular, then came arrowing down.

'Come on!' said Ben. 'It'll be carrying a message from the Dodman and we've got to know what it is.'

They reached the very last boulder that would afford them cover, but it was too far away from where the mynah bird had come to rest for them to hear anything except the thud and shuffle of feet, the breathing of vast lungs and the roar of other voices.

Ben tugged at his hair in frustration. 'Stay here,' he warned Ellie. 'And you, Iggy: stay with her.'

'But—'

'Please, Iggy. I'll be okay. Anyway, there's no point in all of us getting caught.' And before anyone could stop him, he was gone.

He almost got trodden on by a diplodocus which wasn't looking where it was going; and luckily, because it wasn't, it didn't see him. He dodged sideways to avoid the swinging, spiked tail of a stegosaur and ran slap, bang into the backside of a triceratops. It turned around, very slowly, and surveyed him with its tiny black eyes. But although a triceratops has the most enormous skull, it has a very tiny brain, and so by the time it had got around to thinking, *I wonder what on Eidolon that was?*, Ben was long gone, hiding behind the trunk of a burned-out tree. He looked up at it. Then he stuffed the waterproof bag down into his jumper and started climbing, slowly and quietly. It was like climbing the giant ash tree on the edge of Aldstane Park, the one like Yggdrasil out of the old Norse legends. The one Silver had had such trouble climbing because of her flippers. He remembered how she had jumped off the overhanging branch and how he had caught her, and the memory brought tears to his eyes. 'You are my hero, Ben,' she had told him. But the situation they had faced then had been nothing compared to this.

He tried not to think about what would happen to him if he was seen, and applied himself instead to searching for the selkie in a sea of monsters. He gazed and gazed till his Eidolon eye hurt; but if Silver was anywhere amongst them she was well-hidden.

Something vast loomed up in the thickest part of the throng and the eoraptors and velociraptors, the stegosaurs and allosaurs, goblins and goat-men and sabre-tooths all made way for it. Ben gasped. It was the scariest-looking dinosaur he could ever have imagined: a vast tyrannosaur, towering thirty feet high with a massive skull, bone-crushing jaws and cunning eyes. The mynah bird had landed on one of its outstretched, clawed hands.

'Greetings, General. I bring word from the Dodman. *Squarrrk!*' it declared, and the army fell silent.

'Speak on, bird,' the tyrannosaur rumbled. 'Tell us what our master has to say.'

'He says, *squarrrk*, that tomorrow at noon there will be a wedding feast at Dodman Castle and a coronation: for tomorrow he shall be crowned King of Eidolon. You and three of your chosen commanders are invited to attend.'

There was a murmur at this news. Ben frowned. 'But who would marry the Dodman?' he said, to no one in particular.

'Sssssssss!' hissed Boneless Bob. 'Ssssstupid boy! How does the Dog-Headed One become King?'

'I don't know,' said Ben.

'By wedding a Queen.'

'But—' Ben's heart thumped. 'What, you mean *Mum*?'

'Yessssss.'

'But he can't. She's already married.'

'I'm sssure he won't let that sssstand in his way. Looks like you're about to get a sssssstepfather.'

Things in Ben's world were getting worse and worse.

The tyrannosaur grinned widely, giving everyone an unwelcome view of its masses of sharp, shark-like teeth. 'Excellent. I like a good feast!'

'But,' the bird continued, 'you must bring a gift: a tribute fit for a King.'

'What sort of gift?'

'He said "be imaginative". *Squarrrk!*' The mynah bird unfurled its wings. 'Tomorrow at noon. With your tribute. Don't be late!' And with that it launched itself into the dark air and flapped away again.

'What shall we take him?' the tyrannosaur mused.

'Gold!' called one of the dragons.

'Jewels!' cried another.

The lizard-king rolled its eyes. 'Pah! You dragons are so predictable. Can you think of nothing but treasure? He can't eat gold and jewels at a feast, can he?'

There was a brief silence, then a flurry of suggestions:

'Goblin pie!' yelled a troll.

'Fried troll's feet!' retorted a goblin.

'Roast brontosaurus with all the trimmings: garnished with dragons' eyes and stuffed with stegosaur steaks,' an allosaur suggested wickedly.

The tyrannosaur laughed. 'Have you ever tried brontosaurus? They taste like mud, my friend, roasted or raw. Awful. No, that would never find favour with such a sophisticated traveller as the Dodman. He's been around, the Dog-Headed One. He's eaten the best that Eidolon has to offer: and I even heard he's supped in the Other World—'

'How about vampire vindaloo?' growled a sabre-toothed tiger. It had once got lost in the wild road system and found itself in the Other World, where it had sampled a few sheep on Bodmin Moor, before nipping into a local town and falling into company with a pair of urban foxes who knew of all sorts of good things to eat.

'Sweet and sour satyr!' suggested its mate, warming to the theme.

'Mmmm, interesting.' The tyrannosaur stroked its chin thoughtfully, and the satyrs started backing away and making excuses about other places they needed to be.

A small figure appeared suddenly on the lizard-king's

shoulder. It was small and hairless with big pink triangular ears and eyes of a virulent yellow. It was wearing a harness of leather straps which were fixed to the wide collar the tyrannosaur wore about its neck, as if it were a pet, but also a prisoner.

'If it please you, ssssire, I have an excellent idea,' it hissed into the tyrannosaur's ear.

Ben stared. He knew that creature: it was the Sphynx, the horrid bald cat that belonged to Awful Cousin Cynthia and spied for the Dodman. The waterproof bag under his arm rustled, and Boneless Bob's head popped out.

'The Ssssphynx!'

Ben transferred his gaze to the witch's familiar. 'You know him?'

'He's my brother,' Bob said. If a serpent could show emotion, it seemed anxious. Its orange crest rose and fell uncertainly.

'There's not much of a family resemblance,' Ben said unbelievingly. 'I mean, you're a snake and it's a . . . well, a cat, sort of.'

Bob gave him a pitying look. 'You don't understand much about this world, do you? Does Old Creepie resemble your mother? No, well, shush, I want to hear what he has to sssay.'

The tyrannosaur reached up, grasped the hairless cat and held it up before its face. 'Out with it, then, spy!'

The power of the lizard-king's bad breath made the Sphynx's eyes cross. It struggled against the scaly grasp, then went limp. 'I saw a quetzalcoatlus land a few moments ago,' it gasped. 'It was bearing a very tasty-looking prize.'

The tyrannosaur's eyes gleamed. 'What was it?'

'A sssselkie-girl. Her name is Ssssilver, and she is a friend of the Queen's ssson. I am sssure she would make good eating.'

The lizard-king considered this for a moment. Then it rumbled its appreciation. Its voice boomed out across the camp. 'Bring me the selkie. Now!'

There was a lot of flapping and squawking behind the tyrannosaur; then the crowd parted to reveal the most massive, hideous-looking bird. Forty feet long and a dozen high, it lumbered towards the lizard-king in a fashion that reminded Ben of the bell-ringer in a production of *The Hunchback of Notre Dame* he had once seen; but it was much, much uglier than even Quasimodo. It had a long head with a bony crest, a horrible long beak and not a feather in sight. Its leathery wings were half-folded and it used its pinions to propel itself awkwardly across the ground. Ben soon saw why: in one of its great claws it held its prey.

Silver.

Dwarfed by the monstrous bird's mantled shoulders, she lay there in her girl form, her pale hair spilling down to the ground, too frightened even to cry out, her liquid eyes huge in her face.

The tyrannosaur strode forward. It bent its vast head to examine the object, poked her once in the stomach and grinned from one scaly ear to the other. 'Excellent!' it roared. 'A bit small, but very succulent. Give her to me!'

But the quetzalcoatlus wasn't giving up its prize that easily. It glared up at the giant lizard with its small, bright eyes.

'Mine,' it stated, and its beak clacked sharply. Speech was difficult for the flying creature: it had a long way to go on the evolutionary ladder.

The tyrannosaur regarded it magnanimously. 'Yes, it's yours. But if you give the selkie to me, Montezuma, you shall accompany me to the feast tomorrow night and take the credit for catching it. It will be a great honour for you.'

The huge bird turned its head and looked suspiciously at the lizard-king first with one beady black eye, then with the other. Then it shook its beak. 'Me. Eat now.' And it lifted back its bony head as if to deal the selkie a killing blow.

'No!' The shout had escaped Ben before he could prevent it. His hands flew to his mouth as if to stuff the word back in again, but he was too late.

Beneath the tree, a satyr stared upwards. Ben flattened himself against the trunk. The goat-man squinted. The cold yellow, vertically-pupilled eyes scanned the branches. He looked straight at Ben for a heartbeat, then his gaze passed over what he had taken to be a burr in the wood, and he shrugged. 'One of those wailing banshees,' he announced to his friends, and they returned their attention to the quetzalcoatlus, relieved that someone else was going to be the victim.

'Last chance, Montezuma. Will you give me the selkie or must I take her from you?'

'Mine! Mine! Mine!' The creature stamped its clawed feet in fury.

The tyrannosaur moved with lightning speed, and suddenly the flying lizard had no head. There was a vile crunching sound and then Ben could see a huge lump moving down the monster's gullet. The rest of the quetzalcoatlus collapsed in a heap. Before the goblins could move in on her, the lizard-king scooped up the selkie and held her up for inspection.

For a horrible moment, Ben thought it was going to give in to temptation and bite her head off, too; but the tyrannosaur merely weighed her and then pronounced, 'She's not very big; a mere morsel for me. But she's big enough to feed the Dodman.'

Ben's eyes filled with tears. 'I have to save her!'

Something caught him by the sleeve. When he looked down, he found Boneless Bob's fangs clutching the fabric. He prized them off, wiping the snake-spittle away with the other sleeve in case it was poisonous.

'She's my friend. I have to do something.'

'Let me go and I will save her for you.'

Ben stared at it. 'Why would you do that?'

'I have my reasonssss.'

'How can I trust you?'

'You can't.'

'Then why would I let you go?'

'Look, I have an idea, okay?'

'But if I don't keep you safe, Maggota will harm my family.'

The snake's crest flared up around its head like a huge orange collar. 'If you want to ssssave your friend, you'll just have to take that rissssk.'

Ben looked at the tyrannosaur and the selkie in its awful grasp; then he looked at the horde of dinosaurs; then he looked back at the snake. He couldn't move very far amongst this army unhindered, but a slithering sneak like Boneless Bob could. They'd probably regard him as one of them. A monster. They were probably right.

'Okay, I agree,' Ben sighed at last. 'I must be mad.' He shook the serpent out of the makeshift bag and watched as it coiled and uncoiled itself on the branch of the oak tree, flexing its sinuous spine this way and that.

'Thank you. I'll ssssay one thing before I go. Gordon Gargantua.'

Ben frowned. 'What does that mean?'

'You'll know when the time comes.' And with that it wound its way smoothly down the tree trunk and disappeared in a flicker of red and white and orange into the dark mass of monsters below.

Within moments it had fetched up at the feet of the tyrannosaurus.

'Greetings, General Tyrant Megathighs.'

The general looked down. 'Who are you?'

The Sphynx on his shoulder stared so hard it looked as if its yellow eyes would fall out.

'Ask not who I am. Ask what I can do for you.'

'And what can you do for me, worm?'

'It would be inadvisable to give the selkie to the Dodman while she's alive and kicking. She may look delicioussss raw, but selkie-meat is notoriously tough. If you boil her she will become a sssseal: and where is the magic in that? And if you roast her you will spoil her delicacy. It isss a conundrum. But I can help you sssolve it.'

'And how might you do that, worm?'

'I can bring you the best chef in Eidolon.'

'A chef?'

'A troll, my lord.'

The Sphynx's ears pricked up. It remembered the troll. Specifically, it remembered being traded by the nasty prince for the worthless Wanderer. It wasn't sure it ever wanted to see that troll again: it might decide that hairless cat made the best accompaniment to Seared Selkie.

'And where is this troll?' The tyrannosaur scanned the massed ranks of his army. He could see at least a dozen, right off. But they all looked far too stupid to be chefs.

'If you release the Sphynx, I will bring him to you.'

The lizard-king's little eyes narrowed. 'Why?'

'He issss my brother.'

The tyrannosaur laughed. 'As if that means anything. I ate *my* brother!' And it threw its head back and laughed. All around, the other dinosaurs bellowed their approval of this 'joke'. Then it reached up and broke the leather strap which attached the Sphynx to the vast collar around its neck.

Not quite believing its luck, the Sphynx sat there, blinking.

'Go wait for me in the oak tree behind those satyrsss, brother,' Boneless Bob hissed. 'I shall be back in three shakes of my tail.'

It wriggled at speed into the thickest part of the crowd and disappeared.

The Sphynx didn't need telling twice. It leapt down from the shoulder of General Tyrant Megathighs III and belted through the ranks like a skinned rabbit. Three seconds later it was sitting on the same branch as Ben, its sides heaving.

Ben regarded his new neighbour with distaste. 'Just don't say anything,' he warned. 'We're in this together, now.'

The crowd parted to make way for a gigantic troll. It had noxious green skin, a quiff of purple hair and a lot of yellow teeth that stuck out at all sorts of angles. Ben recognised it immediately. It was hard to forget. He watched as the troll greeted the tyrannosaur and bent its hideous face over Silver.

'. . . lots of choices,' it was saying, and started counting them off on its warty fingers. 'Selkie stew, selkie and goblin bake, selkie stuffed with liz—' It hesitated. 'Ah, probably not a good idea in the circumstances . . . Selkie, coriander and prune tajine; selkie sticks and chips . . . ah, I have the very thing! Coronation selkie! Perfect! Just the thing: you sear the meat then cook it very gently for a long time in a saffron-flavoured sauce, add some sultanas and a few fairies' eyes for luck, and hey presto!'

'Now look here, whatever your name is . . .'

'Gordon,' said the troll, and the hairs on the back of Ben's neck rose all of a sudden.

'Gordon. Just take her and do what you have to to make it a really special dish. Because otherwise my colleagues and I will be eating roast troll tonight, do you understand me?'

The troll nodded vigorously. It was a bit bemused as to how all this had happened. One moment he had been checking his store cupboard and listing the ingredients he need to stock up on (cats' tails, minced mermaid and green lentils); the next he had been running as fast as his huge feet could carry him at the behest of a small red-and-white snake. Still: it wasn't every day the troll got his hands on a fresh selkie. Pretty little thing, too. He took her eagerly from the tyrannosaur's claws, and then found himself sent by his summoner in quite a different direction from his cave and kitchen. It was a nuisance, but there didn't seem to be anything he could do about it.

Ben waited until the troll turned away and headed in his direction. As it came abreast of the satyrs he yelled: 'Gordon Gargantua!' and the troll fetched up against the tree with a tremendous thud that shook Ben and the Sphynx right off their branch. The hairless cat did what cats do: twisted in mid-air and landed neatly on its feet; but Ben hit the ground so hard that all the air was knocked out of him.

'Pick me up,' Ben wheezed, 'and run!'

'What?' said the troll. 'You'll have to speak up. I'm a bit deaf.'

His fall had attracted the attention of a dozen sharp-sighted trolls, the satyrs and an inquisitive velociraptor.

'I said, "Pick me up and RUN!"' Ben yelled, using up every scrap of air in his lungs.

CHAPTER TWENTY-ONE

The Getaway

'Run till I say stop!' Ben instructed the troll: it was the only order he could think of for the time being.

Gordon Gargantua was not built for running: it is not a sport at which trolls excel. They have stout bodies and legs like tree trunks, very good for long-distance walking or for stomping on creatures which have annoyed them, but not the best for evading a horde of fleet-footed dinosaurs and goblins. Ben, straddling the troll's thick, warty neck, drummed his feet against Gordon's shoulders. 'Faster!'

The Sphinx, determined to make good its own getaway,

had fastened itself to the seat of the troll's capacious trousers and was clinging on for dear life.

Silver, held tight in the crook of Gordon's arm, turned to look up at Ben. Her eyes shone. 'Thank you, Ben! I don't know how you managed to save me, but thank you!'

'Don't thank me yet,' he warned her. 'We still have to escape.'

Their hunting instincts triggered by the sight of something running, a pack of velociraptors and eoraptors had taken up the pursuit, followed by a dozen curious goblins. None of them were much interested in taking down and eating a troll: but it looked as if chasing it and frightening it to death might be good sport and a change from all the dull waiting around.

Gordon swatted away a small dinosaur that had got too close and it went flying head over heels amongst its fellows, causing several of them to stumble and fall. This just served to make the rest of them more determined to harry the troll: they redoubled their efforts, making little clacking noises deep in their throats which Ben took to be some sort of growl or threat.

'Through these boulders,' he told the troll. 'Follow the dried-up riverbed towards the trees there.' That was where he had left Ellie and Iggy. He hoped fervently they had stayed where he had told them to: there would be no time to search for them, for he saw when he looked back over his shoulder that the chase had now been taken up by a pair of allosaurs, who were outstripping the smaller dinosaurs and the goblins and looked hungry enough to eat them all – troll, boy, selkie and hairless cat – without a second thought.

The troll lumbered painfully through the boulders, driven by the force of Ben's compulsion, knocking his elbows and hips all the way in the narrower stretches. The clatter of his big bare feet scattering rocks underfoot counterpointed with his grunts of pain and the soughing of the air in and out of his mouth. Gordon Gargantua was not in good shape. At one point he clutched his chest with his free hand and Ben was afraid the running had given the troll a heart attack, if trolls had hearts, that was. But, 'Stitch!' moaned Gordon, massaging his ribs. 'Oh, let me stop!'

'We can't!' Ben yelled in his less-deaf ear. 'Keep going!'

Other creatures had joined the pursuit now: a pair of sabre-toothed tigers loped along, as curious as any cat as to what was going on; and a lot more goblins had joined the pack, including a particularly evil-looking one with only one ear.

This goblin peered hard at Ben, then announced, eyes wide with amazement: 'I know that little beast. It's the Queen's son!'

This news travelled fast amongst the pursuers. Ben could hear snatches of their breathless conversations –

'– are you sure, Bosko?'

'– Isadora's elf-boy . . .'

'– halfling prince . . .'

'– reward from the Dodman . . .'

'Oh no,' Ben groaned. He thumped Gordon on the shoulder. 'Can't you go any faster?'

Gordon turned a pair of bloodshot, watering eyes upon

him. 'If you wanted a faster getaway vehicle you should have summoned a blinking dragon!' he wheezed. 'It's not fair: I was just minding my own business . . . few household chores . . . sweep out the cave a bit . . . hadn't planned on running a blinking marathon . . .' Then it couldn't say any more because the ground rose suddenly and it was all it could do to keep moving at all.

Ben stared around at the rocks. He had been sure this was where he had left Ellie. It was so dark he could hardly see a thing and the boulders all looked so similar. He risked a shout.

'Ellie! Iggy! Where *are* you?'

Nothing.

Typical. His sister never did what she was told.

Something caught his foot and yanked it so hard he almost fell off. He looked down and found one of the goblins climbing up the troll's back, flourishing a wicked little curved knife. He caught its arm and managed to wrench the knife out of its grasp; then kicked out frantically and caught it a blow on the shoulder, but still it kept coming. With a yowl, the Sphynx jumped on its head and raked at its face and the goblin fell off, howling.

The unpleasant yellow eyes gleamed in the moonlight. 'You owe me one, Isadora's ssson,' it hissed.

Ben nodded. 'For now,' he said.

An eoraptor attached itself to the troll's right leg. Silver grabbed a dead branch, snapped it off and battered the thing till it fell away, chattering furiously.

'Ellie!' Ben yelled again, and this time he thought he heard a reply somewhere to their right. 'That way!' he instructed the troll, and hauled on its hideous purple hair as if on a horse's bridle to make it change direction.

There was a shriek and a horrible snarling noise, and then the moon came out from behind a cloud, and there was Ellie backed up against a tree, surrounded by a band of velociraptors which were gazing at her rapturously, obviously looking forward to a tasty snack. Above her, Ignatius Sorvo Coromandel sat on a branch, his fur bushed out till he was twice his normal size, hissing and spitting and howling imprecations but being of very little practical use.

'Gordon Gargantua: grab that girl and that cat and let's get out of here!'

The troll waded into the midst of the velociraptors and laid about them with Silver's stick till they turned tail, and watched vengefully from a distance away, waiting for the rest of the pack to catch up. Gordon picked up Ellie, set her on his shoulder and reached for Iggy.

The little black-and-brown cat retreated till he was squashed up against the tree trunk. 'Are you crazy?' he asked Ben. 'You're sitting on the troll that tried to cook me: or didn't you realise? Do you want to be put in a pot and made into prince rissoles?'

'Haven't got time for this, Ig: get down here.'

Iggy shook his head: then he stared past the troll and saw what was following it. About a hundred hungry-looking dinosaurs and goblins. 'Oh.' He closed his eyes and jumped on to Gordon's head, scrabbled desperately in the snakelike hair, then fled down his neck to Ben. The next thing he saw was the Sphynx. All his fur that hadn't been standing upright now rose as if electrified. 'The world's gone mad. What's *he* doing here?'

The hairless cat snarled at him. 'Jussst keep out of my way, Wanderer.'

Ignatius Sorvo Coromandel gave the Sphynx a hard look, then turned his back on him. 'Suits me.'

Gordon Gargantua ran. He ran until his legs felt like lead; till he thought his heart would burst. It was all very well for the elf-boy to keep apologising, but it didn't help that he kept drumming his feet and yelling, *Faster!* The troll was beginning to feel as if his body was no longer his own. Under normal circumstances there was no way he would entertain the idea of running twenty yards on his own, let alone the mile or more they had already covered with him carrying an elf-boy, a girl, a selkie, and two cats.

A few of their pursuers had got bored with the chase and fallen away, and some of the dinosaurs seemed to have used up their best turn of speed and were lagging; but the goblins just never seemed to tire.

At last they came into a clearing and Gordon simply fell down in a heap. Ben and Ellie and the cats went flying; but Silver found herself trapped underneath him.

'Get up!' Ben cried desperately. 'Get up and run!' But all that happened was that the troll's legs waved pathetically in the air as if miming the motion of running.

'Can't,' he groaned, and lay there, panting.

Ben scanned the midnight air for the Mother of Dragons, but all he could see was unrelieved blackness.

'Mummu-Tiamat!' he yelled. But there was no answer.

The goblins were closing in; and if they stayed here any longer, the dinosaurs would catch up too, and then they'd all be eaten alive. Had it really come to this? There was just one possibility, and he knew it was a slim one. There was nowhere large enough here for the Mother of Dragons to set down in; and getting to the edge of the Wildwood before the goblins overtook them would take a miracle. But it was the only chance they had.

'Iggy: climb the tallest tree you can find and try to signal to Mummu-Tiamat. We need her to pick us up. Say . . .' he paused, thinking, 'say "the Prince of Eidolon requests a great favour from you; and he will be indebted to you forever if you grant it." Or something like that. Be respectful. But make her come!'

Ignatius Sorvo Coromandel regarded him with glowing amber eyes. 'I hate climbing trees.'

'Ssssssss!' laughed the Sphynx. 'And he calls himself the Wanderer!'

The little black-and-brown cat drew himself up to his full height (about twelve-and–a-half inches) and growled. 'We still have scores to settle, Baldy, and if you want to do it now, that's fine by me.'

'Iggy! Stop it: there's no time for this now. Please, try to find Mummu-Tiamat. We're depending on you.'

Put like that, what could Iggy say? His fur subsided. 'Okay,

okay, I'm going.' And he took to his heels and fled into the depths of the Wildwood.

Ellie had managed to extricate the selkie from under the troll's groaning bulk.

'We'll fight them!' Silver said through gritted teeth. 'They're not taking me again without a fight.'

'Nor me,' said Ellie fiercely, though she didn't feel very fierce.

They armed themselves with the biggest sticks they could find.

They did not have long to wait. Moments later, the monsters appeared. At once, an eager pair of goblins broke ranks, dashing in and trying to snatch Ben, but Silver thrashed out with her stick and one of them fell away shrieking and clutching its head. Three velociraptors crept around behind the troll and tried to bite it; which galvanised Gordon to lumber to his feet. He grabbed two of the raiders and banged their heads together so hard that they couldn't walk straight when he threw them down again. The third retreated.

Now the sabre-tooth tigers decided to try their luck. They slunk along on their bellies, haunches waggling as if ready to spring; but the Sphynx positioned itself in front the others and hissed something at them in a language Ben couldn't understand. The tigers blinked their huge amber eyes, then sat down and started to groom, like a pair of domestic cats caught doing something they shouldn't.

But there was nothing the Sphynx could say that was going to put off Boggart and Bosko and the rest of the goblin troop.

Ben saw them conferring; then a great roar of laughter went up and they started closing in.

Ben turned to scan the forest behind them. 'Oh, Iggy, where are you? Where's Mummu-Tiamat?' But nothing stirred in the canopy, and with a sinking heart he turned back to face the pack of marauders.

Ignatius Sorvo Coromandel was not the best tree-climber in either of the two worlds. He didn't mind the going up too much: but he didn't like teetering on the top of a tree; and he *definitely* didn't enjoy the coming down, which often entailed an awkward falling run and a less-than-elegant jump: which was fine on a fifteen-foot cherry tree and not such a good idea on a hundred-foot Wildwood oak. That thought was always in the back of his mind as he made the ascent. It made him nervous and tense and his muscles moved jerkily, making the branches rustle and vibrate just when he didn't want them to. At one point he almost managed to shake himself off; then he got the wobble under control and continued upward, pulse racing. The other thought that fluttered around in his head was that he wouldn't be able to see the dragon, or if he *could* see her, that he wouldn't be able to make her come to him – after all, she'd said she didn't care at all about him or the snake, so why should she listen to him at all? And if she didn't come he'd be stuck up a tree and his friends would be lost to the goblins and dinosaurs, and it would all be his fault.

The branches began to thin out, and he was just about to pounce out of the canopy into the clear air towards the top of the big oak when he saw something outlined against the moon. At first he thought it was an odd branch sticking upwards instead of outwards; then it moved. It was tall and thin and strange-looking and then it turned slightly so that the moonlight limned its features and he saw that it was a pterodactyl trying to tuck its head under its wing to roost for the night.

Ignatius Sorvo Coromandel cursed his luck. Of all the trees in the forest to have picked to climb. He froze against the trunk, wondering what to do. Should he make his way down again and try another tree; or wait and hope that the monster would fall asleep? Either would take more time than he had. It called for desperate measures. Positioning himself so that he was hidden by the last of the oak's leaves, Iggy dug all his claws deep into the trunk and began to shake it. At first, the movement was barely noticeable; then the tree's top began to sway as if caught by the lightest of breezes. Iggy began to feel dizzy but he pushed harder and harder. The pterodactyl stirred. It brought its great heron-like head out from under its wing and looked around with its tiny beady eyes. Iggy hoped it was as unintelligent as it looked. If it worked out that none of the other trees was swaying it would start looking for the cause. Which wasn't very far away and rather edible. He pushed this thought aside, closed his eyes and shook the tree with all his might till he thought his backbone might snap with the strain of it. The topmost branch started whipping from side to side as if a brisk wind had got up. Then momentum took over and the swaying increased. The pterodactyl squawked its displeasure. It spread its wide wings for balance and clacked its bony beak. Then it took off into the night, complaining as it went, to look for a more comfortable spot to get some rest.

Iggy climbed slowly to the crook of branches the pterodactyl had vacated. His head was spinning and his stomach felt as if it were at sea. He stared out into the night sky. Something was moving out there: something long and bulky – a huge object planing silently through the dark air.

It was now or never. He took the biggest breath his little lungs could manage. 'Mummu-Tiamat! Mother of Dragons!'

The great shape seemed to pause in its flight, then it sideslipped and began to make its way towards him. Iggy's heart lifted. He might just turn out to be the hero in this drama after all.

'You may as well give up, Elf-boy!' one of the goblins snarled.

'No point in you *all* getting badly hurt for no reason,' another shouted.

'Nah, give up peaceably. Shame to spoil good meat!' suggested one of the allosaurs. And they all sniggered.

'It'll be you who gets badly hurt!' Ben yelled back hotly. 'I can promise you that!'

The laughter became a little more nervous. Then Ben heard one of the goblins tell its neighbour, a sly-looking velociraptor, 'That's the Prince of Eidolon, that is, Queen Isadora's get. We capture him, the Dodman will be well pleased.'

'You'd better watch out,' another said. 'He's got magic, he

has. The last time I saw him he had a dragon with him. Poor old Boggart got burned all down his front.'

'Least it wasn't his back. He's no coward, our Boggart.'

'He's no beauty, either. Some say the burning was an improvement!'

The goblins were in high spirits at the thought of capturing a princeling. And they'd eat the selkie straight off: no point wasting a nice fresh seal-girl on the Dodman, especially cooked in a nasty sauce. The girl: well, the girl was another matter.

'Poor old Bosko didn't do so well out of his encounter with Isadora's offspring, did you, Bosk? Heard you wailed like a banshee when the Dodman took your ear.'

A smaller, one-eared goblin hissed at this and tried to stab the speaker with its dagger. There was a brief and vicious fight, which Bosko won, against the odds. He leered in the direction of Ben, Ellie and Silver.

'See this?' he called, indicating the ragged flap on his head. 'I look like this because of you lot. Lucky little princess still has two nice pink ears, thanks to me, though I reckon one of them would suit me very well. In fact, I quite fancy a matching pair – get rid of this old thing.' He turned to the allosaur behind him. 'What do you say, Pertinax, will you keep her ears for me when you chew up the rest of her, eh?'

The allosaur grinned horribly at Ellie, showing off its best assets: a lot of very white, very pointed teeth.

Ellie shuddered. 'Nobody's having my ears!' she shrieked. 'Or any other part of me. And if any of you vile creatures comes anywhere near me I'll hit you so hard you won't know what day it is!'

'Ooh, "vile creatures",' said a velociraptor to its neighbour, not taking its eyes off her. 'Is that what we are?'

Bosko turned to one of the other goblins, mock-puzzled. 'What day is it, Bumface?' he asked theatrically.

Bumface shrugged. 'No idea.'

Bosko laughed. 'So much for that then, girlie. Now, let's be having yer ears!'

And they started to close in.

As the dark shape sailed closer to the tree, Iggy frowned. He was beginning to have second thoughts, though it was a bit late for that. He didn't remember the dragon having such a long tail. And its body was, well, fatter. He opened his eyes as wide as possible to get as much moonlight into them as possible (for this is how cats' eyes work; unlike humans, who tend to squint) and felt a shudder of dread run through him. There were two figures on the back of the Mother of Dragons, if that was who it was coming towards him, at speed now. But they had left her alone. Or rather, *she* had left *them* . . .

Perhaps, Iggy rationalised to himself, perhaps she had gone back for Zark and Darius. But he wasn't managing to convince himself. He got ready to bolt down the tree.

But then the shape glided into a ray of moonlight, and he found he couldn't move his feet. He couldn't move a single muscle; not even his tail. He was transfixed.

'Hello, Iggy,' said a voice he almost recognised.

CHAPTER TWENTY-TWO
The Elf-girl

Ben was beginning to panic, though he wouldn't admit it to himself, let alone anyone else. There were so many of them. If it had just been goblins, he'd have been less worried: though goblins were vicious, they were also rather stupid, and could be easily frightened. But it didn't look as if anything would frighten the velociraptors or the allosaurs; and the great, armoured triceratops which had just lumbered up to join them looked like a bulldozer. If it tried, Ben thought, it could crush all three of them, and Gordon Gargantua too, without even knowing it.

The troll had got to its feet. 'Now what?' it asked Ben.

Its great hairy mitts hung limply by its sides, and its face was hang-dog. It was just awaiting instructions, Ben realised, still under the compulsion of his summoning even though it was exhausted.

'Try looking really scary,' he told it in a low voice. 'Roar at them a bit, or something.'

The troll frowned. Then he screwed his face up in an alarming fashion and emitted a huge belch. It smelled awful; but the goblins didn't seem much impressed.

'Is that the best you can do?' jeered one.

His neighbour let rip a monstrous burp, and they all laughed, and the next minute they were all burping and farting and roaring with amusement. The allosaur took a deep breath and it seemed as if all the air that had ever been in its stomach came flying out at once. The force of the blast actually knocked down several goblins.

The Sphynx bolted up a tree and sat there, shivering. It would wait this out and side with the victors. It was beginning to look pretty obvious which they would be.

Gordon Gargantua began to cry. Tears like giant raindrops ran down his face. 'I don't want to die,' he said. 'There are so many more recipes in the world. So many more interesting things to eat.'

Ben didn't know what to say. 'Just . . . just sit over there,' he told the troll as kindly as he could manage. It was clearly going to be of little further use to them.

He flourished his stick and the curved knife he had taken from the goblin who had climbed the troll's back. He glared at

Bosko. 'Your dinosaur friends look hungry!' he shouted. 'But with my magic knife here I can cut you so you never stop bleeding; and how do you know they won't then all fall on you and attack you like sharks at the smell of so much blood? I've heard that's what carnivorous dinosaurs do.'

The goblins had a brief discussion as to what 'carnivorous' might mean, came to the conclusion that they had no idea, and that it was just a big word for showing off, and turned defiant faces to Ben. 'Nah: that's Putrid's knife, that is,' said one of them. 'It ain't magic at all.'

Without warning several of the goblins flew at Ben, spitting and snarling and lashing out with whatever weapons they carried. Ben parried one dagger with his 'magic' knife and watched with satisfaction as it skated up the blade of the dagger and caught the goblin a nasty blow on the forearm. It fell away, howling that it was going to bleed to death, but another goblin took its place at once, and Ben found himself cutting and thrusting with both dagger and stick. Another goblin went flying as Silver gave it a tremendous blow.

'Iggy!' Ben yelled into the night. 'Mummu-Tiamat!'

But if anyone replied the response was lost in the ferocious howls and roars of their attackers. They had been driven back several paces now: soon their backs would be up against the forest trees and they'd have nowhere else to go. Things were looking grim. A vague plan began to form itself in Ben's head. It was a truly desperate measure, one that should be taken only if all else was lost. It would be his one chance to save Ellie and Silver.

He fought on desperately, and hoped against hope that some miracle would happen.

Iggy stared and stared, unable to believe his eyes. Of the three figures in front of him, he recognised only one; and it wasn't the one who had greeted him. The one he *did* recognise was hard to mistake. She was vast and terrifically ugly, with wild orange-and-black dreadlocks, bald bits where her hair had been burned down like corn-stumps, and a face covered in warts and wens. As far as he could recall, her name was Grizelda. And the last time he had seen her had been she had been driving a chariot drawn by the Gabriel Hounds through the air above the lake at Corbenic Castle, fighting against his friends, on the Dodman's side.

The second figure was a slight, pale elf-girl with brilliant, uptilted green eyes and hair so blonde it was almost white. This was the one who had called him by name; and he had no idea who she was.

The third creature was a monster of terrible proportions: a huge flying dinosaur with the flat, black eyes of a predator and a forty-foot wingspan.

It was most certainly *not* the Mother of Dragons.

They had beaten off dozens of the goblins; but it made no difference. Ben's arms felt as if they were on fire, the muscles hurt so much. He tried to take no notice, but the blows he was landing were less and less effective. Soon they would be overwhelmed, for the canny dinosaurs were waiting only for the stupid goblins to break down their defence. Then they would close in for the kill and Ben knew that there would be nothing he could do about it. He glanced around at Ellie and Silver and saw how exhausted they were. It was now or never.

He caught Gordon Gargantua's eye. 'When I say the word,' he hissed, 'you run. You pick up Ellie and Silver and you run as far and as fast into the forest behind us as you can.'

The troll looked forlorn. 'I'll try.'

'You'll do it,' Ben said fiercely. 'Because if you don't I shall order you to pick a fight with that huge allosaur over there, and it will rip you limb from limb. Do you understand me?'

He whacked another goblin's dagger away, and the shock from the blow ran up his arm, making it so numb he almost dropped the stick.

'Did you hear that, Ellie, Silver?'

They nodded mutely.

'You get as far into the Wildwood as you can. Dodge in and out of the trees and keep shouting for Iggy and Mummu-Tiamat. They will rescue you, I know they will. You'll be okay.'

'But what about you, Ben?' Silver cried, her eyes huge.

'Don't worry about me,' Ben said grimly. 'I've got a plan.'

'I was looking for a very large dragon called Mummu-Tiamat,' Iggy said nervously.

'And what would a cat be doing consorting with dragons?'

'Arranging a rescue mission,' Iggy said, trying to sound official. 'For my friends. They're surrounded by—' he was about to say 'monsters' but realised just in time that she was actually sitting on one, and might not actually be on their side. 'By ene-mies,' he ended carefully.

'Enemies? Oh dear.' The girl frowned. 'What sort of ene-mies?'

'A lot of goblins, and satyrs and . . . er . . . dinosaurs.' There was no avoiding it. 'There's a whole army of them down there. The Dodman's army.'

'I see,' the elf-girl said. 'Well, we can't have that.' She put two fingers in her mouth and whistled loudly, and seconds later another large shape hove into sight.

This time it *was* the Mother of Dragons; and she had come to the elf-girl just like a well-trained dog coming to heel. Iggy felt even more nervous.

'Mummu-Tiamat,' the girl said. 'We are going to need re-inforcements. I have something I need you to do for me.' And she leant forward and whispered something which Iggy couldn't quite catch, though he tried very hard.

At once, the great golden dragon turned and flapped urgently away.

Iggy's eyes boggled. 'You gave the Mother of Dragons an order and she didn't burn you to a crisp?'

The elf-girl regarded him with her extraordinary green eyes. 'Of course not. How absurd. Now then, Ignatius Sorvo Coromandel, please get on my pterosaur and we can go and save Ben and Ellie and Silver.'

Iggy's head was in a whirl; and not just because of the casual use of his true name to compel him to leap from the top of a hundred-foot tree into thin air. Luckily, he landed foursquare on the back of the pterosaur, in the space between the elf-girl and the giantess. He was about to ask a very important question when the air was stolen right out of his mouth by the sudden downdraught of the dinosaur's descent.

Ben could put off the evil moment no longer. 'Goodbye, Ellie,' he called. 'Good luck.' He risked a glance at the selkie. 'See you again, Silver.' He tried to smile but his mouth wasn't working properly. It seemed to know better than the rest of him that it was unlikely he would ever see either of them again.

He took his welling emotions out on a goblin, giving it such a whack that his stick broke in two. So that was that. He took a deep breath.

'Run, Gordon Gargantua! Take Ellie and Silver and run!'

The troll lumbered to its feet in a disjointed, puppetlike sort of way, picked up its passengers and pushed aside the goblins who got in its way. These went flying into the goblins attacking Ben and caused a very useful diversion. By the time they had extricated themselves, the troll had vanished into the dark forest and Ben was dashing full tilt in the opposite direction, yelling: 'Come on then, you slackers! Catch me if you can!'

He slammed into an unwary satyr and it fell over backwards, hampering the allosaur who had had a clear run at Ben. The allosaur growled and promptly bit the satyr in half. Out of the corner of his eye, Ben glimpsed the cloven hooves vanishing into the monster's maw. His heart raced. He was going to die just like that. He could imagine the jaws closing on his midriff, their crushing force, the teeth penetrating his skin, the chill as it severed his top half from his bottom half . . .

It made him accelerate. His feet hammered the ground. He was running faster than he had ever run in his life. Which wasn't really surprising, given the circumstances. When he'd run the hundred metres at school and got beaten by most of his class he hadn't had a pack of vicious monsters on his heels. If he had, he'd probably have broken the county record.

A velociraptor came at him and he ducked sideways and dodged around a rock; a goblin tried to jump on him but he hurled himself out of its way. Something attached itself to his leg. Without a thought, he kicked out and bashed it against a boulder and felt it fall away. A vampire bat tangled itself in his hair and he swatted at it in disgust.

Then something landed on him hard, pinning him to the ground.

'Gotcha!' snarled a voice.

As soon as the pterosaur landed Iggy was eager to be off it; but he didn't seem to be able to move his feet.

The elf-girl turned around. 'Off you go then, Iggy. Go and find them. We'll be right here.'

This seemed to break the compulsion. Iggy didn't need telling twice. He belted through the trees, yelling, 'Ben! Ellie! Silver!'

At last, someone called him back. 'Is that you, Iggy?' It was the selkie's voice. There was a lot of crashing through the undergrowth and then suddenly there was the troll.

'Thank goodness,' sighed Iggy. And he sat down and gave

himself a quick impromptu grooming. It was good to look your best when taking the credit for saving the day.

But Gordon Gargantua ran right past him. The ground rumbled as he thundered along. Ellie called something as they overtook the little cat, but Iggy was in the middle of washing his ears at the time and didn't quite catch it.

'Eh? Hang on!' yowled Iggy. 'I'm here! Come back!'

Indignant, he got to his paws and stalked after the troll, muttering as he went. At least they were safe: that was the main thing, and there didn't seem to be anyone in pursuit.

By the time he reached the edge of the forest where they had landed, the troll was doing his best to run right past the pterosaur too. But the elf-maiden put up her hand. 'Halt, Gordon Gargantua.' And the troll came to such an abrupt standstill that Ellie and Silver were catapulted right off it.

Ellie sat up and brushed at the knees of her jeans. Then she looked around. When she saw the massive dinosaur with Grizelda on its back, she shrieked.

The elf-girl laughed.

'Oh, Ellie, don't be such a scaredy-cat.'

Ellie narrowed her eyes at the elfin creature, but it was still hard to make her out in any detail. 'Who on Earth are you?'

'Good question: well phrased. Who am I, on Earth and in Eidolon? Well, can't you guess?'

Ellie put her hands on her hips, cross now. 'Look: we haven't got time for riddles right now. My brother is back there fighting off a horde of monsters single-handed. Can you help us rescue him?'

'Ben isn't with you?' The elf-girl's face crumpled. 'That spoils everything. I was looking forward to telling him about the wild roads.' She turned to the selkie, who was looking very forlorn. 'Hello, She Who Swims the Silver Path of the Sea. It's a pleasure to meet you at last. I've heard a lot about you. From Ben.'

'Please,' said Silver. 'Please, whoever you are, help us. We must rescue him.'

'Well, get on board then, all of you. Gordon, come here and help them up.'

The troll did as he was told.

'Gordon?'

He looked up. Then his face split in a huge grin. 'Grizelda!'

'It is you!' The giantess grinned back, which was not a pretty sight.

The troll, however, seemed transfixed.

'Wait for me!'

Everyone turned hopefully; but it was not Ben who had shouted but a small, hairless cat.

The elf-girl regarded it solemnly. 'Cousin Cynthia's familiar,' she said accurately. 'How interesting. Have you decided to change your wicked ways?'

The Sphynx gazed at her, slack-jawed. The skin at the back of its neck began to ruckle: if it had had hair there, it would have stood on end. Its eyes went very wide. Then its haunches quivered low to the ground and it started to back away.

'Ah, Abu al Hôl, Father of Terror: which of your nine lives are you up to now? Can you afford to waste one?'

The Sphynx sat down. It looked terrified.

'Come up here,' the elf-girl bade him. 'I have uses for you, little spy.'

Against its will, the hairless cat found itself bounding up the pterosaur's haunch. It sat down beside its summoner and its skin rippled with fear.

Ellie and Silver exchanged glances. Whoever this tiny, fragile-looking creature was, she seemed very impressive.

'Corinthius, up and away!'

The winged dinosaur bunched its leg muscles and leapt into the air.

CHAPTER TWENTY-THREE
A Tribute Fit for a King

The witch appeared in a whirl of teeth, hair and rotting-meat perfume. In one bony claw she still clutched a half-drunk cup of tea.

'You took your time!' the Dodman roared. He stared around behind her. 'Well, where are they, then?'

'They?' Maggota batted her hideous eyelids at him.

'Don't play the innocent with me. I sent you to fetch them. Where are they?'

The witch wagged a bone-white finger at him. 'Third and last time, Dog-Head. Be careful you don't annoy me too much and waste your last chance. The children: ah yes: the children.

Shall we say I experienced a little local difficulty with the children . . .'

'You've lost them!'

'Not . . . exactly.'

The Dodman stamped his dog-feet in fury. 'I am surrounded by idiots and incompetents!' He gritted his teeth. 'I have one last task for you. It shouldn't be too difficult, even for you. Fetch me Clive Arnold.'

The witch rolled her eyes. 'Well, you might have said before and saved me the effort. I've only just taken him back to the Other World.'

The Dodman frowned. 'What do you mean?'

The witch waved her free hand. 'It's far too complicated to go into now.' In fact, it was plain embarrassing. To explain what had happened would be an admission that her powers were not what they were. And that would never do. When she got her hands on the baby, she would show them all!

'Clive Arnold. Nothing more?'

'Clive Arnold. Now.'

The witch drained her tea, tossed the empty cup to the Dodman and was gone before he'd even caught it. He turned it over in his hands, sniffed at the dregs suspiciously. Was it magic; or poison?

The pterosaur put down neatly in the clearing where they had fought the goblins and dinosaurs, its nose almost touching the trees on one side and its tail on the other. But other than a broken stick and a scrap of bloody fabric, they found no sign of Ben.

No one was left there: except for a goblin sitting against a tree, moaning and nursing its broken leg.

The elf-girl slipped down from the flying dinosaur and approached it. The rising sun limned her in golden light: the goblin shielded its cat-slit eyes, then hissed.

'Putrid Agaricus!'

The goblin paled at the use of its true name: up till then it hadn't even known it had one.

'Tell me where the boy called Ben is.'

It narrowed its eyes at her. 'Why d'you want to know?'

'He's family.'

The goblin hawked, spat, then bent its head to examine the result. 'Blood may be thicker than water; but snot is thicker than blood,' it said cryptically.

'Tell me!' the elf-girl shouted, and the goblin clutched its shattered leg.

'He ran. He bashed me, and he ran, that way –' and he gestured towards the rocks '– and the others all chased him.'

'And what lies that way?'

'Why, our army, of course. What planet have you been on?'

'Till most recently Earth. Mainly.'

The goblin frowned. 'Earth?'

'The Other World, I believe you call it.'

'You don't want to go there. I've heard it's full of all sorts of monsters.'

The elf-girl laughed. 'That's what they say about Eidolon.'

She went back to the pterosaur and spoke to the Sphynx. 'Abu al Hôl, I have a job for you: just the right task for a spy.

Run into the enemy camp and find Ben. Tell him this from me . . .' And she hollowed her hands around one of its big triangular ears and whispered something. Its yellow eyes flared.

'Then come back here immediately. Do you understand me?'

The Sphynx nodded once, very fast. It couldn't wait to be away from her disquieting presence.

'If you are not back here by the time the sun clears those trees, I will summon you. And you will be sorry.' And she reached out to lift it down from Corinthius's back.

The hairless cat recoiled from her touch then hurled itself to the ground and fled. They watched it go in silence. Then:

'Who *are* you?' Ellie asked curiously. 'I mean, you seem familiar in a weird sort of way, but also very strange.' She squinted, trying unsuccessfully to focus on the elf-girl's face.

'Don't you recognise me?'

'I . . . er . . . I don't think we've met before.'

The green-eyed girl laughed.

'Don't you know your own sister, Eleanor Katherine Arnold?'

Ellie frowned, wondering if she'd heard this right. Then she thought: *Perhaps Mum had a secret child in the Secret Country.*

'You don't seem very happy to see me again,' the elf-girl pouted. 'I suppose I have changed a bit. I was a lot smaller the last time you saw me. When Maggota Magnifica stole us away, and you dropped me in the wild road.'

Ellie felt dizzy. 'That's . . . that's . . . impossible. You can't be Alice: Alice is a baby.'

The elf-girl clapped her hands. 'A baby! I *was* a baby: that's true. Oh, but that was ages ago. I've been all over the place since then. The sights I've seen!' Her green eyes shone vividly in the dawn light. 'I've been to the pyramids and Knossos; I've been to Tibet and New York and Marrakech; I've been to the bottom of the sea and the middle of the Rub al-Khali and to Samarkand and the top of Cloudbeard. It's been fascinating.'

'But . . . it was only two days ago that we lost you.' Ellie was bewildered. 'How could you go to all those places in two days?'

'The wild roads, silly. They go everywhere. And they're full of magic.'

'Oh, I see,' said Ellie faintly, though she didn't.

'And now I'm stuffed with magic. Magic and experience. You have to grow to make room for it all,' Alice said wisely, as if it were the most normal thing in the world. In two worlds.

Ellie just didn't know what to say. Or think. It was the selkie who said, all in a rush, before bursting into tears, 'Well, I hope all that magic and experience is going to save Ben. Because he's the bravest person I know and he doesn't deserve to die among a pack of the Dodman's monsters.'

'Nobody deserves that,' Alice agreed solemnly, and green fire flashed in her eyes.

'What have you got there? Leave it alone!'

Reluctantly, the velociraptors fell away. One of them wiped its mouth reflectively. Blood stained its sharp white teeth. The boy tasted good: it was a shame to give him up, even to the General.

'It's just a boy, Lord Tyrant. Nothing you'd be interested in.'

'I'll be the judge of that. Let me see it.'

The tyrannosaur dragged away those who were too slow to respond and tossed them aside. Ben lay crushed and bitten on the ground, barely breathing.

'It's just a scrap of a thing, General,' the velociraptor wheedled. 'Let us eat him.'

'It's the . . . Queen's son!' puffed a goblin, dodging in between the tyrannosaur and the boy. 'He's our prisoner. The Dodman will reward us for him.'

Tyrant Megathighs III bent his fearsome head to regard the goblin eye to eye. 'I think you'll find he's my prisoner now, goblin. Step away!'

Bosko glared back, greed making him brave. 'The Dodman is my master, not you. And I declare this boy as our tribute.'

'Ah yes, the tribute. Where is my selkie?'

Bosko was at a loss. He looked to the other goblins for help: they looked away. 'I . . . er . . . it wasn't my fault!'

'And the troll?'

The allosaur, Pertinax, shook its head. 'It ran, my lord. It took the selkie and the girl, and ran into the Wildwood.'

'How could you lose anything as big as a troll? Are you an army of dimwits? You shame me. You shame yourselves. You shame our leader.'

And with that, he picked up Ben and stalked away, calling

back over his shoulder, 'Pertinax, Ancasta: you will come with me.'

The allosaurs looked at one another. What did he want with them? They could not imagine it was anything good.

When the Sphynx returned, it was not alone. Draped around its neck and body like a weird, ragged scarf in lurid hues of red and white and orange was Boneless Bob.

Alice folded her arms. 'There you are! I wondered where you'd got to. Well, where's my brother?'

'Is he alive?' cried Silver.

'The General has him prisoner.'

'Who's the General?' asked Ellie.

'A huge tyrannosaurussss rex,' hissed Boneless Bob.

The selkie moaned. She would not forget that monster in a hurry.

'They're taking him to Dodman Castle,' added the Sphynx.

'He's going to be a wedding presssent!' said the serpent, its neck-frill flaring.

'A tribute for the King,' the hairless cat corrected.

'Who's getting married?' Ellie asked curiously. She wasn't interested in the 'King' bit, but she liked weddings, and had already planned out exactly what she was going to wear and who she was going to invite (and, more importantly, who she wasn't) to her own. She didn't have a boyfriend yet, and had in fact only ever kissed one boy properly, when tipsy on cider and blackcurrant at Katie Manning's party: but that was a minor detail.

The snake hissed with laughter; then stopped suddenly as Alice narrowed her eyes. 'Queen Isssadora.'

'Mum? But that's impossible: she's already married. To Dad.'

'The Dodman doesn't care about that.'

Ellie shrieked. 'She can't marry the *Dodman*!'

Alice's pale pink mouth set in a hard straight line. 'No, she certainly can't.' She turned to the pterosaur. 'Corinthius, we have a journey to make.'

CHAPTER TWENTY-FOUR

Killing Time

Clive Arnold was asleep when the witch came for him. It was 6.30 in the morning and he'd been tossing and turning for the two small hours he had slept, his head filled with fears for his family and with bad dreams.

In one dream he'd been walking alone in a wood on a bright, sunlit morning, and heard singing. The song had made his pulse race; he did not know why. He ventured further into the wood, in pursuit of the singer, and then suddenly he glimpsed her, dancing barefoot, her eyes closed and her pale hair flying. Legs trembling, he had walked towards her, on tiptoe, trying to make no sound and hardly knowing why. Like this, he came at last into the little clearing where she danced, and just as he appeared, her eyes flew open. They were eyes of the most startling green; and at that moment he felt that all the breath had been sucked out of his body.

In the dream it was Isadora; and then it wasn't Isadora. She was a Queen, then a woman; a Queen, then a woman. She bloomed with health, then became frail and ill. It was as if someone was flicking a switch back and forth, showing one image, then another. He called her name, and she stared at him as if he were a monster, and when he called out to her, to re-assure her, she screamed, and he took a step towards her and found himself falling, falling, falling . . .

. . . and then he wasn't falling any more but flying, like a bird, with the wind pressing against the bare skin of his face and arms. For a moment or two it was exhilarating. He felt a tremendous sense of freedom, of possibility: that everything was going to be all right. Then he looked down. The ground beneath him was a *very* long way away. Somehow, he could tell this even though he couldn't really see very well. In his dream, he shook his head, because his eyesight was perfectly good: he didn't even own a pair of glasses. A little voice in the back of his head reminded him that his eyes only worked in his world. And then he woke up.

He *was* flying. That much was clear. And not in any aircraft, either. He looked down: nothing but a blur of clouds and the misty green-brown of land a long way below. He tried to look up, but it was hard to move his head. Something was hauling at it. He wrenched his neck sideways and stared. And stared.

Maggota grinned back at him. She was very close: horribly close. So close he could see her in all her full and gory detail.

'Welcome back to Eidolon, Clive dear,' she purred, and some maggots fell out of her snakelike hair on to him.

Luckily, the wind blew them off his face before he had a chance to retch. Which was just as well, since if he had thrown up it would have gone all over him and spoilt his clothes. Except that he wasn't wearing clothes, as such. He glanced down to find that he only had on his pyjama bottoms. Perhaps he *was* still dreaming after all.

The witch's insistent tug on his hair (which was how she was pulling him along) dispelled this vain hope.

'I do hope you don't mind the lack of ceremony,' she went on. 'It's all been a bit of a rush.'

'I don't understand,' Mr Arnold moaned. 'You took me home. We even had a cup of tea, and then you . . . you disappeared. I thought you'd gone for good.'

'For good?' Maggota laughed. 'I never go for good. For bad, for kicks or for laughs; but *never* for good. Good is for fools. You and your family seem very attached to the idea of good: which is why none of you are likely to survive in this world. Or the other. Really, you haven't got the sense you were born with. If, indeed, you were born with any.' She clucked her tongue disapprovingly. 'I mean, really: inviting me in for a cup of tea, after all you've learned about inviting a witch over your threshold!'

Clive Arnold closed his eyes. 'It was just good manners,' he said faintly.

Maggota laughed. 'You see? There you go again: such reliance on the concept of good. Good and goodness: the weakest of the weak.'

'You're wrong. It's the strongest force there is.'

'Well, all it's going to do is get you killed.'

'*Killed?*'

The witch gave him a ghastly grin. 'It's really best not to ask.'

They started to descend and the wind rushed past Clive Arnold's ears like a hurricane. He opened his eyes and saw a large building rushing towards him. Dark shapes moved around on top of it, but when he tried to focus on them his head hurt and he had to close his eyes again. Which was probably a good thing, since the shapes were dinosaur guards – a troop of velociraptors and a squadron of pterodactyls, patrolling the battlements and keeping watch for any unwanted visitors.

The next thing he knew was hitting the ground with rather more force than seemed necessary, and being tugged down a flight of seemingly never-ending steps, up which roiled blast after blast of different smells. Some were delicious and made saliva gather in his mouth; others made him want to gag.

'Ah,' said Maggota knowingly. 'It seems we're just in time.'

'In time for what?'

'The wedding feast.'

Clive Arnold frowned. 'What wedding feast?'

'No need for you to concern yourself with that,' she said

briskly. 'Because, though it can't take place without you, you're not actually invited.'

The kitchen staff at Dodman Castle had been up all night and were now at their wits' end. The Dodman did not keep a very orderly kitchen at the best of times, and he wasn't known for his management skills. Hence, those who 'ran' the kitchen tended to be the wilier goblins who knew that working there meant having access to the larder and avoiding getting trampled on by dinosaurs; and a couple of trolls who'd decided they'd rather cook than fight. Unfortunately, the goblins had had rather too much access to the larder and had been stuffing their faces on a regular basis, becoming decidedly tubby; and leaving very little in store. When the Dodman had come storming into the kitchen the night before to announce that there would be an enormous feast the next day, he'd found most of his staff snoozing off the remnants of the last roast ox, their guilt made all the more obvious by the pile of bones they'd fallen asleep on. It had not made him very happy. He had kicked awake the three worst offenders – the appropriately named Gutty, Grabbit and Butterball – upended a tureen of cold gravy on the snoring trolls and informed them all that unless they had a spread fit for a King arrayed in the throne room by noon the next day he, personally, was going to see to it that his guests fed upon roasted troll stuffed with Gutty, Grabbit and Butterball.

Muttering unhappily, Butterball had taken the keys and gone to inspect the larder. He had returned shortly afterward (wiping his mouth surreptitiously) and reported that it now contained only three dried fairies, a couple of boiled wood-sprites, some rotting apples and a mermaid which was beginning to smell. (And if a goblin says something is beginning to smell, you had better believe it's more than half rotten.) None of which was going to make a feast.

They put their heads together. Gutty suggested running away. One of the trolls nodded; the other punched it on the arm. 'He'll only summon us back. And then he'll be really, really angry. And you know what happens then.'

They all fell silent. Till last week there had been seven of them working in the kitchens. The Dodman had fed the other two to the Gabriel Hounds after he'd caught them frying fairies.

It wasn't the cruelty that bothered him: it was the waste of their magic. He had decreed that all fairies, sprites and other creatures of magic were to be killed by him personally before they were cooked. It was the only way he ate now: biting off their heads and draining their magic. The goblins had come to be grateful that they had no magic in them: it didn't seem to do you any good round here.

Then Grabbit had had a brilliant idea. They might not have anything useful in the larder: but the dungeons were stuffed full of captives taken in the war against the Queen's forces . . .

Isadora woke before dawn, stirred by the aroma of something truly terrible. She tried to stretch, and found that she couldn't: the Dodman had left her bound by sturdy leather cords around her wrists, telling her that if she was so attached to her throne, then attached to it she should be. She looked at the complex knots and wondered whether she even had the strength to summon up the magic to unravel them: decided that she didn't, and fell back against the carved wood. Her nose wrinkled.

'What is that dreadful smell?' she whispered, to herself.

'Roasting centaur,' came an indistinct voice by her feet.

She looked down to find her niece, Cynthia, awake and staring at her upside-down with eyes that reminded her uncomfortably of boiled gooseberries.

'I beg your pardon?'

'You should,' Cynthia said rudely. 'You *should* beg my pardon: leaving that Book lying around so temptingly; and the crown, too. How could I resist stealing them? It's all your fault. If it wasn't for you I wouldn't be here in this horrid cage.' And she started to cry.

Isadora forbore saying that it was Cynthia's greed, ambition and naivety which had got her into the cage, since pointing it out would only upset her more. And really, was it the child's fault if she had inherited these characteristics from her greedy, ambitious and rather stupid parents? Aleister had never been the sharpest needle in the pack; while his wife Sybil had all the imagination and individuality of a traffic warden: which was exactly what she had been when Aleister had met and married her. She sighed.

'Roasting centaur,' Cynthia said again, more clearly, 'and the last of Cernunnos's wolves.'

Isadora closed her eyes. 'How . . . terrible.'

'Oh, you'll be surprised at what you'll eat when you're really hungry. I went three days without a bite to begin with. But he just force-fed me. With juiced fairies,' she added malevolently, as her aunt's eyes opened wide in horror. 'Not that he cared whether I lived or died. Just to keep my magic up. So that I could read the Book of Naming for him.'

'So it's you who summoned his monstrous army?'

Cynthia nodded. 'Well, not all of them,' she added modestly. 'Some of them just joined up for the chance to kill dragons and for the promise of land.'

'What land?'

'Oh, they want all the land east of the Fire Mountains, where they've been at war with the dragons for ages, but I don't think he ever promised them anything specific. They're not very bright, most of these dinosaurs.'

'But I only ever had two dragons at my command. They killed Ishtar. I don't even know what happened to Zark, except that he didn't come when I called for him.'

'Good!' declared Cynthia. 'They'll be the ones that wrecked Mum's Range Rover. Serves them right.'

The Queen sighed. It seemed she was wrong: there was no good left in her niece at all.

'Does he really mean to kill Clive?' she said suddenly.

Cynthia wriggled and turned over with difficulty. 'He will stop at nothing to get what he wants.'

'And what *does* he want?' It was a question into thin air: she did not expect an answer.

'Everything. Your throne. Your realm.' She paused. 'You.'

Isadora shuddered. She had never felt so powerless in her life. Not even when she had been so ill in the Other World and had been taken to hospital: even then, there had remained a small well of strength at the core of her, the willpower to survive. For the sake of her family. And where were her family now? She had not the least idea. An enormous tear spilt down one cheek and rolled off her chin. It fell, like the patter of a raindrop, on to Cynthia's forehead. There was a moment of silence in which Isadora managed to stifle a sob, then the little witch said, very softly, 'If you got me out of here, I could help you.'

'And how would you do that?'

'Let me out and I'll show you.'

Isadora smiled. 'You must think me very foolish.'

Cynthia considered this. 'Not really. Just too good for this world.'

'There was a time when that would have been a compliment.' The Queen closed her eyes, concentrating. She had no expectation of help from her niece; but she did not approve of keeping anyone or anything in a cage, no matter how annoying they were. At last she felt her magic return.

She freed her own knots first, then, panting, bent to examine the cage's lock. One of the Gabriel Hounds growled a warning, but she paid it no heed. The tumblers in the lock clicked over one another, realigned themselves and abruptly the hasp sprang open.

Cynthia stared at it, unbelieving. Then she reached out of the cage, removed the lock and wriggled free. She gazed at her aunt in surprise. 'I didn't really think you'd help me. After all, I haven't . . . I haven't been . . . very nice to you.'

Isadora smiled. 'There's no point in adding to the distress in the world. Even the tiniest improvement is still an improvement. I'm not asking anything from you in return. Everyone should get a second chance. What you choose to do with your freedom is up to you. Everyone has a choice as to how they act in the world. In *either* world.'

Cynthia regarded her aunt suspiciously, not at all sure what to make of either the sermon or her newfound freedom. In the end, she bobbed her head awkwardly, then dashed for the door.

The hounds watched her go curiously, but a look from the Queen kept them silent.

She had not freed Cynthia a moment too soon: the door at the other end of the hall burst open and in strode the Dodman, with her brother Aleister clutching at his elbow. Behind them was a frightful apparition with wild red hair, a mouthful of fangs and a clawed hand which was propelling along the fourth member of the group.

'Clive!'

Isadora fairly flew the length of the throne room. Goblins, hounds and sabre-toothed tigers scattered from her path. Evading the burning gaze of the dog-headed man, she ran to her husband and threw her arms around his neck.

'Oh, Clive, I'm so sorry!'

Clive Arnold blinked. He held his wife at arm's length, where he could see her better, and gave her the bravest smile he could muster. Given the circumstances (being hauled from his bed in the witching hour, hurtled through space into another world and presented to a monstrous figure which looked as if it had a dog's head – a fact he attributed to his terrible eyesight in this place) it was a bit of a wobbly smile, but it made Isadora's heart turn over.

'Don't be sorry,' he said softly. 'Whatever happens, I know it's not your fault.'

'Oh, but it is. It's all my fault. If it wasn't for me you wouldn't be here. None of this would be happening.'

'If it wasn't for you, none of my life would have been worth living.' And he touched her tear-stained cheek with a gentle finger.

'The children?' Isadora whispered. 'Are they—?'

Clive Arnold braced himself. He had no idea where in either world Ben or Ellie were; and no idea how he was ever going to tell her about Alice. As it happened, he didn't have the chance to say anything.

'Ah, how touching!' The Dodman's growl was bitter. 'Make the most of your last few seconds together.' He turned to the boggle-eyed goblins. 'Shall we give him to the sabre-tooths?' he asked with a cruel smile.

The goblins chuckled at this. It would probably be entertaining; but ever so messy. This thought gave them pause: who would have to clear up the mess? They would. It wasn't even as if they'd get a chance of leftovers: the tigers never left anything worth having. Once they'd had their way with the human, there wouldn't be as much as a little finger left.

The Dodman strutted to the cage. 'Now then, Cynthia,

what are the names of these sabre-tooths again?' He stopped in mid-strut. He stared at the empty cage. Then he picked it up and shook it, as if his captive had somehow managed to shrink herself to almost nothing and hide in a corner of it. Then he stared around the throne room. The goblins wouldn't meet his eye. The hounds shuffled nervously. Only the tigers regarded him unblinking.

'Where's my little witch?' he roared. Then something else struck him. 'And where's my Book?'

Maggota clapped her hands together in sudden delight. 'You really, really shouldn't underestimate us witches, Rex, dear.'

He glared at her. Then he transferred his gaze to Isadora. His teeth flashed dangerously. 'This is *your* doing!' he accused.

She returned his look coolly. 'I know nothing about the Book's current whereabouts,' she replied truthfully.

'I don't believe you!' He stamped his feet. 'Damn you! Nothing will stop me!' He caught hold of the nearest goblin, wrenched its nasty little curved knife away from it and flourished it so that the blade glinted in the light. Then he ran at the little group, pushed Isadora roughly aside and grabbed painful hold of her husband.

Clive Arnold had had enough of being towed around by the hair. It wasn't as if he had much of it left, and he was quite attached (literally) to what remained. He balled a fist and slammed it into what he hoped was the dog-headed creature's massive chin.

Unfortunately, because the Dodman was so much taller

than he was, and because he couldn't really see what he was hitting, it was not much more than a glancing blow. It did, however, surprise the Dodman so much that he let go of the man, and bit his own tongue. So hard that it bled. Blood oozed out between his black dog-lips and dripped down on to Clive Arnold's head. Within moments, he was the most ghastly sight.

Everyone held their breath. Then Isadora hurled herself between them, shrieking, 'Don't kill him! I'll change the law. You can have the throne: you can have it all; just don't kill him!'

In response, the Dodman merely snarled. 'I *shall* have it all and I don't need your permission or your precious law to take it!'

Maggota pulled the Queen aside. 'There really is no point in prolonging the agony, my dear. Accept your fate. Accept his fate –' she nodded her crescent moon of a chin at Clive Arnold '– and let it go. You should have understood you could never marry outside Eidolon and expect to keep any of it. Such a waste of your magic. Such a trial for the rest of us.'

Isadora turned. 'My marriage and my children have been no waste of my magic or my life,' she said furiously. Then her eyes narrowed as she recognised her old teacher. 'So it's true what they say: that Eidolon does hold a mirror up to the nature of its folk, Maggota of the First Order. Your inner wickedness has made itself very evident indeed over the years.'

'Hoity-toity!' clucked the witch. 'You won't be saying things like that when he's got you chained up in your chambers and I'm the only company you've got.'

Isadora's eyes glittered. 'As if I would ever again wish for your company!'

'Now, now: be polite, or extracting your magic from you may not be as painless as you'd prefer.'

'Faithless old crone! How could you ever choose to take the side of such a creature as him? One set on rooting out and destroying all the magic in our world? He will destroy you, too, you fool!'

Maggota raised an eyebrow. 'Be careful who you call a fool, Isadora, lest you be the thing you decry. You forget who you are talking to!'

'Enough of this!' the Dodman roared. And he fitted the claws of his huge left paw over the crown of Clive Arnold's head and pulled it back, exposing his pale and vulnerable throat. 'Say goodbye to your first husband, Isadora. At least you won't be widowed long!' The blood sprayed from his mouth as he chuckled and raised the curved blade.

At that moment, something whizzed through the air of the throne room. It seemed to have come from nowhere and it moved so fast it was impossible for anyone without good Eidolon vision to be able to tell what it was. Certainly, Clive Arnold had no clue: all he knew was that at one moment the dog-headed monster had been hauling his head back so hard he thought his neck might break, and the next he found himself staggering forwards into his wife's arms, inexplicably free. There was a great deal of commotion; a lot of barking and snarling (and not all of it from the oddly pale dogs that seemed to litter the hall) and a shout of triumph.

'Cynthia!' cried Isadora, her amazement clear in her voice.

The little witch hovered well out of the long reach of the Dodman's grasping claws. She had gratefully retrieved the broomstick from where it had been thrown on the woodpile outside. In her lap, she cradled a large leatherbound volume. This, she was currently flicking through with some urgency, using the knife she had whipped from the Dodman's outstretched hand as a bookmark.

Dragons, Trolls, Goblins, Dinosaurs, Nymphs, Fairies, Sprites, Centaurs, Selkies, Merfolk, Banshees, Vampires, Elves. . .

'You're not in here!' Cynthia accused the dog-headed man furiously. 'How can you not be in here?'

He'd never left the Book of Naming in her possession long enough for her to discover this lack before. He'd always watched her too carefully for that, and she knew that while the words were no more than a meaningless jumble to him, he would certainly spot a picture of himself if she came to that page.

'Well, of course he's not, child!' Maggota chuckled. 'He's not really *from* here.'

At this, the Dodman spun around. Red lights lit his black eyes from within, like demon-fire. 'What do you *mean*, I'm not really "from here"?' he roared. 'I've lived here all my life!'

The ancient witch looked crafty. She hadn't yet decided which side she was on, or how to use the knowledge she had tucked away up her sleeve (which was long and ratty and full of spiderwebs).

'Then how can I kill him if I can't Name him?' shrieked Cynthia, incensed.

'Now, now, Cynthia, dear,' her father exhorted nervously. 'Stop your little game now. Delightful prank, ha ha! But time to make your peace now, eh? Say you're sorry and give the Dodman his knife back, let him get on with the business at hand.'

'The business at hand? You mean killing Uncle Clive? Or Stupid Uncle Clive, as you always used to call him?'

Old Creepie looked distinctly discomfited by this awkward revelation. 'Sorry, old chap,' he said to Clive Arnold, as if somehow calling him names was much more serious than suggesting he be murdered by a monster; but Mr Arnold merely laughed.

'That's all right, "old chap",' he returned sarcastically. 'We always called *you* Awful Uncle Aleister.'

'And for good reason,' Isadora said grimly. She pushed her husband firmly behind her. It wasn't his fault he couldn't function well in the Secret Country: if he lost his temper and struck out again he was as likely to floor her as he was to hit the Dodman. 'Give me the knife, Cynthia.'

The little witch looked at her distrustfully for a moment, then zipped neatly down and dropped the blade into her aunt's hand. Isadora held it in front of her purposefully, though she wasn't quite sure what she was going to do with it. Then she summoned the best of her magic, cloaked her husband with as much invisibility as she could muster and drew herself up in front of him, offering the Dodman the most regal image of herself that she could possibly project.

CHAPTER TWENTY-FIVE

A Meeting of Monsters

It was into this bizarre scenario that Tyrant Megathighs III suddenly appeared. A huge leg (as befitted his name) arrived first, followed by his massive head, crouched to fit through the main door to the hall (which, although designed to permit the entrance of ceremonial coaches and sedan chairs, had never been designed to allow a tyrannosaurus rex to pass with ease); and at last the rest of him followed after some clever contortions. He was accompanied by the allosaurs Pertinax and Ancasta, with their captive in tow behind them. The tyrannosaurus rex's massive bulk seemed to fill the hall. Its head grazed the ceiling. Cynthia retreated into the farthest corner, where her eyes gleamed out of the shadows like a particularly malevolent spider.

The Dodman turned at the intrusion, his expression forbidding. 'Get out!' he yelled. 'You're too early.'

The tyrannosaur was taken aback. Had it not been expressly invited? And while the sun had not been directly over the castle, the smells of the feast being prepared were undeniable. The dog-headed man was often in a vile temper of late; but it knew how to win his favour.

'Sire,' it growled, bowing deeply. 'I have brought you the tribute you demanded.' And it waved the allosaurs forward.

They had meant to garland their tribute in flowers since, as Ancasta pointed out, you should always wrap wedding gifts nicely; but most of the flowers in Eidolon had died the moment their Queen had been taken captive, and so they had resorted to what they could find on the outskirts of the Wildwood, amongst the trampled vegetation and the burned trees. Thus it was that Ben Arnold, Prince of Eidolon, stumbled into the throne room wound around with stinging nettles, ferns and thistles, his arms and legs bound by chains of twisted ivy.

There was a thin cry, and the goblin knife Isadora had been holding clattered to the ground and skated away across the floor.

The Dodman's grim expression changed to one of beaming munificence. 'Ah,' he breathed. 'Tyrant, you have outdone yourself!' He strode forward to inspect his gift.

Ben looked up at the dog-headed man defiantly, and willed himself not to be frightened. Even though the Dodman loomed eight feet tall, and had the head of the ugliest dog imaginable, the first time Ben had encountered him he had been working behind the counter in a Bixbury petshop and had looked like a rather ordinary sort of person (apart from his teeth). The last time he had seen the Dodman, in his current form, the nautilus had been waving him around in one of its tentacles. He might be a monster; but he was not *that* scary. His knees stopped knocking abruptly. He summoned his courage, and took a deep breath.

'Don't you dare touch me!' he said furiously. 'You've got no right to be here. This is my mother's castle; my mother's realm. You have brought war to a peaceful world, destroyed the magic that makes it special, killed hundreds of innocent folk, compelled others to do things you haven't got the guts to do yourself, and for what? To be King of a ruined, miserable place, surrounded by goblins and monsters who don't follow you because they like you or believe in what you stand for, but because they're scared of you or held by the magic of their true names.'

At this, the two allosaurs exchanged a glance. With a self-righteous expression, one said quietly to the other, 'I told you so.'

'But what happens when the compulsion of their summoning wears off?' Ben continued bravely. 'Who's going to stick around then? And where does that leave you? A King with no subjects. A King of a wasteland, of a kingdom that's blasted and wrecked. Is that what you want?'

For a moment it seemed that the Dodman dwindled. In a

fairytale, he would have been diminished by the power of the prince's fervour, revealed by these clear and ringing words as the mean and insubstantial villain that he was. Shame would have shrunk him to nothing. But this was no fairytale; and the Dodman had no shame. Instead of diminishing, he seemed to grow, his evil cast about him like a great cape of darkness. He drew back his black dog-lips to reveal an array of long, sharp, white dog's teeth. Then he threw back his head and howled, an eerie sound that echoed around the rafters and shivered the marrow of every creature in the hall.

'Yes!' he hissed. 'Yes! That's exactly what I want. I hate all you little bright, shiny, happy, magic-filled creatures. I hate the world you've made. I want to see it in shreds, in ashes. No one cares about me, so I care for no one. Your mother ruined my life. Now I'm going to ruin everything and everyone she ever cared about.'

A terrible, heavy silence fell. The sound of pages being frantically riffled in the air above their heads was suddenly very loud. Cynthia was searching, searching, searching . . .

The Dodman fixed the little witch in his sights. Then he turned to the giant tyrannosaur. 'Kill her!' he screamed, pointing up into the dark corner of the roof. 'Kill her and bring me that Book!'

The tyrannosaur seemed to hesitate for a second, as if the compulsion that bound it was wearing thin. Everyone seemed frozen, holding their breath, waiting to see whether the dog-headed man still held his power. Then the monstrous dinosaur sprang into action, crossing the space between it and Cynthia in a single terrifying leap and swiping her off her broomstick and into the air with a wicked, curled claw. Cynthia screamed. It was the last sound she made. Down into the monster's tooth-filled maw she went, head first, her shriek suddenly and horribly cut short by the crunch of its jaws. The broomstick clattered to the floor, followed a split second later by one of her shoes, which had flown off at the impact.

With the other clawed hand, Tyrant caught the falling Book as neatly as a conjuring trick and passed it to the dog-headed man.

Everyone stared in horror. They had all of them seen terrible sights in this war; but to see death come so close and so suddenly in such an enclosed space was shocking. Ben felt as if his ribs had been bound with iron, not ivy; his feet made of lead. He could not move; could not breathe.

Someone sobbed, a racking sound like the swinging hinges of a rusty gate. It was Old Creepie, Cynthia's father. He sat on the floor as if his knees had given way (which they had) and his hunched back shook and shook. Pale-faced, Isadora laid a hand upon her brother's shoulder.

The Dodman regarded this familial act with scorn. His lip rippled and curled. Then he laughed. The horrible sound filled the empty space where Cynthia had been. 'Right then,' he said. 'Who's next?'

His gazed fixed upon Clive Arnold, no longer fully hidden by the shielding magic of his wife.

'Him!'

The tyrannosaur bent to inspect its prey, which was

shimmering in and out of visibility in a most disconcerting way. It swiped a hand down just as the Queen leapt up and pushed her husband sideways. The tyrannosaur knocked them both flying. Clive Arnold landed a little distance away on his backside with a thud, and the spell shattered, leaving him in full view of the beast.

Tyrant grinned and lumbered forward.

'No!'

Without a moment's conscious thought for what he was going to do, Ben hurled himself on to the floor, executed the most perfect commando roll (this being the only way he could move fast at all, with ivy tied around him), grabbed up the fallen goblin knife and swung it in a single, shining arc up and then down.

Goblin knives are very sharp: and this one had been honed on a pair of stegosaurus spikes the previous day. The power of the blow delivered by Ben's desperate hand and the keenness of the blade had driven the knife right through the armoured scales of the tyrannosaurus rex's leading foot and pinned it neatly (and very painfully) to the wooden floor.

Tyrant roared in agony. He beat the air with his scaly fists; but he could not move. At least, not without ripping his foot in two.

The Dodman growled his frustration. 'I am surrounded by incompetents!' He thrust the Book at Maggota. 'Name them,' he instructed her, pointing at the allosaurs. 'They look as if they should be able to take off a head or two without much difficulty. Start with Clive Arnold, then take the boy.'

Even Maggota seemed cowed by the demise of the little witch. Taking the Book of Naming from him, she bent her head over it and her bony fingers moved amongst its pages.

One of the allosaurs stepped forward. 'There will be a lot of allosaurs in that volume, crone. It will take you longer to find our names than it will be to snap your head off, so do not think to try to compel us.' It folded its arms, glaring.

The other allosaur winced. 'Ancasta, do stop.'

Ancasta turned to it. 'Shut up, Pertinax. Shut up and think for just a moment. Did you hear what the Boy said?'

Pertinax nodded unwillingly.

'Do you want to raise your young in a wasteland? Well, do you?'

A tiny, joyful light lit the male allosaur's gaze. 'No, dear.'

'Well then.' Ancasta glowered down at the dog-headed man. 'What you are doing is wrong and I want no more part of it and neither does my mate. There's been enough pointless bloodshed. We're leaving.'

And she turned to go.

'No!' roared the Dodman, quivering with fury. 'Tyrant, drag that pathetic pin out of your foot and kill them. Kill them all!'

The tyrannosaur made a terrible, agonising lurch.

CHAPTER TWENTY-SIX

Alice

The gigantic tyrannosaur ripped its foot clear of the dagger and hurled itself at the two allosaurs. There was not a great deal of difference between their sizes: Tyrant topped his erstwhile captains by maybe five feet, but his jaws were massive, and he was both enraged and compelled by his Naming. The hall thundered as they roared and stamped, moving around one another, half-crouched, like professional wrestlers. The goblins pressed themselves against the walls to avoid their lashing tails, a blow from which could club a dozen of them immediately insensible. The sabre-toothed tigers, deciding that discretion was the better part of valour, snaked furtively between the dinosaurs' feet and fled out into the courtyard. The Gabriel Hounds, meanwhile, clambered upon one another for a better view, baying for blood.

Into this chaos stepped a small, pale figure, weaving a path between the stamping feet and swinging tails, the claws and jaws and roars of the duelling dinosaurs.

In a high, clear voice, she addressed the chief offender: 'Tyrant Megathighs III, desist!'

The huge tyrannosaur hesitated, blinking.

The Dodman barked out a laugh. 'Whoever you are, dwarf, you should know you cannot compel a creature which has already been Named. This dinosaur is under my control!'

If this were the case, Tyrant did not appear to realise it, for his little clawed arms had dropped to his sides and his eyes had swivelled, puzzled, to survey the tiny girl. She smiled at him. His jaws worked, as if they were munching something (perhaps the last strands of Cynthia); then he returned a toothy grin.

The Dodman was horrified. What was going on? 'Get out!' he shrieked. 'This is my throne room; *my* castle; *my* fight. You weren't invited!'

'Oh, I know,' said the elf-girl sweetly. She turned her lambent green gaze upon the amazed spectators. 'But I decided to drop in anyway.'

Isadora's eyes – the same colour as those of the elf-girl – went very round. How could this be? In any other world she would have thought her sight deceived; but this was Eidolon, and magic was suddenly running strongly in her veins. Besides, a mother always knows her child. 'Alice,' she breathed at last.

'Alice!' And she ran across the throne room with her arms out-stretched and swept the tiny blonde creature into her embrace.

Ben stared and stared. *Alice?* But Alice was a baby, and lost, lost in the wild roads. He rubbed his eyes with his free hand and stared again. The green-eyed girl winked at him: just the sort of wink his mother used to give him, and something inside him (who knew what?) recognised his little sister. Though she was not so little any more.

'Hello, Sonny Jim,' growled a gravelly voice at his feet. Ben looked down and found a small black-and-brown cat gnawing through the cords of ivy that bound him. 'It *is* Alice, you know. Weird but true.'

The Dodman turned his fiery gaze upon Maggota. 'I've had quite enough of this,' he snarled. 'Name her and have her throw herself off the battlements.'

The elf-girl extricated herself from her mother and her crys-tal laugh rang out. 'Go on, then, Maggota Medusa Magnifica. Name me!' And she giggled and giggled as if this was all part of the best game in the world. In any world. Which, perhaps, it was.

Maggota Magnifica dropped the Book of Naming with a clatter. It landed on one of her long, bony feet, and must have hurt quite a lot, because it is a very big book, but she didn't wince or make a sound. Instead, she just stared at the blonde-haired child in awe, and not a little fear.

Alice shrugged. She waved a finger and the Book came flap-ping towards her like some great, ungainly bird. 'I don't think we'll be needing you any more,' she told it sternly, tapping it once on the spine. The Book snapped shut and vanished in a cloud of dust.

The Dodman took one look at this small act of magic, turned and ran. The door at the other end of the throne room heaved itself shut before he could slip through it. He spun around, arms splayed against the wood, chest heaving. His eyes bulged.

'Beetle, Brimstone, Batface and Bogie, take her prisoner and bring her to me!'

The goblins sneaked a peek at the little elf-girl, then at the rage-filled face of their master. She didn't look as scary as the dog-headed man, and surely four of them could deal with her? They advanced cautiously, wary of magic tricks.

'No, you don't,' Ancasta said sharply. She scooped up Bogie and Batface, one in each clawed hand, then gave her husband a meaningful stare.

Pertinax, who had never much liked goblins, and found working with them rather beneath his dignity, picked up Beetle and Brimstone and held them at arm's length, where they kicked feebly.

Alice clapped her hands. 'Thank you; but there's no need to hurt them. There's been too much of that going on here.' She turned back to the main door. There, peering in rather nervously, were a selkie, a rather short-sighted girl, a hairless cat and a striped snake; as well as the sabre-toothed tigers, for they suffered from the relentless curiosity of all their kind and could not bear not knowing what was going on.

'Come in, come in,' Alice declared cheerfully. 'Everyone's welcome!'

'No they are NOT!' roared the Dodman, for whom the situation had passed from the surreal to the plain embarrassing. Even if he managed to kill the little creature and its mother, there would be talk the length and breadth of Eidolon about this incident: how a little blonde-haired child had appeared out of nowhere and marched right into his castle – his heavily guarded castle – and ordered his own particular bodyguard of monsters around, made fun of him, *ridiculed* him. He would be the butt of a thousand jokes; he would be a laughing-stock. Enraged beyond measure by this idea, the Dodman hurled himself across the chamber at Isadora.

'Mum!' Ben warned, but she was enraptured by Alice. She turned too slowly and found herself suddenly in the Dodman's arms. No tender embrace this, but a hard forearm across her throat so that she could barely breathe, and one of her arms twisted painfully up her back, imprisoned there by a savage paw.

He snapped his claws at the ghost-dogs, and like dogs everywhere they responded to the master they had always known and jostled around the Dodman and his prisoner, haunches quivering, tails held low. They didn't bark (for once) but maintained a puzzled, attentive silence. *What now?* they seemed to ask. *We will do whatever you ask of us, but we don't understand any of this at all.* Ghosts of any kind do not retain much of what little intelligence they had in life: all they keep is a remnant of what they were, a tiny essential flame. Ghost-dogs are simpler than most: they require only food and fighting and a master's orders in order to carry on their reduced existence.

'I am going out to my army now, and I am taking her with me,' the Dodman announced. 'You can keep this filthy castle. I never liked it anyway. But if you make one move, one little step towards me, or even waggle your little finger to make a spell, I will snap her neck like a stick.' And he thrust his long jaw at Alice provocatively, as if daring her to laugh at him.

Alice wasn't laughing now. Her pale, glowing face had become grave. For a moment, she looked as if she had never been a baby; had never even been human. Her eyes became the deep marine green of a storm at sea; her features sharp and taut. The playful child was gone; replaced by an eldritch creature aeons old.

Then, like waves erasing patterns on a beach, the ancient being was gone. She gestured to the door. 'Go, then. Go and find your army. They are waiting for you.'

'Alice, you can't—' Ben started, but she silenced him with a look.

With the Gabriel Hounds snapping and snarling around him, threatening to bite anyone who tried to harm their master, the Dodman made his way to the courtyard door, his captive held tight against him.

Ellie and Silver pressed themselves flat against the carved statues as he passed. Ellie gazed at her mother, tears running down her cheeks, but in response, Isadora turned her head a fraction, gave her the tiniest smile and dropped a lazy eyelid, as if she didn't mind at all that she was going to die, now that her kingdom was passing into the keeping of her youngest, strangest child.

The sabre-tooths growled at the ghost-dogs; but they did nothing to hamper their progress, and after the odd procession passed them by, they turned and followed them.

As if a spell had been broken, Ben took to his heels. He ran the length of the throne room, down the long, dark passage-way beyond and out into the courtyard. 'Mum! Mum, no!' he cried. And then he stopped. When he had entered the castle, just a little while ago (though it felt like an age) as the captive of the tyrannosaur, the courtyard had been full of the Dodman's minions. There had been goblins on guard with pikestaffs, dinosaurs plated with armour, pterodactyls patrolling the air and a squadron of trolls manning the bridge across the lake. On the iron spikes above the main gate a row of heads leered down into the courtyard, no doubt removed from prisoners taken in battle, all dark and rotting like over-ripe fruit.

Now, it was like walking into a completely different world. The goblins were still there, but they were all sitting quietly cross-legged on one side of the courtyard, as if they were at a Sunday school outing, watched over by a group of centaurs. Their weapons lay stacked in a neat pile well out of reach. There wasn't a dinosaur in sight, except for Ancasta and Pertinax and the tyrannosaur, who had followed everyone out-side to see what was happening.

And when Ben looked up expecting to see the spiky out-lines of prehistoric birds in the sky, he saw instead a dozen or more dragons quartering the air above the castle. Between them, sunlight sparked off the wings of a myriad of fairies and wood-sprites. A lot more of them appeared to have survived the Dodman's ravages than anyone could ever have hoped.

On the bridge which spanned the lake from castle to shore the guard trolls had either thrown down their spears or were leaning on them chatting good-naturedly to Gordon Gargantua and Grizelda. A phalanx of dragons was marching across the bridge now, led by –

'Zark! Oh, Zark!' Ben felt his grin stretch right across his face.

The little dragon was thinner and his glowing red scales looked duller than they had been even when Ben had found him in the Other World, but his eyes were shining, and no longer crazed with grief. He held up a claw to salute Ben and puffed out a little smoke, just to show he still had it in him. Beside him, with one hand on Zark's shoulder, walked a centaur, his dark head thrown back, his carriage proud, a bow slung across his back and a short sword in his hand. It was Darius; yet despite his warlike appearance, no blood stained the bright metal of his sword.

The Dodman looked wildly about him, trying to take all this in. His jaw dropped in shock. He came to an abrupt standstill as if he had been shot. Tremors ran through his muscles, as if even his body was rebelling against him. Taking advantage of the sudden laxness of his grip, Isadora elbowed him hard in his stomach, and when he grunted in pain, twisted out of his grasp and ran to Ben's side. He barely seemed to notice he had lost her. He turned around and around and saw grinning faces wherever he looked. He closed his eyes, squinching them tight shut, then opened them again, in case it had all been an illusion, or a nightmare. But the scene that met his bewildered gaze remained the same. He looked for an escape: saw none. Every exit was blocked by Wildwood creatures or dragons; and he could not swim. He threw back his head and howled like the dog he was.

CHAPTER TWENTY-SEVEN
Transformations

The dragons have come! This was the thought that played over and over in Ben's head. They had come from all over Eidolon, and no one had compelled them. Or rather . . . He shaded his eyes and gazed up into the blue air again; and there she was, a great glorious golden zeppelin of a dragon.

'Mummu-Tiamat!' he cried, but she had already dipped a wing and was spiralling down.

She landed in the courtyard, making it suddenly rather crowded. She lowered her head first to Queen Isadora, then to Ben. 'I hereby repay my debt to you, Prince of Eidolon,' she told him, rumbling a laugh. 'It was your sister Alice's idea. But

I knew what your heart's wish was even though you never said it aloud. And having witnessed your bravery in going to save your friend, I could hardly refuse.'

Ben was overcome. It was, indeed, exactly what he was going to ask as his boon: that she bring her dragons to fight for his mother in this war. Except that it had seemed too great a thing to ask when he saw Ishtar dead and Zark mad with sorrow. He didn't know what to say. It was more than he could ever have hoped or dreamt. He blushed. 'Gosh, thank you,' he said at last. And no one even seemed to have been hurt. 'How——?' he began.

It was as if she could read his mind. Perhaps she could, which was an uncomfortable thought. Her golden eyes whirled. 'How did we make the Dodman's army capitulate without spilling an ocean of blood?'

'Well, yes.'

'Perhaps you should ask your charming sister, since she had a hand in it.' The Mother of Dragons nodded to his right, and he turned and found Ellie there beside them.

'Ellie?' How on Earth could useless Ellie have changed the minds of a thousand dinosaurs?

'I used the word "charming" for a reason,' added Mummu-Tiamat, reading his thoughts again.

'Alice came and rescued us on her pteranodon, Corinthius, which she said she found wandering in the wild roads. With Grizelda, of all people. Apparently, Uncle Aleister made them pull up the Aldstane and then they couldn't get back into Eidolon the usual way and they tried a different way and got lost, and that's when Alice found them, after I'd dropped her when we went through the Minstrels—'

'What?' cried Isadora. 'I don't understand—'

Even Ben was frowning. He waved a hand. 'Never mind about all that now, Mum. We'll explain later, but it'll take a while. Get to the dinosaur army bit, Ellie,' he suggested.

Ellie grinned at them. For some reason she didn't seem to be sneezing or squinting any more, Ben noticed. Something had changed in her. And was it his imagination, or were her eyes just a little greener?

'So when we found out they'd taken Ben captive and were bringing him here, Silver and I wanted to come to the castle immediately and rescue him; but Alice was very firm about it. She said we had to deal with the larger situation first, then get down to the details. She's quite scary, Alice.'

Isadora laughed. 'She is!'

'So we got Corinthius to land near the enemy army and Alice took my hand and we stood side by side in front of them all, which was pretty terrifying, I can tell you,' said Ellie, flicking back her hair proudly. 'And then I greeted them and they all sort of stared at me, mesmerised—'

'How come that little trick didn't work when we were beating them off with sticks?' Ben asked crossly. He thought back. Odd, now that he came to think about it, the dinosaurs had left Ellie alone, concentrating their efforts on him and Silver. And he remembered how Nemesis had gazed at her; Mummu-Tiamat, too. But she never seemed to have the same effect on goblins.

Ellie shrugged. 'I don't know. I don't understand any of it.

Anyway, while they were all standing still looking at me, Alice sort of concentrated on them one by one, and then she Named all the clan-chiefs. I don't know how she knew their names, so don't ask me. And then Mummu-Tiamat arrived with Zark and all the dragons, and Darius brought the centaurs, just to make sure there wouldn't be any trouble.'

'And as witnesses,' the Mother of Dragons added loudly, 'to the Dodman's demise.'

The dog-headed man came slowly out of his trance. He turned his head to look at her. 'So burn me,' he said flatly. 'Burn me and get it over with, you overstuffed lizard.'

Mummu-Tiamat took a deep breath, filling her enormous lungs.

'No.'

Alice stood there between them.

'No,' she repeated. 'It will not end like that. *That* is his way, not mine.' She indicated the line of rotting heads. 'If you must use up the dragon's fire you have just drawn, Mummu-Tiamat, use it for good,' she suggested.

The Mother of Dragons let a single curl of smoke escape one nostril. 'You *are* a strange one,' she said, shaking her head. 'I see a change is coming to the Secret Country.'

'Yes,' said Queen Isadora, taking Alice's hand. 'It is.'

So, instead of burning the Dodman, Mummu-Tiamat incinerated the obscene heads. A swathe of clean black ash drifted down, leaving the spikes on the main gate hot and gleaming.

The Dodman cringed. 'Well, what are you going to do with me, then?' he demanded, his paws balled into fists.

Isadora and her youngest daughter exchanged a glance.

'Hmmm.' Alice stroked her pointed little chin. 'It is a bit of a puzzle, that.' She turned back and called down the hallway, 'Maggota Magnifica, I need your help!'

Seconds later, the bony old witch appeared. Boneless Bob – her beloved son and familiar – was coiled once more around her neck. She regarded Alice and her mother suspiciously. 'What do you want from me?'

'I believe you know the Dodman's true . . . nature,' Alice said softly. 'He appears to be the only being in this world I cannot Name, and I don't understand why.'

At this, a gleam of hope lit the Dodman's flat black eyes.

'Well, now, child,' said Maggota Magnifica, stretching out a vile, bony hand in front of her and examining it carefully. She flexed the cadaverous fingers with their blood-red nails. 'What will you trade me for this most valuable piece of information?'

'Be careful, Alice,' Isadora warned.

Alice smiled. 'The thing you want most.'

'Alice!' Her mother looked seriously worried now.

Maggota frowned. 'The throne?'

'You don't really want that,' Alice said, shaking her head.

Didn't she? The witch mulled this over. It was true: she didn't. She thought again. Then her eyes lit up. 'Ah, yes. Complete sovereignty over witches of every order. That they bow down to me and hail me as First Witch.'

Alice shook her head again. 'No, I don't think so.'

Maggota glared at her. 'What do you *mean*, you "don't think so"? Who are you to tell me my heart's deepest desire?'

Alice gestured with her hand and a tiny silver and pearl-inlaid mirror bloomed in her palm. She held it up to the witch's ravaged face. Maggota cackled. 'You think I'm going to give away my priceless knowledge for a paltry little mirror?'

'No,' said Alice simply. 'You're going to trade it with me for what you see reflected there.'

Frowning, Maggota grasped the child's hand, brought the mirror up to her nose and turned it this way and that, as if to discover her best possible angle. If anyone else had had Maggota Magnifica's hideous mug, thought Ben, and had examined it as minutely as the witch was doing now, they would probably have thrown up, then smashed the mirror into a million pieces; but the witch seemed absolutely enthralled by her own reflection.

She widened her eyes, brushed back her vermin-infested hair, and drew back her poisonous purple lips to reveal her meat-encrusted fangs.

'Exquisite,' she breathed. 'Perfection.'

No one laughed, which was a miracle in itself.

She handed the mirror back to Alice. 'It's a deal,' she said, thrusting a bone-white hand at her. Alice took it, without blinking, and shook it hard. Then she bent upon Maggota her lambent gaze and waited.

Everyone waited. The air felt heavy and still, as if no one was daring to breathe.

'You cannot Name the Dog-Headed One, because he is not a natural being.'

Well, that was just stating the obvious, Ben thought contemptuously. Whatever it was that Alice had given the witch in return for such useless information, he hoped it hadn't been important.

But Maggota had not finished. 'I made him, you see,' she admitted.

'*Made* him?' whispered Isadora faintly.

'Made him,' the witch repeated. 'An experiment. Which got a bit out of hand.' She shrugged. 'I really didn't expect him to turn into such a monster. He was quite sweet, in the beginning.'

'But . . . how?'

'Oh, I borrowed an orphan boy and a puppy from the Other World—'

'*Borrowed?*' cried Isadora, aghast.

'I was going to take them back,' Maggota said defensively. 'But the experiment was such a success and all the other witches made such a fuss of him, I thought, well, I thought I'd keep him.'

Alice gazed at the Dodman, who looked as if he might burst with all the different emotions running through him. 'Did you know?'

He made no response, just trembled from head to toe.

'Did he?' she questioned the witch.

'Oh, no,' she said breezily, waving a dismissive hand. 'Of course not. How could he, once I'd switched the heads?'

Ben felt sick. Did that mean that somewhere there was a monstrous dog running around with a boy's head stuck on it?

'The other creature died,' Maggota carried on, answering Ben's unspoken question, 'so I couldn't really return either of them. But as the Dodman got bigger – older – he became very . . . difficult . . . headstrong.' She laughed. 'Headstrong, ha! And not very nice with the other . . . children.'

'You can say that again.'

They turned, to find Old Creepie standing there, his eyes burning. 'He was horrible to me. Kept biting me, making me do things for him. Bringing him fairies to torture, sometimes making me do it for him. All sorts of dreadful things.'

'You could have refused,' Isadora said gently.

Her brother turned woeful eyes upon her. 'You have no idea,' he said grimly. 'No idea at all.' He turned to the witch. 'It *didn't* die, the other . . . thing. We just told you it did, and you were too busy with all your pupils to have time to see for yourself whether it was true.'

Maggota looked appalled. 'Where is it?'

'In the dungeons,' the Dodman said suddenly. 'We hid it there. It's not seen the light of day since.'

Isadora sat down suddenly and put her head between her knees. 'This is . . . terrible.' After a while, she looked up and fixed the witch with her flashing eyes. 'Maggota, how could you misuse your magic so horribly? It is forbidden to make a living thing. Why, it was the first thing you taught me . . .' She paused, thinking. 'And that is why; because you had already made him and knew what you had done. Is it any wonder he hates all things of magic and has set out to destroy them?' She shook her head wonderingly. Then she turned her pitying gaze upon the dog-headed creature . 'I can't imagine why, after all that he's done, but I feel very, very sorry for him.'

The Dodman stared at her. Then he growled. A white froth

appeared along the line of his long, black lips. 'I don't want your pity!' he howled, and flecks of froth sprayed everywhere. 'I just want you all dead. Every one of you.' And he ran at the Queen as if he would bite her head off.

Alice held out a hand, and he stopped as if he had run into a wall.

'Go and fetch the poor beast you have kept in the dungeons,' she told her uncle. 'Do it now.'

Aleister bobbed his head and scuttled away, taking four goblins with him.

No one said a word while he was gone. Isadora got to her feet and brushed at the wedding dress, now dirty and torn. She walked to her husband's side and laid her head upon his shoulder, and though he didn't have the least idea what was going on, Clive said nothing but encircled her with his arm and squeezed her tight, which was exactly the right thing to do.

Maggota stroked her familiar and stared at the ground, no doubt considering when she might ask for her reward. Boneless Bob's eyes slid back and forth, shiftily.

Ellie hugged herself, since no one else was there to do it for her, and it seemed a bit much to cross the entire courtyard to ask the Horse Lord if he might. She blushed at the very thought.

The Dodman remained motionless, held by Alice's spell, though his black eyes flared with furious light as if his brain was in overdrive trying to make sense of all he had heard. Ben could not take his eyes off him, so fascinated and horrified was he by the witch's tale.

For her part, Alice stayed exactly where she was, thinking hard.

At last Old Creepie reappeared. He looked even creepier than usual, as if struggling under a great weight of guilt, and serve him right, thought Ben. Behind him shuffled the most miserable-looking thing he had ever seen.

It made its way on all fours, and its dog-legs were thin and bowed, shaking with the effort of moving. Its flanks were moth-eaten and ribby, its spine bowed; and its head . . .

Ben had to look away. He knew that if he looked even once into the poor malformed thing's eyes, he would have nightmares for the rest of his life. So he looked down, and found Ignatius Sorvo Coromandel there, looking up at him. He bent and stroked Iggy's head, and Iggy bumped his forehead against Ben's leg, and thus they comforted each other.

Alice was made of sterner stuff. She crossed the courtyard and stood before the other poor monster Maggota had made. It looked up at her wonderingly, its red eyes blinking painfully in the bright sunlight.

'Come with me,' she said gently, and laid a hand on its terrible head.

The dog-man followed her to where the Dodman stood frozen in time. Alice touched each of them in turn. She frowned, concentrating. Then her wide green eyes popped open.

'Alexander George McEwan. Napoleon Rex Barker. Be yourselves.'

A vortex of air enveloped the three figures. Dust whipped around and around, masking whatever transformation was underway at the heart of this storm. There came a noise like a thunderclap, and then silence.

Alice stepped away, leaving behind two figures huddled together on the ground. One was a sandy-haired boy, with pale blue eyes and a dusting of freckles. In his arms a Doberman puppy writhed and yapped.

Four-year-old Alex McEwan stared around uncomprehending. His blue eyes widened till it looked as if they might pop out of his head. Dragons, dinosaurs, horrible little dark green wizened creatures with sharp teeth, horses with men's torsos and heads, a nasty old woman with a hooked nose and a snake around her neck, ugly giants—

It was all too much. He started to wail in anguish.

The puppy, by contrast, seemed entirely unconcerned. Its long pink tongue lolled out of its wide black mouth in delight at all these exotic sights and smells. Its stubby little tail wagged and wagged.

'Right,' said Alice, wiping her hands on her dress. 'Aleister. I cannot bring Cynthia back for you, and I'm sorry about that. This is your chance to make up for what you have done. Corinthius will take you, and little Alex and his puppy Rex, back to Bixbury, where you and Aunt Sybil will look after them.'

'But . . . Sybil hates dogs, won't have them in the house—'

Alice put her hands on her hips. 'Uncle Aleister. Do you want me to do some magic on you? Or on Aunt Sybil?'

'No, no,' he said hastily. 'Er, come with me, little boy, nice doggie . . .'

Alex McEwan stared at the bald, hunchbacked monster advancing upon him and wailed even louder.

'Oh, for goodness' sake,' said Alice. She stalked over to the child and tapped it once on the forehead. It fell immediately into a deep and dreamless sleep. Then she turned to Old Creepie. 'When he wakes up he won't remember any of this. He won't remember anything at all. You are henceforth banished from the Secret Country: your task now is to go back to the Other World and raise him as your own. Make his life as nice as possible.'

'But . . . how will I make a living? We haven't got any money . . .'

'Being happy is not about having money,' Alice said sharply. 'I think you will find that you will manage. And you will like yourself a great deal more if you can do this well. It's a better reward than you deserve.'

'You could sell the Range Rover,' Ben chipped in helpfully.

'Buy something cheaper,' suggested Ellie.

'Maybe a bicycle?' Isadora said brightly. 'They're much more environmentally friendly.'

'A tandem,' grinned Clive Arnold wickedly.

Ben imagined fat Sybil Creepie pedalling away on the back of a tandem and had to muffle a giggle.

Alice looked severely at each of her family members in turn. 'You are not being very nice,' she said crossly.

Epilogue

A few weeks later (though it felt like a lot more) Ellie and Ben were sitting in the treehouse in their back garden at Greyhavens, 27 Underhill Road, Bixbury. A huge sheet of paper was spread out across the wooden floor. Ben had set himself the task of charting the Secret Country. He hadn't told anyone (he knew what they would say) but he meant to go back to Eidolon sometime soon to have an adventure of his own: one that didn't involve hostile monsters, or getting lost. Iggy might well boast that he knew the place like the back of his paw, but Ben wasn't taking any chances. Ellie was helping because she liked drawing and her writing was neater than

Ben's; and Ignatius Sorvo Coromandel was doing what he excelled at – making matters worse – by walking up and down the map, leaving not-very-helpful footprints all over the place.

'Oh, Iggy,' Ben sighed. 'You've knocked over Cloudbeard again.'

'Cloudbeard' was a small cone of cardboard set near the middle of the sheet of paper, and it marked the highest point in the mountain range that Ben had drawn in between the Dark Mere and a wide expanse of ocean. Towards the top of the sheet (depending on which way you were looking at it) there was a long line of silvery-white on which Ellie had written in her best handwriting 'Infinity Beach'. She had also drawn in a tiny hut, although strictly speaking it wasn't actually there any more. For verisimilitude (and just for fun), Ben had added a number of his collection of plastic dinosaurs, which included a bright green triceratops, a post-box red tyrannosaurus rex and some smaller, unidentifiable brown creatures which might (if you looked closely enough) turn out to be cows from his old farm-yard set. They made it look more inhabited, which is what it was, now. Mummu-Tiamat had graciously waived her right to the enormous beach and the swathe of dunes and back-country beyond, ceding it instead, at Ben's suggestion, to the dinosaurs, with Pertinax and Ancasta to have first choice as to which bit of it they wanted to live in. He hoped they would be happy there and raise the babies they had mentioned.

'We're not all monsters, you know,' Ancasta had said, rolling her eyes, when he had thanked her for her intervention in the throne room at the castle.

This left the Eastern Quarter free for the dragons to roam without having any more border wars, and everyone seemed more than happy, for now, with the arrangement.

As for the castle . . . Ellie had drawn in the island in the middle of the lake where Corbenic Castle used to stand, before it was renamed Dodman Castle, and became the centre for all the cruelty emanating out across the Secret Country. Their mother and Alice had decided to dismantle the castle. 'There is too much pain here,' Alice had declared. 'I don't want to live in a place where each stone has a memory of horror.'

Isadora had agreed, even though it had been where she was raised. And since she would be leaving Alice to be the Queen of Eidolon, despite her apparently tender years, and would only be visiting the Secret Country from time to time, it was only right that Alice should decide exactly where and how she wanted to live.

Surprisingly, Alice had declared she didn't want a castle at all, but was going to spend part of her year in the Wildwood, living close to the folk who had survived the war against the Dodman, and part of the year travelling from one province of Eidolon to another, to ensure that all was well and that dangerous pressures were not building up between (say) the dragons and the dinosaurs, or the factions of witches down in the south.

Most surprisingly of all, she had reappointed Maggota Magnifica First Witch; and given her the beauty she had shown her in the little mirror. 'Because,' Alice had explained, 'our appearances in Eidolon reflect our inner nature: so now you are a lot nicer to look at, I hope you will be a lot nicer to be around, too.'

Ellie approved of this, though she was a bit jealous, and had secretly asked Alice if she had a spell which could change the length and line of her nose, which she felt was rather too snub to be truly pretty. Unfortunately (or fortunately) for Ellie, a certain Horse Lord had been within hearing of this request, and had immediately stuck his head through the bush which had up till then been shielding him from view and asked Alice on no account to do any such thing, because he liked Princess Eleanor's nose just the way it was.

Which had just made Ellie blush a lot and grumble about people rudely eavesdropping, but secretly she had been very gratified by Darius's remark, and replayed it in her head every night before she fell asleep.

'What I don't understand,' Iggy said, sitting down suddenly in the middle of the map and thus obliterating everything from Corbenic Lake to the sea, 'is what Alice sees in that horrible Sphynx. I mean,' and he licked the side of his paw and ran it rather vainly across his cheek, making the black fur there even more shiny, 'he's extremely ugly *and* a villain to boot. His outside definitely mirrors his inside.'

Ben was silent for a moment, remembering how he had gone back into the throne room after all the drama and found the hairless cat sitting disconsolately beside the broken broomstick. It kept rubbing its little bald head against Cynthia's discarded shoe, and miaowing pitifully.

'I think,' he said carefully, 'that Alice feels everyone should have a second chance. And anyway, she said that a spy always comes in handy, and it was rather a good spy.'

'Hmph,' said Iggy. 'She could have picked me as her familiar.'

He looked very put out about it.

Ben and Ellie exchanged glances. 'Yes, but Iggy: if Alice had decided you were to be her familiar, you wouldn't have been able to visit Ben and me, or go where you want. In fact, you wouldn't be able to be the Wanderer at all,' Ellie pointed out.

Iggy made a face. 'I suppose not,' he conceded, though his vanity was still hurt that the new Queen of Eidolon should have picked a hairless cat over him. He puffed out his chest. 'Anyway,' he went on, 'at least everyone knows now what nonsense that prophecy was.'

'Oh yes?' said Ben politely. He had now heard this theory of Iggy's about a hundred times, but was determined not to spoil the little cat's justifiable pride in his act of courage.

'Well, maybe not entire nonsense,' Iggy conceded, 'but shall we say, not entirely accurate? Beauty's spell to tame – well that must be Ellie . . .' He always said this because it made her smile, and more likely to give him an extra sardine at tea-time. 'And one with the power to name is clearly Alice. Everyone is agreed on that.' Everyone was. 'But all that stuff about one bravely to bring flame: well, that was *me*, that was!'

'Tell me again how you did that, Iggy,' Ben said gently, because he knew it made the little cat happier than anything else he could do for him, except, perhaps, rubbing his tummy after he had overeaten.

'Well, when you sent me to find Mummu-Tiamat and I climbed that tree—'

'And found Alice on Corinthius,' Ellie prompted.

'And found Alice on Corinthius,' Iggy went on. 'It was me who told her about the army and your situation, and it was because of that that she sent Mummu-Tiamat off to fetch the dragons, which is what I take "bringing flame" to mean. So really, it's me who should take the credit for that bit of the prophecy after all.' And he smiled proudly and puffed up his chest.

'Yes, Iggy, you did a very brave thing, climbing that big tree and driving off that nasty pterodactyl and summoning Alice and the Mother of Dragons to save the day,' said Ellie, grinning at her brother. 'Poor old Ben: not a hero after all.'

Ben grinned back. 'That's okay,' he said cheerfully. 'I never really wanted to be a hero anyway.'

Ignatius Sorvo Coromandel sniffed. 'I should think not: you're not cut out for being a proper hero at all. Not like me. Goodness knows what would have become of you if I hadn't been there to save the day.'

'Look out, Iggy!' Ben cried suddenly. 'There's a dinosaur right behind you.'

Iggy's coat stood on end, all the way from his tail to his nose. His ears went flat. He began to tremble all over. Then, with a yelp of terror, he dug his back feet into the map and launched himself for the door like a black-and-brown furry bullet, leaving two paw-sized holes in the map they had so carefully made.

The little plastic tyrannosaur which had been menacing Iggy promptly fell into one of the holes. Ben looked at his sister. Ellie looked back. Then they burst out laughing.

'So much for heroes,' said Ben, and went back to the map.